Tremble

Editing by Steph White (Kat's Literary Services)

Proofreading by Louise Murphy (Kat's Literary Services)

Paperback cover art by Sonia Gx (ArtBySoniaGx on Instagram)

Hardcover cover art by DisturbedValkyrieDesigns

Internal images by Emily (Emilyvxrsss on Instagram)

Contents

Content Warning

There are mentions of family trauma, domestic violence, attempted homicide, suicide, gun violence, a terminally ill parent, therapy sessions, and explicit language.

Chronic illness and mental health representation are a few main themes in ***Tremble*** and will be in each of my books in this series.

This is an open-door romance with lots of consensual spice. If you aren't a fan, this book may not be for you, or you're welcome to refer to the "Table of Cocktents" on the following page so you know which chapters to avoid.

For a detailed list of events, please feel free to contact the author via Instagram DMs or email at Giuliana.Victoria.Author@gmail.com with any specific questions you may have about the contents of this book. While ***Tremble*** is filled with lots of light and laughter, some themes may be triggering for people. Your mental health is always a priority. Never be afraid to ask for specific chapters to avoid or to just avoid reading the book entirely. Please take care of your mental health <3

Table of Cocktents

For anyone who wants to jump straight to the spice, know how far ahead the "good stuff" is, or wants to skip it entirely.

Playlist

On My Mama – Victoria Monét
cinderella's dead – EMELINE
Beg – Leon Thomas & Elle Varner
Pain – Three Days Grace
Baddie – Honey B
Bed Peace – Jhené Aiko (ft. Childish Gambino)
Nights Like This – Kehlani (ft. Ty Dolla $ign)
Love Language – SZA
Collide – Justine Skye (ft. Tyga)
Feeling Myself – Nicki Minaj (ft. Beyoncé)
Hello – Aqyila
Show My Love for You – Demise
Agora Hills – Doja Cat
SLOW DANCING IN THE DARK – Joji
Moment – Victoria Monét
Mad at Me. – Kiana Ledé
Laffy Taffy – D4L
STRINGS – MAX (ft. JVKE & Bazzi)
Too Sweet – Hozier
Can't Help Falling in Love – Haley Reinhart
Every Kind Of Way – H.E.R.
Let Me Love You – Ariana Grande (ft. Lil Wayne)

So High – Doja Cat
Broken Clocks – SZA
Wicked Games – Kiana Ledé
Girl With The Tattoo Enter.lewd – Miguel
Living Dead Girl – Rob Zombie
Whore – In This Moment
All of Me – John Legend
Marry You – Bruno Mars
A Thousand Years – Christina Perri
Steal My Girl – One Direction[1]

---

1. **Playlist**

Signature Fragrance

Aiyana Kaan:
Autumn/Winter: *Hermes Ambre Narguile Eau de Toilette*
&
Spring/Summer: *Thierry Mugler Alien Goddess Intense Eau de Parfum*
Kassian Narvaez:
Dior Sauvage by Christian Dior Eau de Parfum

Tsalagi Names, Terms & Meanings

Tsalagi: The Cherokee language
Ani'-Yun'wiya': This is what many Cherokee people refer to themselves as. This translates to "the real people" or "the principal people."
Etsi: Mom
Edoda: Dad
Uwetsiageyv: Daughter
Uwetsi: Son
Usdi: Baby (Term of endearment)
Udalii: Wife
Gvgeyui: I love you
Didanawisgi: Medicine man
Uktena: Healer
Aiyana: "Eternal flower"
Zuni: "Beauty"
Qaletaqa: "Guardian of the people"
Adohi: "From the woods"

To my fellow smut sluts who just want a partner who's an absolute fucking simp for you, and you alone. This one's for us. <3

Chapter One

Kassian

Friday, November 10, 2023

"You gonna be a good girl for Daddy and suck my cock dry?" I say to the woman currently on her knees, taking me to the hilt, sputtering around my cock. She's attractive, with pretty dark-brown eyes, and she definitely knows what she's doing with her mouth—but the woman I'm really imagining on her knees is Aiyana. I can't get her out of my head, and it's been years. Years since we first started messing around, always careful to never tell Kat. Years since she moved to the other side of the country. I'm certain Kat would have been fine with it, but Aiyana insisted otherwise, so we kept it a secret. Kept us a secret. If there even was an us.

She's sucking me off like a damn vacuum; I've got my fingers in her hair, pulling her to me, urging her to go deeper. She taps on my thigh three times, signaling for us to stop, and I release her immediately. "Sorry, Kas, I don't think this is working. Is your head somewhere else?" she asks me, head cocked to the side in question.

I deflect. "It seems my head was just in your mouth, baby girl." I try to laugh her off, but she gives me a knowing look. Sheila and I have been doing this song and dance for a few months now. She's a really sweet person with a serious daddy kink, among other more taboo ones, but this has always worked for us. We both want casual, so this arrangement has been good for both of us. It's also been a sick sort of self-induced torture because Sheila looks strangely similar to Aiyana, but no one is as gorgeous as her. No amount of similarity will ever account for the snarky, sarcastic woman I've come to love… and lust after. She lands in a few short hours, and my skin is prickly with anticipation. Will she want to try this out? Give a relationship with me a real shot? Do the whole friends-with-benefits thing? Or pretend we were never anything at all and just move on without me? The possibility of never calling her mine has my heart clenching with agony.

I finally answer her waiting stare. "I'm sorry, Sheils, her flight lands in a few hours, and I'm just so nervous, I'm not in this." I gesture between us. "I can get you off real quick though. I just don't think I'll be able to finish. Not with so much on my mind."

She pats my thigh before standing and picking up her clothes, talking to me while getting dressed. "You've been pining after that woman for so long, of course you're not in the right headspace for a quick fuck," she says as she bends over, pulling her jeans up her tan legs. "It's all right, Kas; I really don't think you have anything to worry about though. You're a great guy, and you share a lot of history with her. I'm confident you'll make it work."

She's dressed in light-wash denim jeans and a white lace bra, searching for her sweater as I get up and start dressing myself before answering her. "If I'm such a catch, why aren't you interested in anything more than my dick?" Again, I'm deflecting. A relationship was never on the table for us.

She rolls her eyes at me, calling me out immediately. "Kas, you don't want a relationship with me, and I don't want one, period. You know that, and you're deflecting again. You are a great guy, but you know I've got another three years of medical school before I can even think about a relationship. If all I thought you were good for was your cock, I wouldn't be interested in your long-lost love with the beautiful Aiyana." I swear I hear her mutter "dumbass" under her breath as she finishes getting dressed.

"Now come give me a hug because this is probably the last time we'll see each other." She's laughing at me, and I engulf her in a tight hug, resting my chin on top of her head.

A few moments pass, and she's pulling away from me. "All right, I've gotta head out. I really hope you get the girl, Kas. I'm very invested in my doppelganger's love life, but protect that big heart of yours."

"Will do. Thanks for understanding," I tell her.

"Anytime, Daddy." She lets out a loud cackle, heading out the door and calling over her shoulder, "Bye, Kas! Good luck!"

CHAPTER TWO

Aiyana

I just landed at PHL and picked up the keys to my rental for the week. I'm currently regretting the number of personal belongings I chose to lug around with me. I can't say I packed light despite shipping the majority of my stuff to Kat at our new apartment. I'm just in town for the week to attend a few interviews, but I have a really good feeling about one employer in particular, so I shipped all of my shit to Kat preemptively. That way, I can just cancel my flight back to our old apartment in San Diego if—no, *when* this new job pans out.

I've spent the last five years completing my Master of Science as a double major in biomedical engineering and chemistry and my subsequent PhD. I have all the education and tons of experience for this job, so I'm not worried about it.[1]

What *I am* worried about though is how I'm going to manage to be around Kas for the foreseeable future.

When I met Kat in middle school and decided she was going to be stuck with me for the rest of our lives, I never expected to meet the sweet, nerdy boy next door who happened to be her twin.

Both fortunately and also *unfortunately*, they were always a package deal, and while Kas was a lanky teen, he was so sweet, and I was so gangly that I wasn't judging anyway. I had the biggest crush on him that I had no idea would become unmanageable as we aged, but as the years went on, he became more and more attractive.

Kat and Kas are twins, but they don't look that much alike to me. They share the same wavy, dark hair; cute, rounded nose; and full lips, but Kas has the brightest hazel eyes that lean more toward green. They're Filipino and Puerto Rican, and where Kat definitely sits somewhere in the middle, Kas absolutely has more of their mom's Filipino features. They're both gorgeous in their own right, but I could never see Kat as anything more than a sister to me. Not to say that I haven't been with several women, but I have a type, and Kat isn't it.

Once I've got all my shit loaded into the trunk, I send Kat a quick text letting her know I'm heading to the apartment. I was warned that it isn't an apartment though. Kas purchased a freaking penthouse, and I can't help but wonder if he did it for my benefit. Kat says he wanted to ensure her safety, insisted she was within walking distance to his place, and all that brotherly love crap. But it's a nice thought to consider him wanting those things for me.

I pull up in front of the massive thirty-eight-story building covered in reflective mirrors and leave the keys with the complimentary valet, handing him a few dollars for a tip. I get out and am greeted by a man who's probably in his sixties. He introduces himself as Ralph and offers to have my luggage brought up to our place.

Ralph shows me which elevator to use to access the penthouse. Luckily, the elevator is working this time. Kat texted last week when she first arrived and told me all about the catastrophe she endured her first night—delayed flight, broken elevator, walking up thirty-eight flights of stairs, door key that didn't work, and no one to set up the code for her. She said she spent the night in the hallway. Hopefully, whoever lives across the hall from us didn't catch a glimpse of that.

I take the elevator up, and when I step out, my door is already open, with a bellhop unloading my bags for me. This is some serious five-star service.

I approach the open doorway, and as I do, I hear the door across the hall pop open, and a man who looks like a literal god comes walking out. He's easily six foot six, broad-shouldered, with a head of dark-brown loose waves that any woman would kill for. He has the lightest green eyes I've ever seen, a straight nose, and a chiseled jaw. How in the hell has Kat not mentioned this man before? She must not have met him yet if she managed to skim over that fun little fact!

I pick my jaw up off the floor and finally turn to introduce myself, extending my hand to him. "Hi, I'm Aiyana. My best friend, Kat, moved in across the hall from you last week. I'm in town this week for job interviews, and then I'll be joining her. It's nice to meet you." I give him my best megawatt smile.

He shakes my hand, smiling back at me. He's got kind eyes, and good lord, his hand is big. "Hey, I'm Alessandro. I met Kat last week, actually." I think I see his cheeks turning pink as he looks down at his feet quickly before straightening and meeting my gaze again. *Interesting.* "If you need anything, let me know. I'm just across the hall, and Kat has my number." He smiles and starts heading off with his duffle bag in tow.

My eyes are as big as saucers; *Kat has my number?* She has his number, and she hasn't said anything about him? What kind of parallel universe are we living in that my *best friend* would leave out such important information? We'll be having a very stern chat about this soon.

I opt to send her a string of text messages about the hottie across the hall from us before I start putting my things away. My bed hasn't arrived yet, so I'll be sharing hers until it does, but I can at least get my stuff sorted while I wait to pick Kat up for the hockey game tonight.

Kas plays for the Philly Scarlets as a defenseman, and there's nothing that would make me miss it. Even if it weren't Kas playing, I've been rooting for the Scarlets since I was six years old, attending every home game with my dad. Even the ones with weird hours, my dad would take me out of school and claim we had a family emergency so I didn't miss it. We had a lot of family emergencies, apparently. Honestly, the school admin should've been concerned.

---

1. **On My Mama – Victoria Monét**

Chapter Three

Aiyana

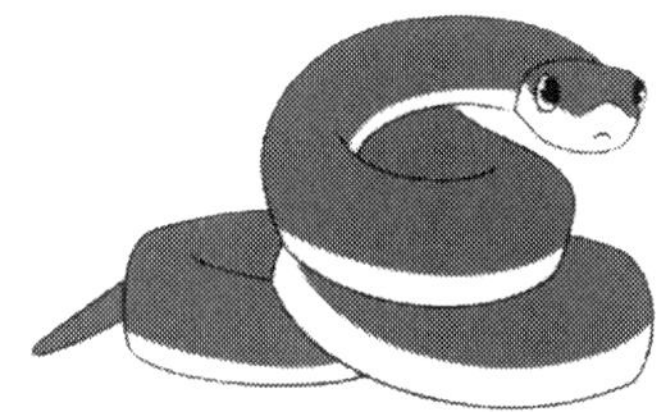

I think I might shit myself. Oh my god, what if I seriously get the anxiety shits before I even get to see Kas? I'm shaking with excitement at the game in front of us, but mostly, I'm a bundle of nerves waiting to see Kas for the first time in what feels like forever.

I direct my attention to Kat when she shouts, "I'm so happy you're here!" She throws her arms around me and squeezes me to her, her hair getting caught in my lip gloss.

"Me too! I've missed you so much! But this conversation will have to wait until after we get back to the penthouse with the dreamy giant across the hall because hockey is on." I direct my sight back to the rink, which is unbelievably close. Kas got us seats just three rows up from the glass, and it's a literal dream come true for me.

"I don't know if you've noticed or not, but hockey isn't 'on' because it's not TV. This is an in-person game." She says it playfully, so I side-eye her and stick my tongue out before turning back to watch the game.

***

A whole bunch of crap just went down that I can't even begin to digest. Our "hallmate," as Kat is now calling him, is a hockey player? And he's on Kas's team? I'm truly delighted by this information because I could use the gossip, but also, Kat could use the lay. And if Kas was comfortable enough with Alessandro to buy us a freaking penthouse across the hall from him, I just know that he's got to be a good guy.

Nothing Kas does is without calculation, so I wouldn't be surprised if he was secretly trying to set them up. *Or maybe, not so secretly.* He's also not the most subtle guy I know.

We're waiting for the guys to come out after their showers, and I see Kas approaching us wearing a charcoal-gray suit with a black shirt underneath, looking like a damn model. When his searching eyes meet mine, his mouth splits into a grin. The anxiety shits will have to wait because my body has a mind of its own.

I catapult myself into his arms with so much force that I nearly knock him on his ass. He's got me locked in one of his tight bear hugs, and our bodies tremble with laughter. My body is nearly in flames from the heat radiating off of him. It warms me to my core, and I'm quickly reminded of why he's always been my very own comfort animal.

Except, he's not a fucking puppy, and I have no business feeling the way I do about him. Not anymore.

Unfortunately for me, though, he's so damn gorgeous, my memory must be blocking some of his shine to protect me from impending doom in the form of utter infatuation. It feels incredible to just be in his arms, melted against him, but we can't stay like this forever. I pull away, taking a few *very necessary* steps back, where the air isn't so suffocatingly full of Kas.

I need space to breathe without his essence fogging up my brain, and he needs to acknowledge his sister before remnants of our past become glaringly obvious between us. We've somehow managed to keep our connection under wraps because getting with my best friend's brother is simply not something I want any part in. Not in this lifetime.

The worst part will always be that it isn't that I don't *want* Kas. It's just that *I can't have him.* And I'll never be able to tell him why.

Chapter Four

Aiyana

Saturday, November 11, 2023

I hop out of my cab after we pull up in front of an Italian restaurant. I'm filled with a mixture of excitement and nerves for my meeting with Rose De Laurentiis, the lead biomedical scientist for BioMedics, a company I've been hoping to work for since high school.

I'm dressed in a slinky black dress with kitten heels. I didn't want to be too overdressed, but I also didn't want to look like I hadn't tried.

I'm not sure what to expect because I've never had an interview with a woman before. The sad truth is that women in STEM are few and far between because the sciences are male predominant, and there's a lot of nepotism involved. The fact that I even got this interview is a huge deal despite my incredible resume, but for it to be with a woman? That warms my heart and leaves me with so much excitement for this opportunity. *I just hope it all pans out well.*

I walk into the restaurant surrounded by limestone walls with round unfinished wood tables, matching chairs, and café lights with grape vines hanging from the ceilings. The hostess greets me and brings me to my table, which is tucked away in a far corner of the restaurant. A petite woman with cherry-red lips and a bubblegum-pink bob is looking over the menu.

As I approach, she peers up at me, her light-blue eyes bright and clear as her lips spread into a warm smile.

She stands, hand extended to me. "Hello, Aiyana, I'm Rose De Laurentiis, though I'm sure you gathered that already. Please, take a seat; it'll just be us for the night." My brows climb up my forehead. I just assumed there'd be others to scope me out or even additional interviewees. A lot of these big companies try to scare off potential employees as a kind of hazing, setting us up by interviewing several of us at one time for a single open position.

"Don't worry; this isn't a boys' club, Aiyana. I conduct all of my own interviews and have zero desire to involve anyone else in the decision-making process for *my* department." Goddamn, this woman is confident and sassy in all the best ways. *I like her already.*[1]

Smiling at her, my nerves begin to calm as I take the seat to her right and quickly begin to relax. "Well, I'm glad I won't have to fight any pretty boys tonight, but I'd have been glad to if it came to it." I wink at her, deciding to just be myself and hoping that's enough to win her over. It's a shot in the dark; she could think I'm inappropriate and hate me, but would I really want to work with someone who doesn't like me as a person anyway? The answer is a resounding *no.*

Apparently, that worked because she smiles at me, her eyes alight with humor. "So, to be honest, you already have the job as far as I'm concerned. I've seen your resume, so I know you're qualified. This interview is more of a formality than anything else. I want to see how we get along and if we both think we'd work well together. If so, I'd like to talk salary and benefits with you and offer you the job tonight. So relax and just be yourself."

I couldn't think of anyone better to work for or with at this rate. She is so unbelievably sweet and carries herself with such grace. She seems like she might be a little socially awkward in situations that aren't directly related to her work, but that's fine with me. I could actually see myself becoming friends with her. She tells me all about her family, her wife, Charlie, and her brothers-in-law. The fact that Charlie's oldest brother is actually Alessandro just reminds me that what they say about it being a small world is true.

The dinner went so well that she ended up offering me the job and a salary far above my asking range. I wasn't lowballing myself either. *I know my fucking worth.*

She told me that it doesn't come out of her paycheck, so why not offer me what she knows BioMedics is willing to pay me if she *also* says I'm worth it? The benefits package is incredible, too, and for the first time in years, I'd have *real* health insurance, not just Kat telling me what to get from the pharmacy and hoping like hell I don't need a prescription.

I can't wait to get started, so after I got home from dinner and gushed to Kat about how it went, I sent out emails to all of the other companies I had interviews scheduled for this week and canceled them all. I just hope the awkward tension between Kas and I can work itself out just as well as this interview has...

---

1. **cinderella's dead – EMELINE**

Chapter Five

Kassian

Saturday, November 18, 2023

It's been over a week since Aiyana moved back, and I've barely seen her.

I've texted her several times, even asking her to go hiking with Kat and me yesterday despite knowing she hates exercise. She said she couldn't because she just started her new job at BioMedics and doesn't want to make a bad impression by asking for time off so soon.

I get it; it's a completely valid reason, but I can't help but feel that she's also avoiding spending time with me.

The thing is, I *know* she loves me too. And I know that I am completely, madly in love with this absolutely fucking incredible woman. So why is she ignoring me?

It can't just be Kat.

There has to be something more to it because Aiyana has never been one to hold back when it comes to Kat. I don't see why she is now.

For five years, I've missed her. And now that she's back, I'm going to show her just how much.

***

I exit the plane when we land in Denver, following behind Alessandro.

I love the guy, but he wouldn't shut up about my sister the entire flight. He's like a love-sick puppy, but I can't blame him. I feel the same about Aiyana, so I gave him a break. He's a really good guy—that's why I set Kat up in the same building as him in the first place and why I invited him on our hike yesterday. He has my full blessing to pursue a relationship with my sister if she wants him to. Some might say I have a bit of a habit of playing matchmaker, but *no one* is complaining. I'm damn good at it, and I just *know* my sister would be happy with Ale. And that's really all I want for her—to be happy and supported in all areas of her life.

As we make our way toward the hotel to drop our bags off, I can't help but wonder what Aiyana's doing. Will she be watching?

I shouldn't care so much, but I do. I *always* care what she's doing. I'm not sure anything will change that. We'll be hopping on the team bus soon for warm-ups at the arena we'll be playing at tonight, and my head should be in the game right now, but it's hard to think straight, knowing the love of my life is just out of reach.

***

I'm drenched in sweat, my heart is pounding, and I honestly don't know how the fuck I'm gonna make it through another twenty minutes of this game.

The team we're up against is playing dirty as hell, and that's just not our style. I play defense, so I'm used to getting pretty roughed up, but the other team's been getting tossed in the sin bin more times during this one game than our team has over the entirety of the season.

It's like they've got a personal vendetta against us or something, but I have no idea what it's over.

They aren't even playing to win. We're still up by two points because they're putting all their energy into fucking around.

***

We won three to one, unable to score any more points in the last twenty minutes, probably from sheer exhaustion at trying to keep from getting tossed around like rag dolls.

I exit the ice, pulling my helmet off and spitting to the side. It's disgusting, but I've had my head banged around so much that despite my mouthguard, I've got a pool of blood-tinged saliva that I can't stand to keep in my mouth any longer.

Coach slaps me on the back, telling me *good game* as I enter the locker room to hop on a bike and get rid of some of this built-up lactic acid before showering. I'm unbelievably glad we're not heading back to Philly right away. I need to crawl into bed and sleep this off.

Chapter Six

Aiyana

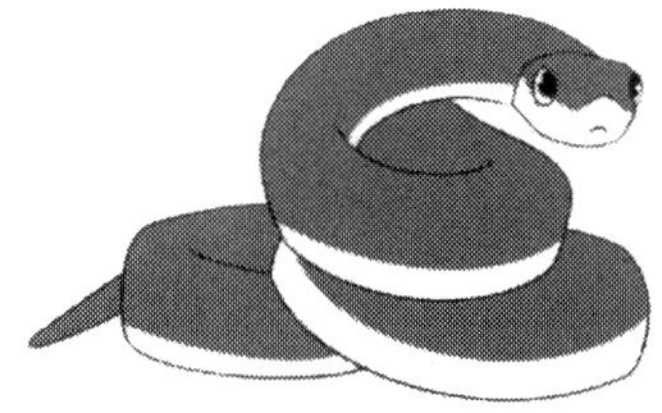

That game was beyond brutal. My forehead is still pricked with sweat despite trying to appear unbothered in front of Kat.

I've never missed one of his games, but I almost wish I had this time. Nausea is stirring in my gut as I mentally replay Kas getting knocked into the boards, punched in the sides, and kneed in the face over and over in my head. Bile rises up my throat, but I work to tamp it down when I see Kat reappear from her bedroom. She had gone to use the bathroom right after the game ended.

I look up at her, plastering a smile on my face that doesn't reflect the nerves I feel running rampant in my gut. "Did Kas text you to let you know what the hell was up with the other team?" I ask, attempting to keep my voice casual.

She doesn't seem to notice, though her brow quirks before answering. "No, he usually doesn't text me right after games." She pauses, assessing me. "But that *was* weird. I wonder why they were being so aggressive." A small flicker of irritation flashes across her features.

Shaking my head, I shrug and reach for my cell on the couch cushion.

I check for any missed messages, hoping for the first time since I arrived back in Philly that Kas *has* texted me.

He's been messaging me daily, sometimes several times a day. I know he's trying to wear me down and figure out how we're going to handle our past bullshit. You don't just leave a man like Kas and never answer for it.

The problem is, I've been torturing myself over that fact for five years. I don't need him to add insult to injury.

I feel sick to my stomach, though, and I've got no missed messages.

I'll text *him*. Just this once.

God, I hope he's not hurt.

I open my messaging app and scroll down until I see his face. He's wearing one of my dad's furs over his head, posing like a model for me. Back when I used to take loads of pictures of him with no qualms.

Those days are gone though.

What do I even say to him? Tell him I'm worried? No, I can't do that. He'll take it as an opening to swoop in and make me fall in love with him all over again.

As if I'd ever fallen out of love with him.

I've been agonizing over what to type for so long that I don't notice Kat flop down on the couch next to me, peering over my shoulder. "You texting Kas?" she asks me with a bright smile on her face.

If she keeps acting like this every time there's a mention of Kas and me together, it'll be impossible to continue convincing him that we can't be together because of Kat.

Something tells me she'd be nothing short of *thrilled* to have her best friend and her brother dating.

I look over my shoulder at her, not even bothering to put my phone away because that would look even more suspicious. "Yeah, that team was rough, so I figured I'd text him to congratulate them on the win."

Her questioning gaze remains on me, but she just turns her attention back to the TV, nodding her acceptance of my answer.

I look back down at my phone and go for a simple text,

Congrats on the win! Hope you're not too banged up.

Minutes pass by with no response, and my anxiety grows. I never have anxiety. Evidently, that doesn't seem to remain consistent where Kas is concerned.

I send another text when it's been thirty minutes with no response, and I've managed to peel all of my gel nail polish off.

Just want to make sure you didn't get too beat up out there.

Rough game tonight.

Well, rough team anyway.

Text me when you can.

Kat is worried about you.

The second text opened up a dam, unable to stop myself from sending another and another... That last text was a lie. She seems completely content, sitting in the corner of our velvet olive-green couch. Coincidentally purchased for us by Kas. I wonder if that was all part of his plan. To put us somewhere close by and fill it with things he bought us so I'd have no choice but to think about him.

The joke's on him though; he never needed to spend the money.

I'm always thinking about him.

Chapter Seven

Kassian

Sunday, November 19, 2023

I'm fucking exhausted, but I feel so much better after that shower.

JJ and I are rooming together tonight, so we make our way up to the eighth floor of the hotel we're staying at for the night. It's nothing super fancy. When we enter our room, the walls are a light beige color, and there are two queen-sized beds with white comforters: the standard.

I dump my bag on the end of my bed, digging around for some sweats, my toothbrush, and cell phone.

My phone's made its way to the very bottom of the bag, and when I pull it out and unlock the screen, I see the most beautiful sight I could possibly imagine. I must've hit my head really fucking hard if I'm seeing Aiyana's gorgeous big brown eyes staring back at me with not one, but *six* texts playing across my screen.

I open the messaging app up and, sure enough, my eyes aren't playing tricks on me. I read each text, and my heart fucking swells. She says Kat's worried about me, but I know that's a cop-out. She'd have texted me herself or called me, or hell, called Ale if she was that worried.

Aiyana was worried about me.

I can't help the cheesy, shit-eating grin that spreads across my face, threatening to leave my cheeks sore tomorrow.

"What's got you looking like the mouse who found the cheese over there?" JJ asks. He quirks a dark brow at me, grinning.

"Aiyana finally texted me," I tell him, and he nods because I've been almost as bad as Ale is, but for years now, so he knows exactly what that means.

I've never told anyone any details; they've got no clue that we spent our entire senior year sneaking around behind everyone's backs or that I've eaten her pretty pussy out so many times I can recall the taste based on memory alone.

I break that train of thought, my dick getting hard just thinking about her and not wanting to deal with that while sharing a room.

I reread her messages, reveling in her concern before finally responding.

I knew you cared, little viper.

Little Viper

I don't. Kat was worried.

Little Viper

I don't care that much, anyway.

Little Viper

Well, I don't *not* care.

Keep telling yourself that.

Little Viper

Even now, at the ripe age of 28, you're still living in the land of the imaginary.

If it means I get to live with you, I'll gladly be the king of the land!

I can't help but continue smiling at my phone. I don't even care that she's denying her feelings for me. *She's replying*, and that's all I need.

Little Viper

I want you to know, I'm rolling my eyes at you right now.

The prettiest eyes in the world. I feel honored <3

Little Viper

You're full of it.

Yeah, well, you keep replying so...You could be full of me too...

Wait, don't take that as a reason to stop!

God, I'm fucking desperate for this woman.

Little Viper

Kas, your desperation is showing...

I
AM
DESPERATE
But only for you, little viper.
Little Viper
You're annoying me. This viper has fangs. You'd do well not to forget it.
I could never.
Go to dinner with me?
Little Viper
No.
So, you'll think about it?
Little Viper
Goodnight, Kassian.
Goodnight, my little viper <3

I can picture her lying on her couch, rolling those gorgeous brown eyes at me. I wish I could kiss her right now.

Chapter Eight

Aiyana

Today is going to be such trash. I had really hoped to get some stuff done around the apartment or, at the very least, relax. But my uterus is leaving no hope in sight of that happening.

I started my period on Friday, and these cramps just won't let up. I just want one normal fucking menstrual cycle that doesn't leave me in a puddle of my own blood like a stuck pig. I climb out of bed, planning to hop in the shower and change before balling up my linens and bleaching everything in sight, but my cell rings before I can make it to the shower.

Kat is still home; I know that for a fact because she hurt her ankle on that hike Kas tried to drag me on the other day. I keep telling everyone that exercise is bad for your health, but they never listen.

Lifting my comforter and shaking it out, all I'm greeted with is the sight of my own blood, no phone to be found, but the damn thing keeps ringing.

I crouch down to check under the bed, and sure enough, it's lying just within reach. It must've fallen while I was sleeping or at least trying to sleep. I grab it and see Kas's face flash across the screen. Panic sears through me, but it's been ringing for so long that I've only got a second to make a decision.

I click accept, and there's silence on his end.

"Hello," I say, annoyance lacing the word. "Is this supposed to be some dumb prank?"

He finally answers, his deep voice echoing over the line, "No, I just hadn't expected you to actually answer."

His surprised delight sends tingles down my spine, but it doesn't matter what he wants. Or what *I want,* for that matter.

"What is it, Kas?" I ask, trying to sound rude as a defense tactic, one that's never worked with him. *I actually think he likes it.*

"You. Always you." He chuckles. I don't say anything to that because he knows I won't, so there's no point in coming up with a response. Doesn't he know how much it kills me that he won't just let this go? I want him so badly that I used to wake up sobbing from dreams about him leaving me, but when I'd wake up and roll over, hoping he'd be lying beside me, I was always hit with the realization that it was never *him* who left *me.* And that alone was so much worse than any nightmare my tired mind could conjure.

The first two years after I left were like that. I got the worst sleep of my life in the beginning.

It hurts me too. He's not the only one. But if he knew the real reason we can't be together, he'd never let me get away with this bullshit. We had both emphasized the importance of open communication. That's something we always had in spades, *but not now.*

He huffs. "I know you started your period the other day, and I'm stopping by to bring snacks and a brace my athletic trainer gave me for Kat. I just wanted to see if you needed anything—painkillers, pads, tampons, chocolate... sushi? Anything."

My chest aches as I hold back a sob that threatens to release itself from my throat. "I'm good, Kas. Thanks though," I tell him, though my body decides at precisely that moment to call me out for being a big, fat fucking liar. I keel over in pain, a cramp wracking my body until my legs tremble with the effort to hold me upright. I release a squeak of pain, and I know he hears it when his tense intake of breath comes over the line.

I'm standing in my room in excruciating pain; my lower back is killing me, my breasts are sore, and my thighs are covered in blood. This is the least sexy I've ever felt, and it only hurts my pride more that arguably the *most* sexy person I know is on the other end of the line.

"I'm on my way," is all he says before the call drops.

Chapter Nine

Aiyana

I finally checked the time when I got off the line with Kas. The team must've flown home extremely early if he's already on his way over. It's just after nine in the morning, and Kat is still asleep. We didn't go to bed until late last night, and neither of us have plans for the day, so she said she's going to sleep in.

I finish blow-drying my hair and braid the black strands back into a single plait, changing into a pair of black leggings and my favorite oversized hoodie. It's one that Kas gave me in our senior year of high school. Well, he didn't *give* it to me, I took it, but he never asked for it back. So I'll consider it a gift.

I finish getting ready for my big day of laundry and being a complete couch potato when my phone chirps with a text from Kas.

Kas

I'm at your door. Open up.

Rolling my eyes, I pad across the vinyl plank floors and open the door to find Kas with his hooded eyes pinched in worry. He's holding several paper grocery bags containing god knows what, so I open the door wider for him by way of greeting.

He lets himself in like he owns the place because, well, technically, he does.

He goes to work, putting all sorts of snacks up in the cabinets, and I take note of what he brought—garden salsa Sun Chips, crunchy Cheetos, and strawberry Pop-Tarts. He moves on to the fridge, stocking it with Sour Patch Kids, sour Skittles, brie, dill pickles, and Fruit Roll-Ups. All of my favorite snacks, most of which are relatively unhealthy, but I've always been a big proponent of food serving more purposes than one. One of which being to feed my bleeding uterus and, of course, my soul.

He even remembers that I like my candy cold.

It must be the hormones because my eyes prick with tears before I practically suck them back into the devious little tear glands they came from. I'm pretty sure it's not actually possible to suck them back in, but where there's a will, there's a way.

When he's finished in the kitchen, he heads toward my room, and my eyes widen with shock. That's bold. Even for him.

I stomp after him, letting out an exasperated huff. When he gets to my room, he takes in the bare mattress as I wait for the sheets and mattress protector to finish washing.

His eyes swing to me and back to the bed before he dumps out the bag of items and gets to work, making my bed.

He's brought a heated mattress pad, a black sheet set, and a soft faux fur blanket big enough to act as a comforter. I'm too stunned to say anything, let alone help him, as he trudges full steam ahead with his plans.

Once the bed is made, I realize he's picked a blanket with a giant purple-and-gold snake in the center, surrounded by a black border.

He's killing me. Slowly, but never softly.

He pulls out the final items from the bottom of the bag. Extra strength painkillers with caffeine because those were the only ones that ever worked for my headaches, and a bag of assorted dark chocolate Lindt truffles.

His eyes finally land on me, his breath hitches, and all of his resolve seems to vanish.

Kas practically hurdles himself toward me, gripping my cheeks as he looks me over, seeing my eyes welling with tears. I've missed him so much; it's like a piece, no, a whole *chunk* of me has been missing without him.

I take the step forward before I can second-guess myself, and his arms instantly curl around me, pulling me to his chest, warming that broken, messy place in the deepest recesses of my heart.

He's twining his fingers into the hair at the nape of my neck, tugging gently as he lifts me into his arms and walks us backward toward the bed after kicking the door shut. We lie there, just holding each other, saying absolutely nothing for the next half hour until I hear the pipes running with water, letting us know that Kat's awake.

He kisses my forehead, the peaceful silence still enveloping us as he leaves me in the bed, cold and lonely despite the heat radiating from the mattress pad.

Will I ever stop missing this man?

Will I ever stop *loving* this man?

Chapter Ten

Kassian

Tuesday, November 21, 2023

We haven't spoken since Sunday, but I can't take it anymore. I've learned how to manage; getting through life without her never became easier, but I cope so nothing seems off to anyone else, but inside, I'm a wreck.

A train heading toward a dead end with no breaks.

I pace the floor of the gym, waiting for my turn on the bench as Kyle finishes his set.

Her birthday is coming up. December twelfth, she'll be twenty-eight, same as Kat and me.

Before I even know what I'm doing, I have my phone in my hand, texting her again.

What are we doing for your birthday?

"You done dicking around or need to send another text?" Kyle asks me in a mocking tone.

I grunt and head toward the bar to finish my workout.

***

It's been hours since I texted her. I know she's working, but her lack of reply still sends me spiraling.

It's not healthy for so much of my self-worth to weigh on whether or not she answers me or pays me any mind.

I should schedule an appointment with my therapist. She's heard all about Aiyana.

Before I can talk myself out of it, I call Dr. Sanchez's office and schedule a virtual call for later this evening.

***

"I really do think you've made some great progress with this call, and I agree. It might be a good idea to start having these visits more regularly again. How do you feel about bi-weekly visits?" Dr. Sanchez asks.

I think about it, trying to make a conscious decision like we've discussed rather than just agreeing to something without any thought put into it.

"Yeah, let's start with biweekly, and if we need to move it to weekly, then we can always adjust. I'll shoot your office my hockey schedule, and you can let me know your availability." I smile at her.

"Sounds good. Enjoy the rest of your evening, Kas," she says before ending the meeting.

That was helpful. I really enjoy speaking with Dr. Sanchez because having an unbiased outward view of a situation is helpful, but so is having someone not involved in my daily life to just act as a listening ear. It's taken years of therapy after what happened with our mom, but I'm finally at a place where I'm confident I'm able to tell when I need to seek help and when I'm able to handle things on my own.

As if she knows I just got off a call discussing her, Aiyana replies to my earlier message.

Little Viper

"We" aren't doing anything.

Of course we aren't. God. I try not to deflate at the thought of not getting to spend time with her, but as I just discussed with Dr. Sanchez, I need to avoid deflecting and trying to bait her with humor.

Okay, let me know if you change your mind.

Little Viper

Really? You're not gonna try to hound me about it or make up some dumb excuse for me to go out with you? Not going to throw some surprise party in my bedroom that I have no way of avoiding?

Nope. I'm working on giving you the space you need even if it's killing me not to see you.

Little Viper

Kas...

Little Viper

You know this isn't about what either of us want. It'll just be too awkward with Kat.

I know that's what you
keep saying, but I'm not buying it. Kat practically glows when she sees us together. I think she'd be thrilled to have her best friend and her brother dating.

Little Viper

I think you see what you want to see.

Maybe so. Just let me know if things change. I've missed my little viper every day for the last five years.

Dr. Sanchez said to try open communication and vulnerability on my part. Both are things that Aiyana and I have struggled with the last few years, even though they were never an issue before she moved.

Chapter Eleven

Aiyana

Let him know if things change?

Clearly, *he has.* We haven't been great about being vulnerable with one another the last few years. Not since my dad realized that things between Kas and I were getting serious after I graduated from undergrad.

He made it abundantly clear that we should be proud to be Ani'-Yun'wiya', that it's important to honor tradition, and that I'm expected to marry someone with a similar cultural background. And I *am* proud to be Cherokee. I'm so damn proud that I let his words worm into me, making decisions for me.

If he weren't so sick, I'd probably tell him my thoughts on his opinion of my love life. I'd tell him they're archaic and that love is about more than just culture, but he *is* sick. And I don't have the heart to say any of those things to him as he continues to become more and more frail every time I see him. Besides, he and Kas have always loved each other, and I don't want to put either of them in a position where things would be strained.

My dad was more of a father figure to Kat and Kas growing up than their own father was. There's just too much at stake for me to put my own wants ahead of those I love.

But I miss him.

Maybe just hanging out with him wouldn't be such a terrible idea. We could be friends?

No, no. I know that isn't true. There's no such thing as just being Kas's friend. Not for me.

So, I finally respond.

Nothing's changed.

Chapter Twelve

Aiyana

Monday, November 27, 2023

The distinct sound of Rose's kitten heels clicking against the linoleum floor tells me that she's approaching my workstation.

"Hey, Aiyana,"—she smiles at me brightly—"could we do lunch together when you're done in here?"

I fight the wide-eyed expression that's trying to make its way onto my face. "Yeah, that'd be great. Just give me five minutes to wrap up in here."

Why would she want to have lunch with me?

I finish up what I'm working on, wash my hands, and head over to my cubicle to grab my purse and cell phone before heading over to her desk, where I find her already waiting for me.

Her pastel-pink hair is down to her shoulders with a soft wave in it, and it contrasts her black dress and matching heels. "Ready to go?" I ask her, and she makes her way around the desk.

"Yep, mind if we go to that little café across the street?" she asks me.

I eye her questioningly. "The one with the incredible calamari?" The only calamari better than the one at Giovanni's is the one Kas used to make me.

"God, yes! That one," she says with a laugh. "I'm glad I'm not the only one who loves it. Okay, it's settled; we'll go there."

We head across the street and make pleasantries, asking about how our Thanksgivings went last week. She spent hers with Alessandro's family, and I spent mine with my parents while Kat and Kas had dinner at this inn they've been going to every year for their Thanksgiving buffet.

We take our seats and order the calamari and a couple of salads before Rose turns her attention fully on me, her eyes glittering with mischief.

"I'm sure you're wondering what your boss is doing asking you to lunch," she says with a chuckle, not giving me time to answer, "and I promise, I'm not usually one to meddle." My eyes go wide with worry. Meddle in *what?*

"Oh, relax, nothing about you. It's just that my brother-in-law won't shut up about your friend Kat, and I'm just wondering if she has any interest in him too. Because if she doesn't, I'd like to steer him in the direction of leaving her be so he doesn't get hurt." My shoulders relax, and I release an involuntary sigh the moment I realize where this conversation is headed. She isn't trying to meddle in *my* life. She wants to make sure her brother-in-law doesn't get hurt. Now, *that* is a conversation I'm willing to have. Because frankly, Kat needs to pull her head out of her very perky ass and put us *all* out of our misery. At the very least, those two need to bone.

Opting for the more PG version of my thoughts, I tell Rose, "Kat *does* like him and wants to date him, but she apparently has some reasoning as to why she thinks she can't." God, that sounds fucking familiar, except I really do have a reason. So far, Kat hasn't been able to provide any logical explanation for why the gentle giant across the hall shouldn't be allowed to make a mess of her body and tell her sweet nothings before bed. "I see how they are together, and I think with a little nudge from me and Kas, she might finally let herself get involved with him. I don't think there needs to be a hard stop from Ale. He should just give her some time to process her feelings. Truthfully, Kat hasn't been in any very serious relationships because she's always been preoccupied with school, and if it wasn't school, it was work. I think she needs to come to terms with how quickly her feelings are growing for Alessandro."

She nods, assessing me and digesting my words before finally answering. "Agreed. Thanks for that," she says, almost dismissively, as if that was all she needed to hear to feel adequately appeased. "My wife, Charlie, begged me to ask you about it. I'm sorry if I've made you uncomfortable at all," she tells me with sincerity in her voice.

I shake my head. "Not at all. I prefer to meddle in other people's love lives than my own," I joke.

She leans back in her chair, relaxing. "I can't say I disagree." She gives me a small smirk.

We finish lunch, and I head back to work.

***

Maybe I should text Kas and see if he can give Kat the nudge she needs to give Alessandro a shot. I mean, didn't she say her biggest concern was causing issues between Kas and Ale?

Hey

Kas

Hello gorgeous.

Could you talk to Kat about Alessandro? She has it in her head that you wouldn't be cool with them dating.

Kas

Sounds oddly familiar, doesn't it?

Kas

But yes, I'll call her tonight.

Thanks Kass.

Kas

That's not a very clever way of calling me an ass...

Kas

Not very nice of you either.

When have you ever known me to be "very nice"???

Kas

I can recall one summer where you were on your knees... praising me with compliments...

Heat rushes through my body, a jolt of electricity heading straight to my clit at the memory. I know *exactly* what summer he's referring to, and he knows it. *Fucker.*

No idea what you're talking about.

Kas

Can you be honest with me for just one second Aiyana?

Why does he want to talk about that summer so badly? As his next message comes through at that thought, I quickly realize he's most definitely *not* talking about *that* summer after all.

Kas

Have you missed me? At all? Even just a little bit?

God, fine. This man just won't let up, and frankly, I'm done denying it, even if nothing can come of the admission. Besides, he'll know I'm lying if I try to say otherwise anyway.

Yes.

Kas

Good.

Kas

Me too.

Kas

Every day.

Kas

Can we please at least be friends? We can just text each other about our day?

He sounds as desperate as I *feel* to be back in his life. And now that we're no longer living on opposite ends of the country? I don't think I can keep avoiding him.

Fine. How was your day?

Kas

Fuck yes!

His excitement at a simple response from me does funny things to my insides.

Kas

Sooo much better now.

Kas

This gorgeous woman I've been obsessed with since middle school finally decided we could be friends. How about you?

I roll my eyes at that text despite the flurry of butterflies fluttering around in my gut. And just like that, Kas has reminded me just how easy it is to get addicted to him.

Pretty good. Got to talk to this loser from middle school that I missed and my boss took me out to my favorite calamari spot.

Kas

Giovanni's Cafe?

Kas

It's by your new job, isn't it?

Yeah, you remembered?

Kas

Aiyana... I got you calamari from that place twice a week in undergrad and tossed it in the air fryer two mins before feeding it to you so you wouldn't know lol of course I remember.

My mouth goes dry with the emotions swarming me. I can already tell what a horrendous idea this was. I don't know how the hell I'm going to keep him at arm's length.

I shake the feelings off. I can't keep pushing and pulling with him. I already agreed to be friends. There's no backing out now, so I've just got to be the adult here. Or try to be anyway. Because if this goes sideways, it won't just be me that pays in the end.

OH

MY

GAWD

You dick!!!

You've had me craving your damn calamari thinking I'd never have it again for FIVE YEARS!

Kas

Give me a half hour to place an order and grab my air fryer and I'll be right over with it.

No! You've ruined the illusion. Besides, it's getting late. I have to call my dad. We'll talk tomorrow.

Night Kas.

Kas

Goodnight my little viper <3

That fucking nickname. It unravels my already fraying edges every time he says it.

***

As soon as I get out of the shower, I unplug my phone from the charger and search for my dad's contact info, pressing dial.

It rings only once before his melodious voice trickles in over the line. "How's my favorite daughter doing? Are you enjoying your new job?"

"Hi, *Edoda*. I'm your favorite because I'm your *only* daughter, and my job hasn't changed since I saw you on Thanksgiving." I laugh, going through the same song and dance as usual.

"Ah yes, thanks for reminding me." He chuckles. "You know, I was thinking..." he tells me, trailing off in thought.

"Oh no, you? Thinking? That's never good!" I joke with him, though he has a penchant for getting us *both* into trouble with his ideas.

"I've been feeling much better lately. Maybe we can go to one of the Scarlets' games together soon? You think Kas could get us tickets?" Anything my father wants, he can have. No request is too big because I'll figure out a way to get it for him for every sacrifice he's made for me.

"Of course. I don't think that should be too much trouble. When do you wanna go?"

"How about the game on Monday? There's less traffic, and they'll be playing that team from Vermont we hate so much." He snorts before letting out a series of coughs that make my chest strain with worry.

I rush to answer him. "Of course, next Monday sounds perfect."

"I look forward to it. Gotta go to bed, though, my sweet child. Your mom is scowling at me." I hear her murmur something snarky at him before she grabs the phone to tell me goodnight.

"Goodnight, *Edoda*, *Etsi*. I love you both."

As soon as we end the call, I consider texting Kas about the tickets, but it's late, and I need a reprieve between conversations with him.

Chapter Thirteen

Kassian

Tuesday, November 28, 2023

The sound of a shrieking rooster drags me from my dream, and I can't say I'm not disappointed as hell at the intrusion. Like most nights, I dreamed of Aiyana curled up in my arms. I just hope that someday soon, I'll be able to make that a reality again.

I grapple for my cell, silencing the alarm. A message from Aiyana is splayed across the screen, and my heart warms in my chest at the sight.

Little Viper

Can you get dad and me tickets for your game next Monday?

Sure, does he want box seats or close to the ice?

Little Viper

Do you forget who you're talking about?

Little Viper

The closer to the action, the better. He wouldn't feel right in a box seat anyway.

Hah, you're right. Two tickets coming right up. Think Kat will want to go or is this just a you and dad thing?

Little Viper

Just us this time. Thanks Kas.

Anything for you.

And I mean it. I'd do *anything* for her.

Though I also love her dad. I haven't gotten to see him this week, and I'm sure if Aiyana knew I went to see her parents each week since she's been gone, she'd lose her mind with guilt. That's why it's just our little secret. He knows how much she'd worry if she thought he needed my help. I'm not sure if he even did, but I'd like to think I was able to help him and Zuni, Aiyana's mom.

They've been better parents to me than my real parents ever were, and I'll be forever grateful to them for that kindness alone.

Chapter Fourteen

Aiyana

Wednesday, November 29, 2023

Kas

Good morning, gorgeous.

Kas

Sleep well?

This isn't part of the rules Kas. No good morning texts.

Kas

I don't remember any rules…

Kas

Was your lawyer supposed to drop off paperwork before we started being friends again?

Kas

I must've just missed her. Let her know she can try again later. I'd be happy to sign this friendly agreement.

You think you're cute, but you're not.

Kas

I'm certifiably adorable.

First rule, no good morning texts.

Kas

Okay, I'll text later for a good night text then.

I swear, with the amount that I roll my eyes at his messages, you'd think they'd get stuck like that. And now, I don't even have the energy to argue with him.

Chapter Fifteen

Kassian

Thursday, November 30, 2023

How was your day?

Little Viper

Good, same as yesterday. Oh and I think Kat's getting close to giving in…

Interesting… Can the same be said about you? ;)

Little Viper

Not a chance.

All right, I'll keep waiting.

Little Viper

Don't hold your breath.

Little Viper

You'll die of oxygen deprivation…

Nah, I'd pass out and my body would wake me up first. But I'm glad you'd be worried!

Little Viper

God, goodnight Kassian.

Goodnight my little viper <3

I'm definitely wearing her down.

Chapter Sixteen

Aiyana

Friday, December 1, 2023

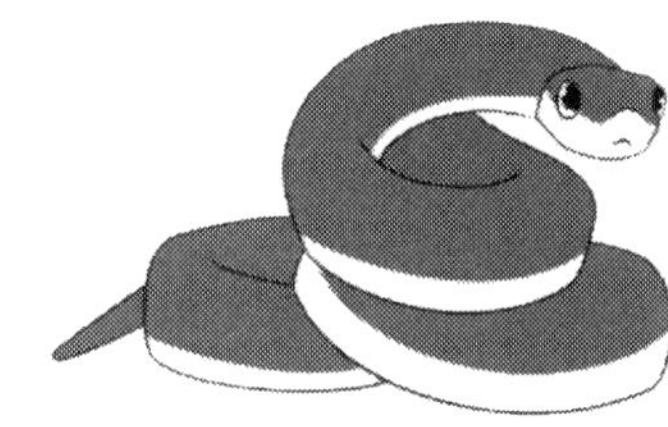

Good luck tonight, don't fuck up. I want to see my favorite team get that damn cup this year, Kas.

Kas

Your favorite team, or your favorite player???

I'm rolling my eyes at you right now.

Kas

I know you are…

Kas

Anything for you though…

Kas

What do I get if we win?

Oh, I don't fucking know Kas…

The satisfaction of winning?????? Isn't that what you're SUPPOSED to do? I'm pretty sure that's your job…

Kas

No kiss then?

No.

Kas

A date then?

You're a child.

I think it over, considering my options. I could continue to say no and let all of our conversations remain in texts… or I could agree to hang out, just as friends though.

It's tempting.

Fine. You make sure you win by at least two points and you can buy me dinner next week. Not as a date. Just you and me watching TV and eating the calamari that you promised me.

Apparently *too* tempting.

Kas

Deal.

Kas

Don't you worry baby, we'll win.

I'm not your baby.

Kas

You're no fun.

Never claimed to be. Now go win the damn game Kassian.

Kas

Ay, ay captain!

What the hell am I going to do with this man?

Chapter Seventeen

Kassian

Saturday, December 2, 2023

I have no fucking clue how we managed that, but we won. By *three* points, and I get to go on a date with Aiyana!

A date that isn't a date, but I'll take what I can get at this point.

God, she's infuriating.

I can't wait to figure out what the *real* reason she claims she doesn't want to date me is so I can fix it.

We won.

Little Viper

I saw.

Dinner tonight?

Little Viper

I'm busy.

Okay, tomorrow?

Little Viper

Still busy.

Monday?

Little Viper

I'll be at your hockey game with my dad… you forget?

Good point, when works?

Little Viper

I'll let you know.

I'll be waiting…

Chapter Eighteen

Aiyana

Monday, December 4, 2023

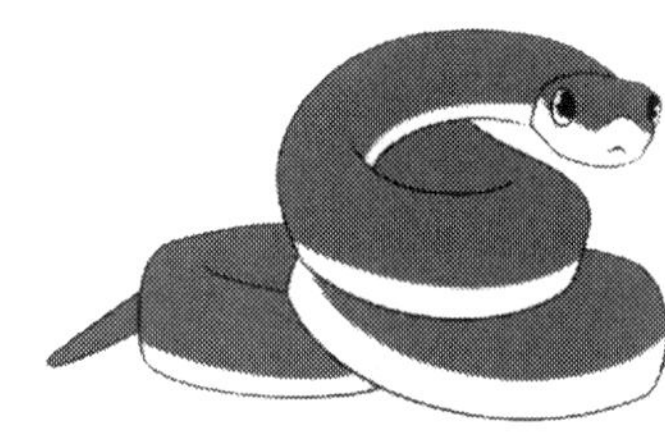

"Oh my gosh! That was incredible! I'd forgotten how great it feels to be this close to the ice." My dad is beaming over at me, the joy on his face melting the cold outer edges of my heart.

"It *was* incredible." I smile at him. "I'm glad you could come, *Edoda*."

"Me too. You think Kas has time for his favorite old guy?" he asks, his words filled with hope.

"I'm sure, and we can wait in the tunnel for him to get out." He hops up immediately, hurrying down there, knowing the way better than anyone.

We chat about our plans for the holidays as we wait for the team to come out. Apparently, my parents are going on a cruise for the holidays instead of hosting at our family home like usual. I'm bummed out because I was looking forward to being back for it this year, but I do my best to hide the disappointment on my face. My parents deserve to enjoy their time together. You never know when it'll be your last day with a person, and Dad's health isn't getting any better.

We both redirect our gazes toward the locker room doors as the team starts to pile through, and as soon as Kas spots us, he comes barreling toward us. Instead of stopping to hug me first, his arms snake around my dad, lifting him off his feet in one of Kas's signature bear hugs. I watch as he expertly avoids knocking over his oxygen tank before placing him back on his feet.

"Mr. Kaan, how've you been?" he asks before looking over at me, a twinkle in his eyes that lights me up inside.

My dad pats him firmly on the back, smiling from ear to ear. "You haven't called me Mr. Kaan in years, Kas. Don't get formal with me now."

They go back and forth with one another until the tunnel is nearly cleared out, and Kas offers to walk us to my cherry-red pickup truck. I love that old thing.

When we get to the parking lot, Kas helps me set Dad's oxygen tank inside the seat before hoisting him up and walking me around to the driver's side. Before I can open the door, he pulls me into a hug that has me melting against him, the smell of soap and leather mingling on his skin.

"Goodnight, my little viper," he mumbles into my hair before releasing me. Even I can admit to myself that it was over too soon. His hugs are the best I've ever gotten.

"Goodnight, Kas," I whisper as he walks away, unsure if he even hears me.

***

After dropping Dad off, heading home to shower, and climbing into bed, sleep evades me.

Memories of Kas and I flood my brain—us as kids, meeting for the first time, my intense crush on him throughout middle school. The love notes we'd pass back and forth in high school, sneaking around under the bleachers and in our backyards during our senior year of high school. Spending all of our free time when Kat wasn't around in undergrad together.

My heart aches with longing for that.

I do owe him that dinner...

I pull out my phone and send him a text before I can reconsider.

Dinner after your game on Friday?

And thanks for tonight. Dad really enjoyed himself and he loves getting to see you.

Kas

Friday sounds great!

Kas

Anytime, baby. He's my favorite guy!

Kas

Goodnight my little viper <3

Just this once, I'll ignore his *baby* comment.

Goodnight Kas.

Chapter Nineteen

Aiyana

Thursday, December 7, 2023

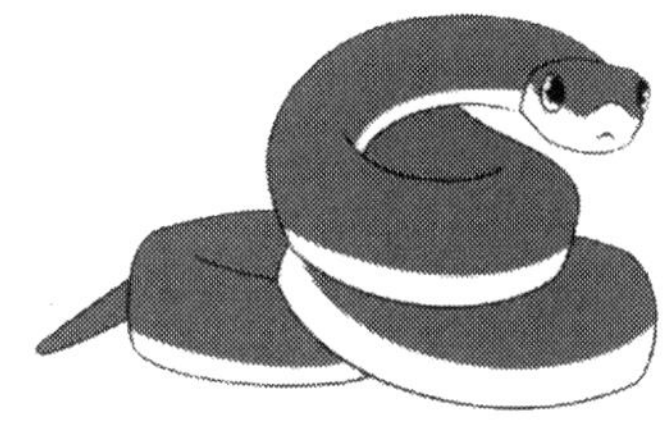

I can't say I'm unaware that this could blow up in my face because I'm *fully* aware, but tomorrow, when Kat's distracted, sounds like the best possible time to get this over with.

Besides, now that I've made Kas a promise, there's not a chance in hell he'd let me back out.

Your sister just told me she has a date tomorrow night at Rocco's.

Kas

Dinner at my place then? I don't want to crash her date, especially if she takes him home… gross!

Your place is good. No funny business though Kas.

Kas

Me? Funny business? I would never.

Goodnight Kassian.

Kas

Goodnight my little viper <3

I can't believe I'm agreeing to go to his place. Especially with no buffer. *I'm so fucked.*

Chapter Twenty

Kassian

Friday, December 8, 2023

I'm practically trembling with excitement. We're on our way to winning the Stanley Cup, and with another win under our belt tonight, we're getting closer to securing our spot at the top. No losses yet isn't too shabby. And to top it off, I get to have Aiyana all to myself tonight, which is arguably the most exciting part.

I called Giovanni's this morning and placed an order for pickup right after the game, and as soon as Aiyana texted that she was coming over, I placed an overnight order for an air fryer to my apartment.

I might not be able to win her over with my charm, but surely my calamari should work.

God, I'm just glad I had the time to clean up my apartment before heading to the game tonight.

***

I've picked up the calamari from Giovanni's, as well as a bunch of other dishes I know she loves, and I'm hightailing it back to my place before she gets there because I *know* she'll leave if she gets there before I do.

As I pull in, I see her beat-up old pickup truck parked outside of my building.

Shit.

My tires shriek across the pavement as I stop beside the valet, jumping out and tossing him the keys with some cash.

"Thanks!" I shout over my shoulder at him as I sprint to the elevator. My arms are full, and if it weren't for the adrenaline rushing through my veins, my earlier exhaustion would probably be dragging me down by now.

I click the button for the penthouse, enter my code, and send up a silent prayer that she didn't have any issues getting in. I told the front desk to send her up if she did get here before me. Hell, I told them to send her up absolutely any time she wants.

To be clear, I'm hoping after tonight, that'll be all the time.

I'm nearly out of breath, and my chest is heaving as I try to regain my composure, and when the doors slide open, Aiyana is standing there, in my living room. Wearing *my* jersey.

Fucking hell.

I give her a relaxed smirk; at least, I hope it looks relaxed because I'm the furthest thing from it. "Hey, little viper, you look good in my jersey," I tell her with a wink.

Her eyes swing over to the boxed-up air fryer that arrived just before I had to leave the house.

"You got an air fryer." She says it flatly, her brows pinched together.

"Well, yeah. How else was I supposed to make my famous calamari?" That gets a giggle out of her, and it's like seeing heaven, or maybe tasting a burger for the first time. It's so damn good; my entire body feels intoxicated with the sound.

"I still can't believe I never noticed that you were literally buying fucking carryout all that time." She shakes her head, smiling down at her feet, and a weight lifts off my shoulders. I was worried this would be awkward, but as it seems, when it's right, it's right. And Aiyana is so fucking right for me; it's almost laughable that she can't seem to see that.

"Give me a tour of the place, Kas," she tells me, smiling with mischief.

As much as I want to figure out what she has planned, I also recognize that I need a minute to calm my frantic heart rate. "Okay, just give me one second to set up this air fryer."

Chapter Twenty-One

Aiyana

Kas looks absolutely delicious in the charcoal-gray suit he put on after his game, and as much as I know I'd love what's underneath even more, it's good to have those extra layers between us.

"There isn't much to see—my place has fewer rooms than yours because it's just me here, but it's got more space."

He leads me to the living room, where there's a massive black leather sectional with faux fur throw blankets in varying shades of gray, and as is the theme for these penthouses, huge floor-to-ceiling walls of windows give us a gorgeous view of the skyline. The biggest difference is that his view is three times the size of ours. He's also got a couple of small silver side tables next to the couch, a matching coffee table, and an area rug.

Aside from a few pieces of furniture and a wall-mounted TV, the room is pretty bare, but the deeper I travel into the room, the more nervous I get.

To the side of the TV is a collage of framed photos. More than half of which contain pictures of me. My skin feels tingly, and anxiety begins pooling in the pit of my stomach. Nothing like a little humor to ease the awkward air surrounding us. "Dang, Kas, are you stalking me or something? This looks like a shrine."

He's watching, his hooded eyes locked on me, taking in my every breath, assessing me. A small smile turns his lips. "I'd pray to you any day, little viper."

I redirect my attention to the kitchen, stalking out of the room, hoping that he'll follow, and thankfully, he does.

"The only other space here is my room, and it's up the stairs." I follow him up the metal winding staircase to the loft-style bedroom. It's very him, much warmer than the living room.

He has photos lining the walls and a large bed in the center of the room on a platform base that I'd recognize anywhere. He built that with my dad in undergrad. Spent an entire summer working on it, staining it that deep mahogany brown, the color of my eyes, he used to tell me.

I take in the smattering of colors, mostly dark, like black and dark wood.

I turn to head back down to the kitchen, but he catches my chin, tilting it up between his forefinger and thumb. He smiles down at me, and those hazel eyes remind me of the lakes we used to risk our lives to swim in each year. "I've missed you, little viper," he tells me in a hushed tone, almost a whisper.

I cast my eyes downward, averting his searing gaze. *I can't breathe when he looks at me like that.*

He releases my chin as if nothing had happened at all, and we head downstairs toward the kitchen, where he warms up all of my favorite dishes, including the calamari.

He works in silence, neither of us speaking as we watch each other, stealing a glance here and there. The silence is comfortable, no longer awkward and tense.

When the food is warmed up, he makes us each a plate and leads me to the couch.

Kas plops down, placing the plates on the coffee table, and I sit down on the other end of the couch, as far away from him as possible. I can't trust myself around him.

He gets up, grabs a silver-gray blanket off the back of the couch, and lays it over my legs before handing me my plate and setting my water on the table next to me.

When I'm comfortable, he takes his seat again, relaxing into the dark cushions of the leather couch before seemingly deciding to abandon any inhibitions he may have been holding onto. "Alright, baby, tell me why you supposedly can't be with me."

I'd say I'm fucking shocked, but I'm not. Despite that, my eyes are bugging out of my head. Meanwhile, he just managed to say that with a straight face. I had no delusions about where this night was headed, but I'd at least thought we could make it through our meal before he started hounding me for answers to questions he doesn't really want the answer to.

"Jumping right in, huh?" I ask, attempting to deflect. He doesn't warrant that with a response, simply digging into his food and waiting for the real answer. I huff, annoyance lacing my words. "I already told you, Kas. It would be awkward with Kat, and even if she would be fine with it, what happens if and when we break up?" The words spewing out of my mouth feel like venom on my tongue. If he had me, he'd never let me go, just like a boa constrictor.

He's shaking his head at me slowly as he chews, working his jaw in a way that has my eyes snagging on his stubble, swallowing the bite of food as my gaze trails down his neck, watching his Adam's apple bob.

"If I had you, I'd beg you to marry me, and you know it. I've known it since we were fourteen." I'm nauseous. There's something about knowing something in theory and actually hearing it in reality that has the power to turn everything on its head. The thought of never getting our fairy-tale ending has wrecked my dreams every night for years now.

I finally take a bite of food, starting with the calamari, and the moment it hits my tongue, a wave of nostalgia hits me as the memories of all the times he made it for me in undergrad come flooding in. A moan slips past my lips, and a smirk lights his face.

"Just give me a chance, and I could have you moaning like that every day, little viper." He's grinning at me, but his gaze is heated, and it gives me an idea.

A really, really bad one, but *what the fuck*. I'm going to be hurting my own damn feelings till the end of time anyway, and when he finally moves on and marries someone else, someone more deserving than me, at least I'll have these memories to carry or at least *drag* me along.

I try to keep my voice light and cheerful, but I feel anything but. "What if I let you?" His dark brows shoot up his forehead, jaw slack before I continue. "Make me moan, that is." His face takes on a strange scowl, something between intrigue and disappointment.

He takes a moment to mull it over before answering. "Like a friends-with-benefits situation?"

A nod is my only response.

"Okay." My eyes light up. Could this really happen? "But,"—and there's that dread seeping in again—"no one else gets to have you. You're mine and only mine."

"Well, obviously, Kas." I roll my eyes at him. "I'm so busy with work that I barely have time for one fuck buddy"—he cringes at the name, but I forge on—"let alone multiple."

With a quick nod, as if a very important decision has just been made, he says, "Good, same goes for me obviously. You should know, though, I'm absolutely going to use this as a way to win you back." His voice is full of hope. "Now eat up, little viper. You're gonna need your energy." He smirks, digging into his food, and I can't help the twinge of excitement that flows through me.

Chapter Twenty-Two

Aiyana

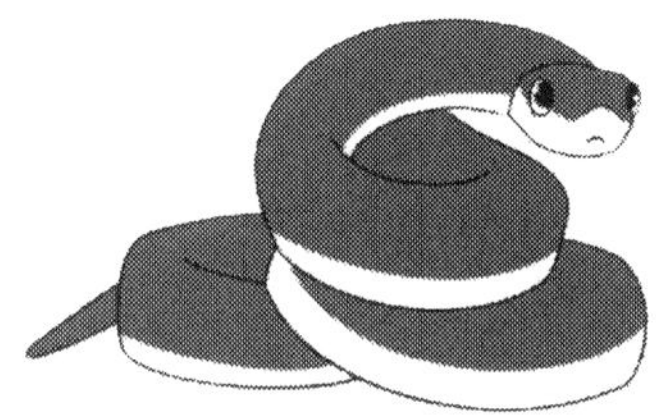

We finish eating dinner, and I check my phone, noticing that Kat just texted. "Sounds like things aren't going well on Kat's date; she's gonna head home soon," I call over to Kas from where he's standing, cleaning up the kitchen.

He looks over his shoulder at me, worry pulling at his eyebrows. "Does she need a ride home?" he asks, *always the doting brother.*

Shaking my head, I tell him, "No, she said she's gonna take a cab home." He nods and puts the last plate in the drying rack before wiping his hands on a dishcloth and stalking toward me.

My pulse is skyrocketing, and I can hear my heartbeat in my ears; it's getting louder the closer he gets. His eyes are dark and dangerous as he extends his hand to me. "Come upstairs with me?"

My body has a mind of its own as I take his hand in mine and nearly sprint up the stairs with him.

The moment our feet hit the top of the stairs, Kas twirls me around so my back is flush with his chest, and his hands are *everywhere*. His nose is gliding up the side of my neck as he breathes me in, his hands keeping me close, touching and kneading my heated flesh. I feel like I'm on fire, being flayed open with his every caress, and we aren't even naked yet.

"God, you always smell so good," he groans into my ear, nipping on the sensitive skin of my throat and winding his fingers in my hair, pulling my head back to give him better access.

I'm a live wire, my body strung so tightly that I can't get myself to move. All of my senses are flooded, overwhelmed by Kas.

We're really doing this.

"How do you want it tonight?" he asks me, his voice husky as his hands stop on my hips, holding my ass to his erection and sending a jolt of pleasure straight to my clit. The familiarity of this, of him... of *us,* leaves my stomach in knots at the twinge of sadness that spirals through me. I'm filled with so many conflicting emotions, and yet, every thought in my mind surrounds Kas in one form or another.

He nips my neck, drawing me back into the moment, and I'm hit with the realization that he just asked me a question. I don't even remember what it was, so I answer in a lust-induced haze with a noncommittal, "Huh?" I sound exactly as dazed as I feel.

I lose all sense of time and place when I'm with Kas. *That's how it's always been.*

He grips my hair harder, a tremble racing through my body. "I asked," he says, voice rough, "how you want me to fuck that sweet little cunt of yours. Your pick, little viper." He bites down above my collarbone, sucking on the tender skin immediately after.

"Dealer's choice," I whimper. For once, I feel unable to make a decision myself. When it comes to Kas, I'll take it however he wants to give it. Sex with him has always been incredible, even when we were inexperienced twenty-year-olds with absolutely no idea what we were doing. And no man, or woman for that matter, has ever compared.

He lets out a dark chuckle, sliding his hands up my spine before pushing me to my knees. I fall, catching myself with my hands, but *I know exactly what he's decided on.*

Chapter Twenty-Three

Kassian

Saturday, December 9, 2023

I almost feel bad, having pushed her a little harder than I intended, but when her bottom lip juts forward as she crawls around to face me, eyes full of desire, I know she doesn't mind one bit.

"There she is," I taunt. "There's my little viper. You gonna be a good girl and choke on my dick like you used to?" My body is already humming with need. I don't know how the fuck I'm planning on lasting with her finally in front of me, wanton and practically begging for me.

Heat simmers behind her eyes as she undoes my pants and pulls them down my thighs along with my briefs. My cock juts out, lightly smacking her cheek, and she giggles, the sound making me feel light as a feather.

Aiyana wraps her hand around the base, giving me a tug that elicits a groan from deep in my chest. Her smooth palm wrapped around my shaft feels like silk, and I could die happily in this moment, *right here.*

Her other hand moves to gently cup my balls as she directs the head into her mouth, teasing and tasting, her tongue flicking the overly aroused skin at the underside of my dick.

It feels so fucking good. My ass clenches as blood rushes to my engorged length, and tingles zip up my spine as I get lost in the sensation. She increases her pace, sucking me more deeply, her head bobbing as I thread my fingers through her dark strands, my periphery going black, and I'm seeing stars.

My dick twitches in her mouth, and she's slobbering all over me, drool spilling out of the sides of her mouth. I'm eager for release. Hell, watching Aiyana suck down every drop of my cum is something I'd gladly watch every day, but I love taunting her. "The only time you ever did listen to me was when my cock was in your mouth, huh?" She lets out a moan, dropping the hand that was cupping me and snaking it down to her core, rubbing herself through the soft material of her leggings.

I tsk at her, jerking her head back abruptly, and watch as she wipes the saliva off her mouth. "That's not part of our deal. You made me wait *years* before I could have you like this again; that sweet cunt is all mine tonight." Her eyes flash with a wicked expression, but she gives in, standing as I tug her to her feet.

"Undress," I instruct her, already working to tug off the rest of my clothing. She does as she's told, and I think I might be addicted to this submissive side of her. Hell, who the fuck am I kidding? *I'm addicted to every side of her.*

Holy fuck, she looks even more incredible than the last time I saw her like this. I can't help but prowl toward her, gripping her ass cheeks and pulling her up my body. Her lithe, tan legs wrap around my waist as I walk her backward before dumping her body into the center of the bed.

Chapter Twenty-Four

Aiyana

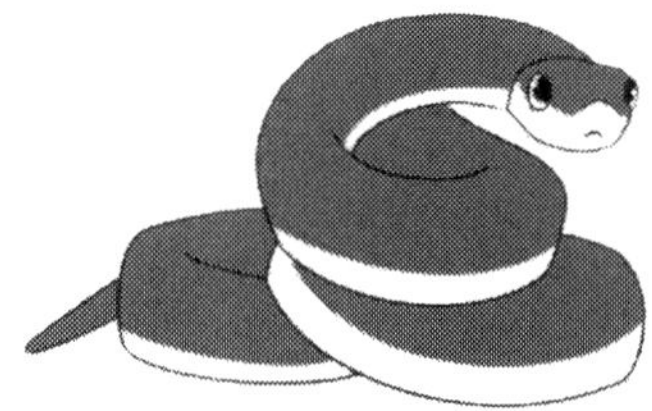

I'm fighting to control my breathing, my heart racing so fast I think it might burst. Kas slides himself down my body, lifting my leg, fingers wrapped around my ankle as he kisses up the inside of my calf, splaying me open for him. My body is trembling under him, and I don't know what's worse—him stopping or never letting go of this hold he has on me.

When he gets to the apex of my thighs, he turns his head, rubbing his stubble along the skin, breathing me in as his eyes fill with hunger. He swipes a finger through my slickness, holding it up to my mouth, and says, "Suck, little viper."

For what feels like the first time in my life, I do as I'm told, and the salty flavor of my arousal sends a shudder through me.

Kas groans, eyes cast downward toward my dripping heat. He trails his hand back down, tugging on my nipples. I whimper, and he takes it as his cue to absolutely ravish my body.

His tongue flattens against me, swiping through the wetness and making my toes curl with need. I twine my fingers in his hair, urging him on, and he laughs. *Laughs.*

"So goddamn greedy," he chastises before he continues his onslaught, my core tightening, and the walls of my pussy spasm.

"More," I moan. "I need more."

Finally, he inserts two fingers, curling them toward my G-spot as he pumps them in and out of me at a rhythmic pace, flicking and sucking his tongue over my clit, his face buried between my thighs.

My eyes are practically rolling in my head, my back arching as my core clenches, heat unfurling within me. Kas urges me on as I reach the precipice, my body alight, fire searing through me while I ride his fingers.

It takes a moment for the fog to clear, but when I look down, Kas removes his fingers, sucking them gingerly into his mouth and moaning with pleasure. "Fuck baby, I've missed every piece of you." He drags his finger through my overly sensitive folds, sucking the remains of my orgasm from his finger again. "But especially this."

My eyes are wide at his candidness, and a jolt of desire zaps through me again. I've missed him too, though I know I can't say that. I don't deserve to tell him how badly I've needed him when it's my fault that we can't be together in the first place.

"Hey, where'd you go?" he asks me, eyes soft, and clearly, he's aware that my mind was elsewhere for a moment.

I smile back. "Nowhere, just here with you." I pull him down on top of me so his weight crushes me, and he works my arms over my head, securing my wrists so I'm unable to take control.

He nips a trail of small bites up my neck and jaw, placing a gentle kiss on my temple before moving onto my lips. His lips are soft and gentle as he pecks at the edges of my mouth before deepening the kiss. Kas swipes his tongue along my lower lip, and when I reciprocate, he pulls my lip into his mouth, sucking and biting down hard enough to draw blood.

He laps it up, tilting his head into me, and his loose, dark waves cascade over his forehead, and I find myself lost in him... *again.* His tongue sweeps into my mouth, and I moan, struggling to loosen his grip on my wrists so I can scrape my hands down his back.

He pulls away from me, just far enough so he's able to tsk at me, shaking his head before going back to work, lavishing me, *body and soul.*

He's devouring me in every sense of the word. Pulling, sucking, and nipping at my tongue and lips, all while grinding his erection into my thigh, just an inch over from where I need him most.

Kas groans. Pulling back and gripping the base of his cock, he slides it through my wetness, pressing firmly on my clit before backing off to ask me, "Can I fill this pretty pussy with my cum, or do I need a condom? I tested negative at my last physical."

I eagerly nod. "I did too, and I have an IUD. Fill me," I tell him, moaning.

He smirks and pushes in, not going slow but sinking right into me. My walls spasm around him, stretching as he fills me with every delicious inch of his thick length.

"Oh fuck," he groans, his forehead pressed to mine as he thrusts into me relentlessly. I claw my nails up his back, holding onto him as he takes me, seemingly punishing me for the last few years spent without him.

"God," I moan. His dick curves slightly upward, reaching a part of me no one else ever has. I lean into him, my teeth digging into his shoulder, and he pulls my hips closer to him, slamming into me.

My muscles are coiling tightly, heat searing through me as my pleasure builds. My clit is aching for attention, so I flatten out on the mattress and reach between us, drawing lazy circles against it.

He smirks down at me, grabbing my hand. He pulls it to his mouth, sucking in long draws as he continues his steady pace. "I'm in control tonight, little viper. This pussy is mine. You'd do well to remember that, yeah?" he asks me, and a whine slips past my lips.

He pulls out of me abruptly and slides off the bed, but before I can protest, he reaches down to grab his pants, pulling his belt from the loops. Kas looks at me, eyes gleaming wickedly, and reveals a grin that sends a tremble of equal parts desire and fear down my spine.

He cracks the belt, a sharp sound reverberating off the walls as he walks to the end of the bed. Leaning over, he grabs my hips and pulls me to the edge before flipping me over onto my stomach. Reaching for my arms, he draws my wrists together behind me, using his belt to bind them tightly before he finally releases me. He rakes a hand between my thighs and parts me, trailing his warm fingers along my sensitive inner thighs before sinking them into me.

He surprises me—pulling his fingers out, he grips my thighs, widening my stance and opening me to almost an uncomfortably exposed position before he smacks my pussy with the same force as he would my ass cheek. The sting goes straight to my clit, and he rubs it away quickly before slapping my swollen pussy lips one more time.

"Such a pretty cunt. I could stay here all day," he tells me, his voice rough.

I haven't had time to recover yet as I feel him enter me, and pleasure jolts through me again.

Kas's lips part on a sharp inhale, and I feel him harden even further inside me.

I'm moaning, unable to contain the sounds as he buries himself into me, his leather belt digging into my wrists with every thrust, and the pain nearly undoes me, but I'm hanging on, refusing to come until he does. I'm just afraid he's doing the same.

I work to meet his thrusts, even in my precarious position, my abs on fire with the movement. I need to come so badly, but I won't give in.

He smacks the side of my ass. "Always trying to take control, little viper; you think I don't see what you're doing?" he asks, his voice sounding smooth like smoke. He leans further into me, hand wrapping around my throat as he pulls me into his chest. The new angle has me seeing stars, and my walls clamp down on him. "I know your body better than anyone, Aiyana. Come for me, baby." And it undoes me.

The reminder that I'm all his, even when I've tried so hard not to be, absolutely wrecks me.

My pussy walls clench around him, milking him as he slams into me, his body going stiff as his grip on my throat tightens, his lips still hovering over the shell of my ear. "Fuck," he grunts as he fills me with his cum, "such a good girl for me." I ride the wave of euphoria, nearly beaming at his words.

My racing heart begins to calm as does the layer of fog enveloping us in our desires. He releases the belt and gently turns me over. I rest my hands on his shoulders, dragging them down to feel him under my fingertips, finally taking the time to really inspect his body.

Kas is still the sexiest man on the planet, not much could ever change that, but there are some subtle differences about his appearance. Namely, new tattoos.

He has some new ones trailing from his shoulders to his jaw, not covering the front of his neck though.

My eyes scan downward, taking in the smaller tattoos filling in spaces between the older, less crisp ones.

But none of those are what makes my stomach drop to my toes.

I run my palm over the near-black, anatomical heart he has tattooed on his left pectoral, just over his own heart. But it isn't the organ itself etched into his tan skin that turns my world on its axis.

It's the purple-eyed, black viper winding throughout the heart that causes me to suck in a quick inhale of breath.

I can feel his eyes on me, boring into my soul as he awaits my response.

"It's to represent how you, my little viper, have effectively woven yourself into my heart, mind, body, and soul. And I still can't seem to get enough."

I clench my eyes shut, but not quickly enough because a single tear still manages to slip through. I feel the rough pad of his thumb wipe it from my cheek before he wraps me in his warm embrace, maneuvers me under the covers, and tucks me safely to his side.

I knew better. I *always* know better when I make these kinds of decisions based on my own desires instead of the reality of a situation. It's selfish and disgusting, and I'm not sure I'll ever truly recover from the damage I've just caused myself.

But pulling back now will only hurt him more, so I stay, indulging in this fantasy. *Us.*

Chapter Twenty-Five

Kassian

As I start to wake up, I peel my eyelids open, and every emotion from the last several years washes over me in warp speed when I gaze down at Aiyana's sleeping body, pressed snuggly to mine as she drapes herself over my chest. Her inky hair is hanging over her face, her little breaths blowing the strands around, and I can't help but reach over and wipe them out of her face, sinking my fingers into her thick, silky strands.

My chest constricts, knowing that if she were aware of her current position, she'd be hightailing it out of here.

Her fear of commitment has always been an issue for us.

She's the most decisive person I know. When she wants something, she'll fight tooth and nail to have it, but when it comes to us, she's always been difficult to convince.

I don't even think "fear of commitment" is the right phrase because that doesn't seem to be the issue. When we're together, she's always been happy and *sated.*

Growing up, she never hesitated to tell me she loved me, even before we ever started sneaking around. Hell, *she* told me she loved me *first.* Which I've never really gotten over. I'm still just a tad bit salty about that fact.

I wanted to say it first because I think I meant it first.

I'm not sure where she got the idea that we can't be together. Her parents adore me, my sister would be elated to know we're together, and it's not like our desires for our futures are so misaligned that we wouldn't make sense together.

Neither of us has ever wanted children, and with how independent she is, I can't imagine she'd mind me traveling periodically during hockey season.

Besides, I'd give up every goal for her. I recognize how ridiculous that sounds, but she's endgame for me. Everything about her makes my blood fucking sing, and the last five years have only solidified that notion.

I feel her begin to stir on my chest, and as her eyes open, she blinks several times, looking around the room to get her bearings before looking up at me. She gives me a shy smile, and I can't help my reaction to her. I dip my head, pressing a kiss to the crown of her head, and pray like hell that it doesn't send her running for the hills, claiming things are getting too *real.*

To my unbelievable surprise, she doesn't move. Just stays there for a while longer before pressing a kiss to my abdomen and pushing herself up. Her big brown eyes bore into me, and the curtain of dark hair cascades over her shoulder.

"You gonna feed me, or do I have to beg for that too?" she asks with a smirk, my cock saluting her at the thought of her begging me to do anything.[1]

I run my fingers through her hair, gripping it at the base of her skull, and give her a lopsided smirk. "Don't worry, little viper, I'll feed you. You wanna start with my cock?" I raise a brow at her, and she laughs, a full-bodied one that has her head bent backward, eyes squeezed shut, and the bed practically shaking with the force.

She smacks my chest as the sound calms, climbing out of the bed to search for her clothes.

"Real food, Kas. Trust me, you don't want me sucking your dick right now. I'll bite it off." That has me cupping my cock, protecting it from her as we both laugh.

“Good lord, woman!” I all but screech at her between gasps of laughter.

Ignoring me, she starts getting dressed, so I get up, head to the shower, and peer over at her. "Wanna get clean first?" She shakes her head at me, chuckling at my not-so-smooth advances, but she drops her clothes back on the ground and follows me into the shower.

---

1. **Beg – Leon Thomas & Elle Varner**

Chapter Twenty-Six

Aiyana

Sunday, December 10, 2023

It's just before bed when Kas's nightly texts come rolling in. The dread I felt before doesn't follow them, though, and it's a relief.

I know he says he'll use our current arrangement to win me over, but I've made it clear that it won't be happening. He's an adult, and he's choosing to throw caution to the wind. I can't say I'm not at fault if and when he gets hurt because I absolutely am, but I'm also certain he isn't going to be moving on with someone else while I'm even the least bit accessible.

Besides, I'm proud of Kas because he's held off on texting me most of the day, only sending me a few memes here or there.

Kas

So, my sister and Alice got their heads out of their asses…

I know where this is going.

Kas

Why don't you do the same?

Kassian…

We agreed on casual sex.

Kas

YOU agreed on casual sex. There's nothing casual about how fucking wild I am for you.

If you can't handle the rules we've laid out, then we should stop now.

Kas

Fine. I'll be a good boy.

I'll believe it when I see it.

Kas

Speaking of which, I heard you helped Kat plan their first real date… on your birthday?

Kas

So, clearly you're free.

You act as if I don't have any friends aside from Kat…

Kas

You don't.

He's not wrong. I have acquaintances and people I enjoy being around or speaking to, but since moving in with Kat, I never felt the need to branch out. I always just felt at home with her and Kas.

His words don't upset me though. I've never felt I needed anyone else. My parents are the best I could ask for, and Kat and I have been inseparable since the day we met. They're all I need.

Kas

I'll hand over the reins for the evening *insert side eye emoji*

I'm rolling my eyes so hard at you right now.

But sure, you can come over.

Only if you bring dinner though. And it is NOT a date. A girl's gotta eat.

Kas

You'll be eating alright...

I'm done with you. Sushi, pizza, tacos and Thai. Don't fuck it up.

Goodnight Kassian.

Kas

Wouldn't dream of it... Goodnight my little viper <3

Chapter Twenty-Seven

Aiyana

Monday, December 11, 2023

All day long, Kas has been texting me to check in about my birthday.

I've tried getting some actual fucking work done, but between the butterflies flapping around violently in my stomach, feeling more like hornets than anything else, and Kas's incessant texts, I've managed the bare fucking minimum all day.

Kas

We still good for tomorrow?

Yes. For the fifth time.

Kas

Just checking.

I thought you hit puberty already. Stop acting like an angsty teen.

Kas

You're a brat.

See you tomorrow.

Kas

Wait!

Kas

Did you watch the game tonight?

I watch every game.

Kas

I looked good out there, didn't I?

I'm rolling my eyes at you.

Kas

I know.

Kas

Answer the question.

Goodnight Kassian.

Kas

That's alright, I already know the answer ;)

Kas

Goodnight my little viper <3

Chapter Twenty-Eight

Aiyana

Tuesday, December 12, 2023

It's my twenty-eighth birthday, and I'm overflowing with nerves. Not about my birthday. Nothing has changed between yesterday and today, and I'm not afraid of getting old and gray.

Actually, it's quite the opposite. I'm terrified of *not* living a long and fulfilling life. My birthday call with my parents this morning only worked to nestle that fear further into my gut.

But today, that isn't what's got my stomach twisted in knots.

I probably should've thought this through more. Maybe gone to his place instead, but having him come over here gives me an excuse to kick him out, and I need the scapegoat for when my feelings threaten to strangle me tonight.

I pace my room, deciding whether I should cancel, but I hear a light knock at my door before it cracks open, and I see Kat stick her head in. "Hey, happy birthday, gorgeous." She smiles at me.

"Thanks," I tell her. "Come on in."

She takes a seat on my bed, her light-blue shorts contrasting heavily with my dark bedding as she sits with a small box wrapped in pink paper on her lap. "Ready for your present?" she asks me, and I shake my head, laughing at her.

"Always, but you didn't have to get me anything!" I tell her, taking a seat next to her and flicking her on the forehead in the space between her eyebrows. She rolls her eyes at me and pushes the box into my hands.

"Shut up and open it, you miscreant," she says with a chuckle. "Always such a brat."

I smile at that. She's not wrong.

I pull the hot-pink bow off the box and tear the paper, a royal-blue velvet box underneath. I peek up at her from the corner of my eye before lifting the lid, revealing a dainty gold chain with a tiny viper pendant nestled inside. Tears prick my eyes as I toss my arms around her shoulders. "Thank you, Kat, it's perfect," I tell her, my voice threatening to crack.

I end the hug, pulling away to work the small necklace from the box, and she smiles brightly. "Kas actually picked it out."

My eyes widen, but I recover quickly, shaking my head and smiling. "I should've known; you've always been trash at giving gifts," I tease. That's the furthest thing from the truth.

Kat is one of the most thoughtful people I know. She puts a lot of time and thought into every gift she gives, which is why I hate getting her anything. Because I know it'll never be good enough, even though she's loved every last, horrendous fucking gift I've given her.

She smacks my shoulder, getting up to leave the room, but I tug her back to me, dropping her hand the moment she's stopped heading out of the room. "Can I do your hair for your date?"

Her eyes light with excitement. "Yes, please! I'll be right back!" She bounds away, heading to her room. When she gets back, she's got the most stunning emerald-green satin dress on a hanger, and her arms are filled with bobby pins, hair spray, and all sorts of other crap I won't be needing.

"Oh my god, that dress is stunning! You thinking an updo?" I ask her, and she nods. I instruct her to sit and get to work, using a small amount of product to make her smooth hair a little tacky—that way, I'm able to twist it into the perfect bun at the nape of her neck without using bobby pins. I've mastered the art of a beautiful updo, leaving tendrils to frame her face and without a single pin in sight so that at the end of the night, Alessandro can tug on her hair without getting caught in a landmine of pins.

When I'm done, I have her stand, and she takes a look in the long gold full-body mirror. "How? How do you always manage to do that?"

I quirk a brow at her, seeing my own reflection behind her in the mirror. "What? Hair?"

"Not just hair," she says, rolling her eyes as she turns back to face me. "It's like magic. Meanwhile, I could spend an hour on my hair, and it'll look worse than when I started."

"We can't all be good at everything," I tell her with a wink. "Except for me, of course."

"I'm just gonna let that one go," she says as she heads out of my room with her dress in her arms.

Less than thirty minutes later, she's standing in front of me, twirling in the form-fitting dress, her face glowing with the smallest amount of makeup that highlights her honey-colored eyes and high cheekbones.

"You look incredible, Kat," I tell her honestly. My best friend is simply perfection.

In true Kat fashion, she's unable to take a simple compliment without a blush spreading across her cheeks.

"Thanks," she says, casting her eyes downward. "Are you sure you don't want me to stay tonight? We can do whatever you want for your birthday, and Ale and I can just reschedule. I'm sure he wouldn't be upset."

"I'll be fine. I've got my new vibrator, my audio daddies, and food on the way to keep me company. I won't be missing out on anything. Plus, I need to hear if the saying is true..." I trail off, deliberately baiting her so she won't stick to the current line of questioning.

"I know I'm going to regret asking this, but *what* saying?" she says, hands on her hips as if her patience is officially wearing thin with me.

"Big skates, *huge* cock," I tell her, drawing out the word and putting my palms up, separating them by a solid two feet for emphasis.

Her cheeks flame again, and she turns on her heel. "Has anyone ever told you you're a menace?" she calls out over her shoulder, grabbing her bag and heading for the door.

"Only every day of my life, babe," I say, heading back to my room once she slips out the door.

Lying in bed, I question many of the life choices that've gotten me to this very moment.

Mostly, they're bad decisions on my part, but who doesn't love a little chaos? If baby Aiyana weren't such a badass bitch as a tween, I'd never have dragged Kat into my life by her frizzy little ponytail.

The Kat and Aiyana of the past were also late bloomers. And I'm not just talking about our tits.

I guess the complicated part is that without Kas, I couldn't have found Kat. And even if I had, I'm not sure this cosmic pull we have toward each other would've quit until I was in his orbit.

A buzzing sound from my nightstand pulls me out of my reeling thoughts.

And, of course, it's Kas.

Kas

All food items have been secured. On my way. Be there in ten.

Okay.

Ten minutes!? I bolt out of bed, running around my room in search of clothes. What the hell do I wear? Pajamas? Something to cover me up so he won't get so handsy? Do I want to show off for him? Should I dress up?

I stop abruptly, hands gripping the edge of my dresser as I look myself in the face. Staring back at my reflection in the mirror, I say, "This is *just* Kas. Put on what *you* want to wear, and don't worry about him."

With a steadying breath, I pull out a pair of black spandex bike shorts and a matching sports bra. I open the next drawer and grab an oversized Three Days Grace T-shirt I got at a concert with Kas when we were nineteen.[1] It's one of my favorites.

I change into the clothes and head to the bathroom, pulling my hair out of my haphazard bun. I brush my hair before braiding the strands back and out of my face.

Just as I've finished, I hear Kas at the door, knocking lightly before letting himself in.

"Hey, little viper," he calls to me as I head into the kitchen, watching as he hauls an ungodly amount of food onto the counter. "Happy birthday, princess." He smirks, setting the food down and waltzing over to me. He grips my hips in his hands and pulls me in for a crushing kiss that sends sparks of desire zipping down my spine.

I pull back, shaking my head at him, steeling my nerves, and reminding myself that this is *not* a date.

Stepping out of his grasp, I head over to the bags, peeking into each one. My stomach growls, and he chuckles at me. "Go take a seat, and I'll make you a plate."

Heading toward the couch, I call over to him, "You good with watching the New York Monsters game?"

"Yeah, that's Luca's team. I actually have it recording at my place. I wasn't sure what you'd wanna watch," he tells me, piling our plates high in the kitchen.

"Recording? What are you, a hundred?" I ask teasingly.

"Ha ha ha, very funny. We're the same age as of today." He laughs as he picks up the plates, heading toward me, and extends one in front of my face.

I grab the edges of the plate, sitting it in my lap, and I'm giddy with excitement. "Fuck yeah!" I give a little fist pump. I've got a street taco with extra cilantro and onion, white rice with panang curry, drunken noodles with extra tofu and egg, four pieces of a spicy salmon roll, and a slice of cheese pizza with cheese-filled crust on the massive plate. My mouth is watering.

Another reason Kas was always so easy to fall in love with. He never treated me like a dainty, fragile piece of glass. I'm not even five feet tall, but as my parents say, I've got the appetite of a seven-foot linebacker.

Kas looks over at me, smiling as he leans forward to grab the remote and turn the game on.

We eat and bicker, nearly spilling food on the couch and in my lap several times as we get up to cheer every time Luca blocks a shot into his net. I haven't actually met him yet, but Kas has mentioned him once or twice, and he's an incredible goalie. Though the team he plays for is pretty trash. With how close he is to his family, I wonder why he isn't playing for the Scarlets.

As if reading my mind, Kas says, "I wish he could come play for us, but the Scarlets don't want to deal with his bad boy reputation. He's a damn good goalie though. Maybe once he settles down, he can make the switch because his team is trash. He's never gonna go anywhere with them, even if he can block every puck."

"That's a shame. I never did understand why people obsess so much over other people's private lives. Sex is just fun. Who cares what he's doing in the comfort of his own bed as long as it's consensual?" I ask, mostly rhetorically.

"Is sex between us *just* fun, little viper?" Kas smirks at me, setting his now empty plate down on the pecan side table. He reaches over, grabs my empty plate, and tosses it on top of his own before crawling over on top of me, thoughts of the game in front of us officially abandoned.

He slides his hand around to grip the hair at the nape of my neck, pulling my mouth to his in a searing kiss, making my toes curl. His tongue slips into my mouth, teasing and tasting me, and I feel his growing erection pressing against my belly.

I grip the front of his Henley, dragging him into me, fighting for the control I so desperately need, but he runs his hands down my waist and grips my ass, pulling me up and into him as he stands, hauling me off to my room.

He kicks the door closed behind him, and it closes with a loud slam; his lips never leave mine as he nips at my lower lip, sucking me into his mouth. Kas drops me onto the bed, eyes darting to my neck where the tiny viper pendant is now dangling. He wraps his fingers around it, gently rubbing it with his thumb before bending forward and pressing a kiss to it, then releases it. The warm metal rests against my cool skin, and it's like I can feel his fingers there too.

Those gorgeous hazel eyes meet mine as he runs his warm, calloused hands down my arms, sending a tremble through me. He takes my hands in his own, pressing a kiss to each knuckle. I feel any control I had left begin to slip away. I *need* that control. Because without it, I won't live up to my father's expectations of me.

He must feel me slipping away because he grips my chin, tilts my head back, and says, "What do you need tonight, little viper?"

I give him a grin, pushing him back aggressively enough that he wobbles a bit, stepping away from me as I stand. "Strip and get on the bed," I tell him, pointing to the queen-size mattress as I head to the bedroom door to lock it in case Kat gets home early.

By the time I turn around, he's already down to his briefs, working them over his thick, muscular thighs as I approach. "Now lie on your back so I can ride your face while you eat me out like the good boy I know you are."[2] I smirk as his eyes blaze back at me. "It *is* my birthday, after all."

He climbs onto the bed, his head at the foot as he lays there naked and waiting. His thick dick stands fully erect, the curved tip resting slightly on his lower abdominal muscles. The sight of him has me wet and ready. He smirks back at me, watching as I take in every muscle and contour of his immaculate body. "You already know I'm a good boy, for you anyway. I'll eat that pussy like it's my last fucking meal for the rest of our lives if you'll let me."

My cheeks heat, but I feign indifference, having to work extra for the eye roll that comes next, tamping down his massive ego. I strip down and climb on the bed, straddling his face and making sure to position myself toward my dresser and not his massive cock.

Tonight is about *me* and what *I* want, not about pleasuring him, and if I face that gorgeous dick of his, I'll have it in my mouth in no time.

I settle myself over him, and his rough hands wrap around my thighs, cupping my ass cheeks and squeezing with delicious pressure as he pulls me onto his face. I lean forward, gripping the metal bars at the foot of my bed, and he groans loudly, swiping his nose through my dripping heat, putting pressure on my clit. He runs his tongue along my center, diving in, and the flood of wet arousal rushes through me, my body already on fire for him.

He teases me, stroking slowly, then circling my clit, and when the pressure is just right, he pulls away and laps me up, driving me absolutely wild.

"Stop toying with me and make me come, Kassian," I grind out, my hands white-knuckling the bars in front of me as he chuckles, gripping me further onto him.

I hear him reply, "As you wish," just before enthusiastically wrapping his lips around my needy clit, sucking, and giving me the pressure I need. He moves down to my center but angles his head just right so that I can grind that sensitive bundle of nerves against his nose while he parts me and laps me up.

"Yes," I moan, "just like that. Don't stop," I tell him as I ride his face. My legs are wobbling as I fight to hold myself up. I vaguely feel his hands shift, parting my ass cheeks, and he slips a finger in behind me, pressing down on the tight hole, adding just enough pressure that my body quivers over him, and my orgasm bursts through me. My core clenches, fire searing through me. His moans of approval keep my orgasm quaking through me for so much longer than normal, all of my nerves firing, everything overly sensitive as I come down from the high.

Once I've caught my breath, I climb off of his face and slide down his body, lying on top of his chest, unconcerned about my weight crushing him. He's a big boy. He'll be fine.

I give him a lazy smile, ruffling his hair before I pat his cheek. He smiles back up at me, his eyes glassy and hooded.

"Good boy," I tell him, pressing a chaste kiss to his cheek before rolling off of him in search of my clothes.

He sits, shoulders shaking with laughter as I get dressed. "Just gonna ride my face and kick me out, huh?"

I smirk at him over my shoulder. "No one said anything about kicking you out. Though you're free to go—your services have been rendered." I chuckle, and his eyes turn hard for a moment.

He shakes his head, working to get his clothes back on before taking a seat back on the bed, grabbing the remote, and turning the TV on. He pats the space next to him, and I turn off the lights, the glow from the TV illuminating the room.

I'm suddenly exhausted, so I curl into his side after checking my cell, making sure Kat hasn't texted that she needs me for anything. It's just after nine, so the New York game is either over or about to be. He tugs on my braid, looking down at me with a small grin lighting his handsome face. "Anything else you'd hoped to do for your birthday?"

I shake my head. "Nope, my favorite foods and a good orgasm will do. I'm a happy camper." I laugh, but he tugs on my braid more firmly.

"Your orgasm was *just good?*" he asks with a quirked brow, sounding arrogant in a way that only Kas can pull off.

I roll my eyes. "*Really* good," I tell him, laughing.

He pinches my arm, tossing me to my back and tickling me, sending me into a fit of giggles as I wrestle him off. "Fine! Fine!" I concede. "Sooo good!" I tell him, laughing as his eyes light, still tickling me until I'm nearly out of breath.

"I don't know that I'd use the word good," he chastises relentlessly.

"Earth-shatteringly amazing!" I shout, trying to wriggle out of his reach.

He stops, grabs my cheeks, and presses one wet kiss to my lips. "That's more like it." He winks, releasing me and sinking back against the headboard, picking up the remote to search for something to watch.

He settles on a Disney movie, and I relax into him, drifting off halfway through it. When I wake up, the screen is still lighting the room, but I hear something at the door. I push up, rolling over Kas and waking him; he grumbles something at me and sits up. "Where's the fire?"

"I think Kat's back, and all your shit is out there!" I tell him, frantically making my way to the door and unlocking it. I bolt out but then turn back around. "Stay put!" I whisper shout at him, closing my bedroom door as I rush to the entryway. I grab his shoes, keys, and coat and scan the room for anything else that might tell Kat someone's here. I rush back to my room with all of his things in my arms, dumping them on the floor before bolting back out to open the door.

I wrench the door open, not even thinking to look through the peephole. "I thought I heard... Oh, oops." My eyes are wide with shock before I quickly recover, and a wide grin lights my face as Kat tumbles toward me, but Alessandro catches her before her ass can meet the ground. "Carry on, don't have to drop, sorry, I meant stop... don't have to *stop* on my account," I tell them and hurriedly close the door.

I rush back to my room, closing the door and panting a little, my smile so wide my cheeks hurt. "What am I missing?" Kas asks, eyeing me speculatively.

"I just interrupted your sister making out with Ale in our doorway." I chuckle as his cheeks go pink with embarrassment.

He's silent as we hear the door open, and he groans. "God, I hope they don't stay here," he says, and I send up a silent prayer for the same.

"I'm sure she wouldn't stay here when he's got his own apartment across the hall, and keep your damn voice down!" I whisper, and he chuckles.

"Well, if they do stay, I guess we'll just have to tell them about our little arrangement." He chuckles, and anger shoots through me momentarily.

"Kas, we've talked about this," I say as I hear a knock on the door.

"Just stopped in to change. I'll see you in the morning!" Kat calls into the room, and my breath is caught in my throat.

My wide eyes shoot to Kas, and he smirks, opening his mouth to call out to Kat, but I smack my hand over his mouth and shout back at her in an overly cheerful voice that makes me cringe as it leaves my mouth. "Tata, love you, bye!"

"Tata, love you, bye!" she calls back to me, and a moment later, I hear the front door slam shut. My shoulders sag with relief, and before I can drop my hand from Kas's mouth, he licks my palm. I pull it back, wiping my wet hand against my biker shorts, rolling my eyes at him.

"You should probably head out," I tell him, suddenly overwhelmed, wishing I could just tell him why we can't be together so I don't have to bear the weight of that disappointment alone. But he loves my dad, and I just couldn't do that to him. The thought of him resenting him for anything sends a sour feeling to my gut.

"I'll leave if you really want me to, but I promise to keep my hands to myself if you want me to stay." He gives me a shy smile, the one he knows I can't seem to say no to. Not that I truly can't, but that I don't *want* to.

"Fine, stay, but you've gotta go before Kat gets back in the morning," I tell him, voice stern and my eyes squinted.

He salutes me playfully. "Yes, ma'am," he says, then plops back down on the bed.

I head to the bathroom with Kas trailing behind me. He rummages around under the sink as if he's done this a hundred times before.

"What are you looking for?"

He straightens, a hand fisted around a toothbrush. "This." He smiles, grabbing the toothpaste out of my hand and placing a dollop on both of our brushes.

Once we're ready for bed, I can't wait to climb beneath the covers. I'm suddenly exhausted despite my nap.

Kas wraps his arms around me, tugging me to his warm body, and I rest my head on his chest as he pulls the comforter and the blanket he bought me a few weeks ago over us, reaching for the remote to turn the TV off. He kisses the top of my head, mumbling, "Goodnight, my little viper."

I doze off, my dreams filled with Kas.

---

1. **Pain – Three Days Grace**

2. **Baddie – Honey B**

Chapter Twenty-Nine

Kassian

Wednesday, December 13, 2023

It's early when I wake up, Aiyana still lying on my chest.[1] Staying true to my word, I run my fingers along her back, and she stirs from her sleep. When her eyes pop open, she gives me a small smile that lights me up. If every day could start like this, I'd be king of the fucking *world*.

"Morning," she says. I cup her cheek and press a chaste kiss to the tip of her nose and another to her forehead before sliding out from beside her. I head to the bathroom and call over my shoulder to her, "Go back to sleep. I just wanted to let you know I'm heading out."

Her smile falls slightly before she picks it back up, but I don't ask questions, knowing she doesn't want me to.

I use the restroom, swishing mouthwash before I head out, pull my coat on, and slip back into my sneakers. I walk over to her, pressing another kiss to her forehead, and let her know I'll text her later. I lock up and head out, knowing I have a game tonight and should get my house chores done before our away game on Friday.

***

We won tonight's game too, and as I head home, I answer my messages, one from Aiyana catching my eye first, of course.

Little Viper

Good game!

Thanks :)

You watch from home or in person?

Nevermind, I'd have known if you were there tonight...

Little Viper

Couldn't make it in person tonight :(Had to stay late at the lab.

Little Viper

Goodnight Kas

Goodnight my little viper <3

1. **Bed Peace – Jhené Aiko (ft. Childish Gambino)**

Chapter Thirty

Aiyana

Thursday, December 14, 2023

I'm about to head to the cafeteria for my lunch break when I get a text from Kat that has my heart sinking to my toes.

Prior to my dad's diagnosis, messages like this never bothered me, but ever since, I automatically think the worst.

Kat

Call me when you get a chance.

Something about those words in that order always makes me anxious now.

Maybe it's the seemingly countless times I've received a message with those words just before being told my father was sent to the hospital again, or maybe it's just an innate human response, but my thumbs are flying over my screen, calling her as quickly as possible. She answers on the second ring, sounding cheerful. "Hey! I'm sorry to bother you at work, but I have a favor to ask," she tells me quickly, my racing heart leveling out.

"I thought you, of all people, would know better than to send a text like that, Kat!" I shout at her, still a little peeved at the rush of anxiety and adrenaline pumping through my blood.

"Oh god, sorry! I just have a patient who's Cherokee. The hospital's chaplain doesn't have any connections to a shaman who's able to get here today, and she's in rough shape. She'd really like to have one at the hospital. Her family is trying to make it before she passes, but we aren't sure if they'll get here in time, but I'll be damned if she goes feeling alone." Her voice breaks on the line, and my gut wrenches with sadness.

"I'll give my dad a call real quick. I'm sure he'll be able to give me a few names and numbers. Don't worry, I'll have someone down there within the hour," I tell her, knowing my dad will help me make good on that promise.

"You're the best," she says on a sob, and the weight she's carrying makes me want to lift some of it for her.

"Anything for you, babe. I'll call you soon," I tell her, hanging up to call my dad.

He answers before it can go to voicemail. "My favorite daughter!" he says, coughing a few times, and my heart begins to sink again.

"*Edoda*, could you send me the numbers to the *uktena* in the area? Kat has a patient who isn't doing well," I tell him in one fast breath.

He's silent for a moment before answering. "Of course, I'll send them to her now." But I stop him.

"Could you actually send them to me? I want to call them all and see if they're available. I'm on my lunch break, and I don't want her to have to worry about it while she's working," I explain quickly.

"Anything for my two favorite young women," he says with the same charm I've loved my whole life.

"I love you, *Edoda*," I tell him.

He answers, "And *gvgeyui, uwetsiageyv.*" *I love you, daughter.*

He hangs up, and a few minutes later, I receive a text with the name and number of a shaman. I frown at first, worried that he won't be available, but another text comes in.

Edoda

Always taking care of others, let me take care of you this once. I already called, he's on his way to Kat now. I let her know. Eat your lunch.

Tears prick my eyes, and I pull out the leftovers I packed for lunch, eating in silence at my desk.

Chapter Thirty-One

Kassian

Friday, December 15, 2023

Little Viper

Can you give me a call when you get a chance? Nothing bad, just have a favor to ask.

I'm getting ready to board the plane for the game tonight but I can call right now. I'm not against holding up an entire plane for you ;)

Little Viper

Everything's fine Kas. Your sister just had a really shit day and I was hoping we could surprise her? Any chance your coach would be cool with giving us a ride to your hotel and then letting us fly back with you guys tomorrow?

Little Viper

I've got the flight there covered. A friend owes me a favor.

Of course, I'll talk to him real quick.

I get up from my seat just as the attendants are closing the doors. "Sir, you need to take a seat," one of them tells me.

I smile at her. "I just need to speak with my coach real quick, I promise." She nods and heads in the opposite direction as me.

Once I've sidled up next to Coach Allister, I give him my biggest smile, and he looks over at me, groaning and shaking his head. "What do you want, Narvaez?" He's already rolling his eyes, prepared to say no to whatever ridiculous bullshit is about to come out of my mouth.

"My sister had a shit day at work, and her best friend—" He interrupts me before I can finish.

"The one who's got you actin' senseless?" he asks, and I nod, still smiling because he isn't wrong. "Continue," he drawls.

"She wants to surprise her by bringing her to our game tonight. Any chance we could give her a ride back tomorrow?" He looks at me head-on, processing my words and considering. Just as I figure he's about to say no, he gives me one stern nod.

"Fine, but don't ask me for shit like this again. Now get out of my face so we can get this giant tin can in the air," he grunts.

"You got it. Thanks, Coach!" I tell him and haul ass back to my seat before he can change his mind. Grabbing my phone, I shoot Aiyana a text, letting her know I've got the plane and hotel covered.

When I set my phone down, Ale eyes me speculatively. "What's got you so excited?" he asks, his brow raised.

"You'll see soon," I tell him, chuckling to myself, and I can't contain the massive grin that's spread across my face.

"Historically, nothing good has ever come from you speaking *those words,*" he groans beside me, leaning back in his seat.

Chapter Thirty-Two

Aiyana

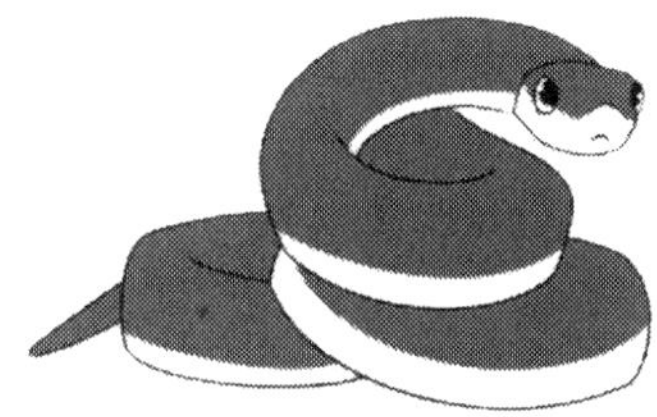

"Well, I'm glad I finally got to meet Luca tonight. I've watched a few of his games," I tell Kat as we head into our room. We landed in New York just before the game started, and Luca picked the four of us up for dinner and drinks at a Korean karaoke bar.

"Yeah, he was really nice, but nothing like I had expected him to be. He and Ale are so different from one another, it's hard to believe they're only a year apart," she tells me.

I nod in agreement, setting my things down on the bed furthest from the door. "Yeah, he's cute though." I wink. "He's the kind of guy I could get myself into a lot of trouble with," I tell her, waggling my eyebrows suggestively.

She laughs. "You definitely could, but Kas would have a cow." My breath gets lodged in my lungs as her words hang in the air, but she quickly adds, "I saw the way he shot daggers at the back of his head when you started flirting with him. I think my brother's got a crush on you." I shake my head, refuting what she's said, but she gets up to get ready for bed before I can say anything back.

***

Not long after Ale came to retrieve Kat for a walk or whatever the kids are calling it these days, I get a text from Kas, just like I had expected.

Kas

Were you flirting with Luca tonight to make me jealous?

I roll my eyes—male egos.

So what if I was, what're you gonna do about it?

Kas

I'll come over there and show you.

Heat rips through me, the thrill of having Kas all to myself tonight sending an ache between my legs.

Kas

You need to be punished for being a bad girl, little viper.

God, is it fucking hot in this room? My skin is on fire, and he isn't even here.

Before I can respond, there's a knock at the door. I get up on shaky legs and head over to it, checking that it's him before answering. He barges through, slamming it shut and locking it behind him.

Kas throws the extra lock over it so no one can get in, even with a key, and wraps a hand around my waist, tugging me to him as his other hand snakes up to cup my breast. He feels for the hard bud and tugs on it, sending a jolt of electricity through me before his hand comes up to wrap around my throat.

He rests his forehead against mine, eyes lit with something simmering beneath the surface as he stares me down in such close proximity.

His grip around my throat tightens, and wetness floods my core, making me contract around nothing. "You think you're so funny, huh?" he asks, humor absent from his voice. It's rough and intoxicating as his minty breath skates over my lips, and my hands instinctively grip his hard biceps.

He tsks at me. "Such a bad girl, little viper. We agreed." The hand around my waist skates down to cup me. "This tight little pussy is all *mine.* So you're gonna learn a lesson about flirting with other men, yeah?" he asks me, and I nod, anticipating the best fuck of my life based on the way his heated gaze is boring into me right now. Rough sex has always been my favorite poison.

He lifts me up, and my legs wind around his trim waist. He walks us over to the bed, depositing me on it before his deft fingers find the waistband of my leggings, yanking my panties down with them as he tosses them into the corner of the room. "Stand up and bend over the bed," he grunts roughly, "and hold on."

God, why is he so fucking hot like this?

I do as he says, my ass facing him as I'm still wearing the jersey I put on for every game. He grips the back of it. "You're wearing my jersey and flirting with another man?" he asks, sounding fired up. Gripping my hip, he releases his hold on my top and angles his cock against my center, foregoing all foreplay, though I'm fucking soaked as is. “Hold on, little viper, you’re gonna pay for that,” he tells me as his hips slam into me, stretching me so wide that I have no choice but to slump against the bed.

“Oh god,” I moan, unable to stop myself. His hand tugs roughly on my braid, wrapping it around his fist as he tugs my head back sharply, the pain searing my scalp and sending another jolt of pleasure to my core.

He’s bent over me, groaning in my ear, his grip tightening with every thrust as I clamp down on his cock, milking every inch of his impressive length. “You like that, huh? Getting fucked like a little slut?” His words should anger me, but I know this game. He’s more than aware of what I like in the bedroom, and for some reason, this is absolutely it.

“Yes,” I shout, moaning as I grapple for purchase in the sheets, trying to anchor myself somehow. “God, yes, fuck me just like that.”

“Are you my little slut, viper?” he asks, his pace becoming erratic. The slapping of our bodies has my chest heaving with need, and his hand slips between us, swirling and pinching on my clit.

“Yes, yes!” I shout. “Yours,” I tell him and release a long moan at my words.

My abdomen is clenching, my core is tightening, and my cunt is spasming around him, his hard pace driving me into the mattress as he literally fucks me into it. He releases his hold on my aching scalp and settles for smacking my ass harder than anyone ever has. It hurts so damn bad, but the pain sends a shiver down my spine, my mind getting lost in the sensations. “Oh fuck, yes,” I moan, “harder, Kas.”

“Say it again,” he groans.

“Harder,” I tell him as he smacks me, relentlessly pounding into me.

“No,” he grunts, “say my fucking name again, Aiyana.”

Oh my god—as my name leaves his lips, spoken like an angry-as-hell prayer, I understand why he wants me to do the same.

My body's on fire, and I'm about to come undone, shouting his name as he goes rigid inside me. "*Kassian...*" The words float away from us, the room going eerily silent as we reach our climax at the same time. It sends me over the edge, heat searing me, making me feel fucking combustible as his hot cum fills me. I feel it pooling out of me, dripping down my thighs.

Chapter Thirty-Three

Kassian

Jesus Christ, I've never come so hard in my fucking life.

Aiyana looks so pretty, bent over the side of the bed, wearing my name on her back as her sweet pussy spills with my cum, dripping down her tan thighs. Her ass cheeks are rosy from being spanked so hard, and her raven-black hair is frizzy in her braid.

I pull out, keeping a hand on her lower back to keep her pressed into the bed. I want to watch as my cum floods out of her, claiming her cunt.

I swipe my fingers through her swollen pussy lips and bring them to her mouth. "Suck," I tell her, still commanding, but the anger I felt before has worn off entirely. I know she's mine, even if she wants to pretend she isn't.

After her plump ruby-red lips suck my fingers, I pull them out, releasing her so she can stand. She turns around, facing me, and she looks like a fucking mess. Exactly how I want her.

She pushes me back, both hands on my chest as her lips purse. "What the fuck was that, Kas?"

She asks me as if it isn't obvious. "You don't get to go flirting with other men, not while I'm the one filling you, and definitely not in front of me."

She puts her hands on her hips, staring me down, "Oh, so now I'm your *property*?" She sounds pissed, and I kind of like it. She's adorable when she's mad.

I chuckle lightly at her, and her eyes flare in response. "Of course not. You're free to do as you want, even if it'll break my fucking heart. But we agreed when we started this that it's just you and me, baby, no one else. So if that's changed, you've gotta let me know so I can walk away before I get crushed again."

Her eyes soften. "Again?" she asks, her voice small, and it makes me want to shake her with how absurdly oblivious she must be.

Instead, I grab her cheeks in my hands, pressing a kiss to her forehead. "Yes, baby, every time you've ever left me, you left behind a giant gaping hole in my heart that no one else has ever been able to fill." I kiss her forehead again, then her eyelids, and lastly, the tip of her nose before tilting her head back, staring at her head-on. "And for the record,"—I muster a small smile as she looks back at me with glossy eyes and a pink-tipped nose—"I've *always* been *your* property."

I bend, kissing the corner of her mouth gently, and her lips open for me. I sweep my tongue in, tangling with hers as her hands come up around my neck, tugging me more closely to her until she releases me, taking a step back and clearing her throat.

"You should head back to your room. I should shower, and Kat will be back any minute."

I nod and get my clothes back on. She walks me to the door, and our fingers graze, but she makes no move to take the touch any further, so I walk to the elevator, unable to push her any further tonight.

When I get back to my room, I send her a text before hopping in the shower.

Goodnight my little viper <3

She doesn't respond for several hours. Finally texting back.

Little Viper

Goodnight Kas

My heart aches. I'd give absolutely anything to have her lying next to me.

Chapter Thirty-Four

Aiyana

Saturday, December 16, 2023

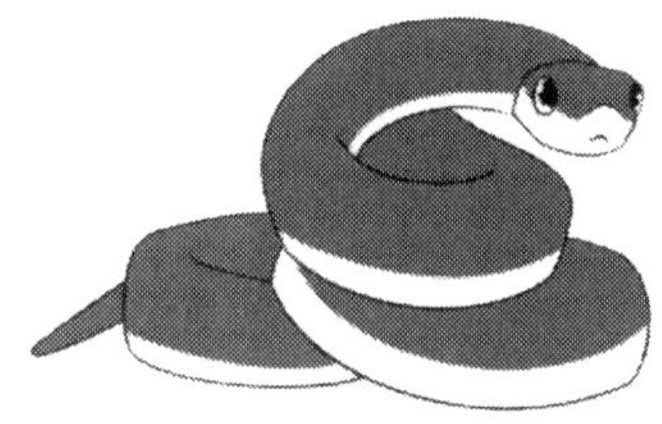

The flight this morning took off really early, and Kat and I sat at the very back of the plane, both of us leaning on one another to sleep in. Kat didn't get back until the sun had started coming up, so at least one of us had a good night.

When we got back home, I placed an online order for more menstrual products, knowing my cycle is about to start, and once it does, I won't be going anywhere.

I make myself lunch and listen to music, writing down some ideas to discuss with Rose about a vaccine we're working on. It's been in process for a while now, but I've been looking into the methodology, and I think there's a quicker way to formulate the product without compromising quality or increasing costs. It could bridge the gap, allowing us to release it to the market sooner so we can help better protect children in endemic areas more quickly.

I send her a text, asking her to remind me to discuss it with her on Monday, and then head to the bathroom to take some painkillers and stuff the massive tampon in to stop the floodgates that just erupted. My body aches all over, the cramps seizing my breath as I keel over in pain. I grab the TENS unit from under the sink along with some alcohol swabs, cleaning the skin and applying the adhesive pads to my lower abdomen before climbing into bed and turning it on the lowest setting. The cramps finally start to settle enough that I can fall asleep. *I need a fucking nap.*

***

When I wake up, I feel nauseous, and my lower back aches from sleeping flat on it instead of curled around a pillow, but it's the only way to keep the TENS unit in place while I sleep. As usual, I trade one pain for another, settling on back pain as the lesser of the two evils.

I'm also pretty sure you aren't supposed to keep them on as long as I do, but when I'm in this much pain, it's hard to care when I've finally found some form of relief.

I can't get out of bed just yet, so I turn the machine off and remove the pads from my stomach before rolling over on my side and grabbing my cell phone.

There's a message from Rose letting me know she's excited to hear my ideas, and I see an email with a calendar reminder for a meeting to discuss them with her. I smile to myself. I got really lucky with this job. Rose has been incredible.

There's also a message from Kat saying she left with Alessandro to go for a run. Sounds fucking horrible. I roll my eyes at the thought.

And the last text is from Kas.

Kas

You need anything this weekend?

Did you sneak into my phone and steal the password to my period app or something?

Kas

I tracked it for years when we were together in high school and undergrad. You don't think I know you've got a 28 day cycle and a menstrual phase of 6 days?

Kas, that's fucking creepy.

Then why is it making me feel all warm and fuzzy inside?

Kas

I'm creepy for you baby ;)

Kas

That sounded better in my head.

Kas

Ignore that.

To answer your question, I'm fine. Thank you though. Gonna head to bed early tonight I think.

Kas

Goodnight my little viper <3

Goodnight Kas.

Butterflies take flight in my stomach when he calls me that, but just like every other night, I take a flamethrower to them and remind myself why they can't be there in the first place.

Chapter Thirty-Five

Kassian

Sunday, December 17, 2023

This morning's practice was brutal, and all I want is to go cuddle Aiyana, but she'd probably lose her shit.

That doesn't stop me from texting her anyway though. I know Kat isn't home because she's out with Ale, so I send her a message, all but begging her to come over or to let me go there.

Pretty please let me take care of you tonight?

Little Viper

Bring ice cream or I'm kicking you out.

Holy fucking shit! She's actually letting me take care of her!

At the same time that this excites me, it also makes me worry. She has to be in a lot of pain to accept help from anyone, but especially me.

Honey lavender from that mom and pop down the road?

Little Viper

And a pint of jelly donut. Make sure it isn't the vegan one. *insert purple devil emoji*

Little Viper

And Kas…

Forget something? Pain meds or tampons? Pads? Tell me what you need, little viper.

Little Viper

Just wanted to say thanks.

Anytime.

I smile at my phone like the corny fuck that I am. I am *so* gone for this woman. Which reminds me, I need to schedule this week's call with Dr. Sanchez.

Chapter Thirty-Six

Aiyana

I'm not a reckless person. I'd even say I'm not usually very selfish either, but when it comes to my heart and Kas's, I'd say I've been a lot of both lately.

And as guilty as that makes me feel, I also recognize that I'm at my happiest when I'm with Kas. *That's how it's always been.*

So when he asked to come over tonight, I jumped at the opportunity. I feel like dog shit and probably look like it too, and all I want is some sort of comfort to get me through the worst day of my period.

I keep my eyes closed, hoping like hell this migraine will start to subside soon. Kas should be here soon, but I don't make any effort to leave the bed. He owns the place. He can let himself in.

I do my best to focus on my breathing, trying to ground myself as my parents have taught me to when I feel like I'm losing control.

But the pain is searing through me from too many places, making it nearly impossible to clear my mind and release any of the agony.

The groans and whimpers of pain leaving my throat sound almost animalistic; I barely recognize them as my own.

"Aiyana." I barely make out my name, hearing it float into the space around me gently, coating my exposed and raw nerve endings like a sheath.

"Aiyana, baby," I hear again; this time, it's closer.

The bed dips behind me, and I'm suddenly enveloped in warm, strong arms, dragging my body back against a hard chest that I know so well.

"Little viper, tell me where it hurts, and I'll make it go away," he whispers against my hair.

"Everywhere," I whisper back, unable to speak at a normal volume. Everything is just too loud.

"Can you sit up long enough to take some medicine?" he asks me gently, and I nod on instinct, sending a jolt of pain through my skull.

I work my hand under me, trying to push up, but Kas can tell I'm struggling. He lifts me, supporting my body against his. "Open your mouth, baby," he instructs.

I do, and a moment later, I feel the tablets he's placed on my tongue and then a straw to drink from. The cool water feels nice against my throat, which is raw from my cries.

Kas lowers me back down and presses a kiss to my temple and then my jaw. "I'll be right back. Just rest and let the meds work."

I try my best to keep quiet as I lie here, not wanting to alarm him any further. Several minutes pass, and the throbbing in my head starts to subside. I'm finally able to pry my eyes open as Kas is making his way back into the room.

His warm eyes meet mine, and a small smile spreads across his lips. "There are those pretty eyes I've missed," he tells me as he sits beside me, placing a cool cloth over my forehead.

"Thanks, Kas," I say weakly.

"Anything for you, my little viper. Can I pull your shorts down a bit? I got some stick-on pads that heat and cool every twenty minutes on their own."

I nod, rolling the waistband of my sleep shorts down for him. He fusses with a bunch of things lying beside him before placing a large white adhesive-coated cloth on my lower abdomen. The gel on the cloth immediately starts to cool the area, and I can't tell if the pain is actually beginning to dissipate or if it's a placebo effect, but I'll take the win either way.

I close my eyes, my tense muscles starting to relax, and a moan nearly escapes me when I feel Kas start to massage my feet, digging deeply into the fascia at my arch.[1] He takes his time, pressing his thumbs in a strategic pattern I'm starting to recognize from the little bit of reflexology I'd learned about from the *didanawisgi* or medicine man I'd grown up around.

While the Cherokee tribe originated in northern Georgia, and clearly, much has changed in the last few thousand years, there are still several elders and their families living near here that my father was able to connect with when my parents moved to the area before I was born. And since Kas and I basically grew up together, for all intents and purposes, he learned some of it too. That was something I've always loved about Kas—his appreciation for my culture and learning about it as much as he could.[2] Whether that was just out of his own interest or for me, I'm not sure, but it doesn't matter either way.

As he holds pressure in those strategic places on the soles of my feet, I feel the smallest bit of tension relieved from my pelvis. He starts working his way up my calves, and a while later, he's massaging each hand, pressing firmly over the locations for the ovaries, pelvis, and lower back.

I breathe a sigh of relief; a solid sixty percent of my pain has resolved in the last hour that he's been here, tending to my every need. Including ones I hadn't even thought to consider.

"You feeling better, gorgeous girl?"

I crack my eyes open and snake my hand toward his until it's firmly in my grasp. "I am, thank you."

Kas leans forward, removing the cloth before pressing a wet kiss to the center of my forehead. "Good, I'll be right back."

While he's gone, I turn on the TV to watch *Gilmore Girls* and set the volume low. Kas comes back holding two bowls and uses his hip to close the door behind him before climbing back on the bed. He hands me a bowl that's piled high with my two favorite ice cream flavors.

Kas leans back against my headboard, stretching out his long, muscular legs. "Oh, fuck yeah, *Gilmore Girls*!" he says around a mouthful of ice cream, doing a little fist pump with his spoon in his hand.

"Don't tell me this is *still* your favorite show?" I joke.

"Hey, it's a fantastic show, and it's timeless. Besides, when you know every word, it makes it easy to have it on in the background when you're getting stuff done around the apartment."

"I'm not arguing; you know I'd *never* argue that it isn't the greatest show of all time. I'm just surprised that *you* still watch it."

Kas rolls his eyes at me and turns his attention back to the TV as he eats his ice cream. "You remember when we'd watch it every day after school because it was the only thing Kat would watch without getting bored and begging us to change the channel?"

"Oh, I remember. I *also* remember you having a hissy fit the one time she didn't want to watch it."

"Yeah, but I eventually gave in." He huffs.

"Because you *always* give in when it comes to Kat." I laugh.

"You and I both know she deserves the world. So who am I to tell her we can't watch *Twilight* for the fifteenth time?"

I peer over at him. "Tell me the truth, Kas. Did you really love *Twilight* and just complain when we wanted to watch it so we'd think you didn't? Or did you *actually* hate it?"

"Oh, I fuck heavy with *Twilight*. Always have." He smirks as my mouth gapes open. "But Edward can suck it. Team Jacob all day, baby!"

Playfully, I smack his shoulder. "God, you're the worst. All that time, poor Kat really thought she was forcing you to deal with another one of her hyperfixations when, in reality, you were just too embarrassed to profess your love for the werewolf."

"That was a selfless act, Aiyana! Kat would've been *crushed* if she only knew her very own *twin* wasn't Team Edward!" He says it dramatically, tossing his forearm over his face as he collapses against the pillows.

"Yeah, well, you're both wrong," I taunt.

He flings his arm back to his side to meet my eyes. "What the hell are you talking about 'we're both wrong,'?" he says in air quotes. "There are literally four fucking books, with the most pressing concern being whether or not Bella ends up with the sparkly pasty dude or the long-haired dog. Please, enlighten me as to how the hell we could *both* be wrong, Aiyana." He sounds exasperated, and I love it.

"You're both wrong because Charlie is clearly the hottest character in any of the movies, and honestly, Bella should've ended up as a throuple with Alice and Jasper. They had good vibes. *Sexy* vibes. That's all I'm saying."

He stares at me, jaw agape as if he's stunned. Finally, he speaks slowly as he says, "I really *wish* I could argue with that logic, but I'm"—he shakes his head—"Well, shit, I'm inclined to agree."

"Hah, told you so." I wink, turning my attention back to the TV as I shovel more of the silky ice cream into my mouth.

***

I've almost managed to forget the cramping pain in my pelvis as Kas holds me tightly against his chest while we mindlessly watch TV for hours. "You know what show I really miss?"

"Not a clue, but I'm sure you're gonna tell me," I say.

"*Flavor of Love.*" He chuckles deeply.

My eyes widen. "Oh my god! I loved that show! 'I've got love for you, New York' was my favorite phrase for a year after watching the repeat season where New York comes back on the show!"

"Oh, I remember. You said it so many times I almost thought my name *was* New York, but when she got her own show, that was just as good, honestly. Though Flav's signature clock around his neck was iconic."

"The first year we discovered that show, you surprised me on Valentine's Day with a massive wall clock hanging from a bunch of tinsel around your neck."

His laugh reverberates through me from his chest pressed firmly against my back. "It took so much tinsel to hold the damn thing up, I had to braid them together, and it took your dad and me an hour to get it hung up in your room afterward because the drywall screws wouldn't hold it."

"Where'd you even get that damn thing?" I ask, realizing I never had before. That clock is still hung up in my childhood bedroom.

"At one of the estate sales Lola took Kat and me to. Honestly, it's probably pretty haunted."

"Well, that would explain why my window was always unlocked in the morning," I tease.

"Nope, that was most definitely just the gangly boy next door who snuck in your window every night to cuddle you to sleep."

"Ooh, yeah, him! I forgot *all* about him," I joke.

"I'd flick you right now if you weren't already feeling so crappy," he tells mc.

"I don't feel as bad anymore, thanks to you," I admit, lifting his hand and running my lips along his knuckles.

When I release his hand, he brings both of them up behind me to gather my hair, playing with my loose strands, and a while later, he starts braiding them back until it's gathered into one long plait. "Hair tie?" he asks, and I hand him the one off of my wrist.

He finishes securing the ends and tosses the braid over my shoulder to hang down my abdomen.

As we lie here, my eyes begin to feel heavy. "I'm getting tired, Kas. I'm going to get ready for bed."

He follows me, getting cleaned up, and joins me back in the bed after turning off all of the lights in the apartment.

I fall asleep beside Kas as he rubs circles along my back until I fall asleep.

---

1. **Nights Like This – Kehlani (ft. Ty Dolla $ign)**

2. **Love Language – SZA**

Chapter Thirty-Seven

Aiyana

Monday, December 18, 2023

Kas's strong arms wrap around me, hauling me onto his chest and almost startling me out of my sleep. Luckily, I realize where I am and whose arms they are before I can scream.

"Good morning, little viper," he says, kissing me between my brows.

"Morning," I answer groggily.

He rubs circles along my spine, just like he did last night. "How are you feeling today?"

"Better. The second day of my period is always the worst."

"I don't remember them being that bad when we were younger. Has the pain gotten more intense?" he asks, peppering kisses over my forehead.

"It has. Not to bore you with the science of it, but if you really want to know, it might be easier if I just explain why the pain is so bad," I tell him, not wanting to get into this if he'd rather I give him a simpler explanation.

"I'd like to know, Aiyana. I've researched endometriosis, but I'm a little confused about some of the details," he says.

Of course he wants to know. Because it's Kas, and he *always* wants to know more when it comes to me. *This* is just one reason why no one else has ever compared. I press a kiss to his chest before answering. "So endometriosis doesn't have a well-known cause, but essentially, the endometrial tissue that lines the uterus is very sticky, for lack of a better way of describing it. For someone with endometriosis, this tissue grows in places that it shouldn't, like the outside of the uterus, the bladder, the bowels, basically anywhere in the pelvic cavity. It creates adhesions to surrounding structures, and since this tissue responds to hormonal changes, when I menstruate, it's kind of tugging on all those structures it's implanted itself in." I exhale a long sigh, sliding off of him to roll onto my back. I rest my hands on my tummy and continue. "Which is why it feels like I'm being torn apart from the inside out."

Alarm laces his words. "And there's no cure for this?"

"No. There are several treatments, but each of them has its own risks. Certain types of birth control can help, but they weren't super effective for me and just made me feel bloated and tired half the time. It was like trading one issue for another. I've had a laparoscopic surgery done—that's the one with the camera and the tiny holes in the abdomen so the surgeon can visualize the insides and remove any tissue that's not in the right place. The problem is that any surgery causes scar tissue of some kind, and you can't possibly remove all of the endometrial tissue once it's spread the way mine has. There's also an injection called leuprolide that's been really helpful for a lot of people, but..." I hesitate.

Kas chuckles beside me, grabbing my hand. "Little Aiyana is *still* afraid of needles, huh?" he teases.

"Oh, shut up." I roll my eyes.

"You don't find that at all ironic? You literally formulate *vaccines* that are given with *needles.*"

"I see the irony. I just try not to think about it too much. Besides, a vaccine here or there is a little different than getting jabbed every month. I've considered it and even scheduled an appointment to get it, but decided it wasn't something I wanted to start, knowing that if it worked, I'd be doing it for the rest of my menstruating life. Which will likely be many, many years from now."

"Are there any other options?" he asks, sounding hopeful. I love that he's always able to keep searching for the positive in a shitty situation.

"An oral version of something similar came out in twenty-eighteen, and it sounds like that has been really effective for a lot of people, but again, I'm tired of options that would have to become a regular part of my life. Ultimately, a hysterectomy may be the best option for me since I don't want any kids. I could still keep my tubes and ovaries so I won't totally screw up my hormones, but at least I won't have a period to keep angering the misplaced tissues. It's not completely effective, and definitely not a cure, but it's something I'm leaning toward more and more with every cycle," I answer honestly.

"I'll support whatever you want to do, Aiyana. And I'll hold your hand the entire time if you'll let me." He rolls over onto his side, pulling me to his chest and squeezing me tightly.

Emotions well in my throat, and a single tear manages to slip out. *I've missed Kas and the comfort he's always been able to bring me.*

"Thank you," I tell him softly, enjoying just being held before I have to start getting ready for work.

***

A smile spreads across my lips as I think about how this day went. Usually, I'd still be pretty miserable by this point in my cycle, and I am, but today was a good day regardless.

I got to have my meeting with Rose this morning. I can't help the smile that spreads across my lips. She was so receptive to everything I said, spending hours going over every detail. She even canceled her other appointments for the day to work on a plan for implementing my ideas as quickly as possible. We'll start on Wednesday if everything goes well with upper-level management, and she put me in charge of it.

I was literally beaming with pride when I called my parents to tell them. They were so excited for me, and Dad nearly demanded that I set up a day for him to tour the site. I promised to get them both visitor passes, which Rose approved as soon as I emailed her about it.

Just before I close my eyes, ready to sleep, Kas texts me as he always does.

Kas

Goodnight my little viper <3

Goodnight, caveman.

I tell him, laughing to myself because he's been acting so possessive. I can't even say I mind it. It's sort of sweet having someone fawn over me.

Kas

Ook ook, hear me roar, I am caveman.

Another text comes through of a photo of Kas pounding on his chest.

Ook ook????

Is that how you think cavemen sounded?

Kas

What the fuck else did they say? They weren't exactly very literate.

Goodnight Kassian.

You're ridiculous.

Kas

Goodnight, again, my little viper <3

Chapter Thirty-Eight

Aiyana

Tuesday, December 19, 2023

"It shouldn't take this fucking long to get home," I groan to myself. *How come no one around here knows how to drive?*

The light ahead of me turns green, and yet, the douchebag in front of me, likely playing on his phone, goes nowhere. I lie on my horn, and he jolts forward, finally moving in the right direction. "Jackass."

Ringing startles me, but I see my mom's name pop up on my phone screen, so I swipe it to answer. Her loud voice fills my truck's speakers. "Hi honey," she says.

"Etsi, what's up?"

"Your father is working on a big furniture project, and he needs help. It's too damn big. Any chance you could bring a friend by and give him a hand tonight or tomorrow?"

Without hesitation, I answer, "Of course, Etsi. I'll find someone and let you know when we're planning on going, okay?"

"Thank you, honey. It's just too big for him, and he's working on it for a friend. He promised to have it done really soon, and it's just too much work on his own."

"No problem. I'll talk to you later. I love you."

"*Gvgeyui*, Aiyana," she tells me before hanging up.

Finally, outside of my apartment, I park and pull up Kas's contact info. He answers on the first ring. "To what do I owe this immense pleasure, little viper?"

I shake my head, knowing he can't see me. "I just got off the phone with my mom—" And he interrupts me.

"Is your dad okay?" he asks, sounding a little frantic.

What the hell is up with everyone doing that lately?

"Yeah, he's okay, I think. He's just working on a really big piece of furniture, and he can't hold it up on his own, and Mom is afraid he's gonna hurt himself. She's wondering if I could come help, and she asked that I bring someone. I know Kat would agree, but she's going out with Ale tonight, and she was always the worst at woodworking of any kind."

"Oh, I remember. All the times she'd spill the cans of stain when we gave her that job because it was the hardest to mess up." He laughs. "I've got a game tomorrow though, but I could go now if you're free?"

I don't really have anything going on tonight, and I already told Mom I could do either night. "Yeah, want me to swing by and pick you up? I can be ready in thirty?"

"Nah, I'll grab you in an hour if that's okay. We both know you haven't eaten, and I was just finishing dinner. I could bring you something if you wanted to leave sooner though." I blush at his thoughtfulness and agree to have him pick me up in an hour before heading upstairs to eat and change. He texts that he's five minutes away, so I lock up and head downstairs to meet him before he can valet and hike up to my floor to get me himself.

I pull open the door to his truck, hoisting myself in and slamming the door behind me. "Hi." I smile at him, buckling myself in.

He reaches over once I've finished, the truck in park as he pulls my lips toward his with his hand on my cheek. He presses a gentle kiss to my lips, and we break apart, someone honking behind us, ruining the moment.

He rests his large, warm hand above my knee, squeezing as we pull out of the parking lot and head toward my parents' house.

When he asks me about work, I excitedly relay everything that's been going on, and he cheers me on. "That's incredible, Aiyana," he says, eyes crinkling with pure joy. "I always knew you were a fucking rock star; I'm just glad your boss sees that too." He looks over his shoulder at me, shooting me a brief smile before redirecting his eyes to the road, and soon, we're pulling onto the long gravel road that leads up back through the woods. We park in front of my parents' small, one-story home—the walls paneled with wood covered in tribal markings my father chiseled in himself.

My heart beams with pride momentarily until I see Kas's gaze fixed on the small home next door. You can barely see it through the thick trees, especially with the sun down and the rain making everything even more dreary. Though with the cold weather and the loss of leaves, you can just barely make out the side of the light-blue house with the caved-in roof. No one moved in after what happened with his parents, not wanting to live in a house with so many unhappy memories.

He's got a faraway gaze, clearly somewhere else entirely. I rest my hand on his thigh and squeeze gently, helping drag him out of the dark recesses of his mind. He looks over at me, mouth slightly ajar, eyes glassy. "Hey, come back to me," I whisper, my voice cracking slightly on the last word.

His eyes cast downward toward where my hand rests, and he covers my hand with his own. We sit just like this for several minutes until the porch light turns on, and my mom walks out, waving over at us, shouting for us to come in.

"You ready?" I ask him quietly. Squeezing my hand, he nods, giving me a small, reassuring smile before unbuckling and hopping out, running around the car as he pulls the hood of his coat up and sprints through the rain to my door to open it for me and help me out.

We head to the door, my mom beaming at us through the rain. When we get to the door, we shake like wet dogs and pull our coats off. Kas's arms reach around my mother's thin frame, lifting her off her feet and twirling her around as she laughs at him, smacking his shoulder like she always does, but secretly loving it.

"My favorite woman! How've you been, *Etsi*?" And my heart cracks right open as he uses the Tsalagi word for "mom" when he addresses her. He's always done that, but the realization that she'll never really be his, not by marriage or blood, weighs on me heavily.

"Oh, shush, you! I just saw you a few days ago." She smacks his shoulder again and laughs, a big smile on her beautiful, tawny face. She turns to me, but her words make me pause. What does she mean that she saw him a few days ago?

Before I get to ask the question that's sitting on the tip of my tongue, she envelops me in a crushing hug just as my dad walks out, carrying his oxygen tank with him. I hear his deep cough before I see him, though, and my heart sinks just a little more.

I smile at them both, bringing them in for a hug together, and when they let me free, Kas hugs my father in the same way he did my mom, lifting his legs just a couple of inches off the ground as if my father isn't a hulk of a man himself. His deep brown eyes, the same as mine, smile back at me as my mom waves us inside.

"Okay, so what are we working on tonight?" Kas asks, and Dad ushers us into the garage, where we find massive slabs of stained wood and tools strewn all around. I think it might be a giant chest of drawers.

"It's a wardrobe for Adohi. He came over after he saw that patient who Kat called about and said he had been meaning to commission a piece from me." He smiles broadly, the wrinkles in his forehead furrowing gently on his tanned face.

"Alright"—Kas claps him on the back—"put me to work." He smiles, and that same crack in my heart threatens to burst open again.

He tells us what to do, and as we work, he drags his oxygen tank around, and I see how cumbersome it's become despite being on wheels. When he needs a break, he pulls a chair next to me, and my mom comes out with electrolyte drinks for us. Red for Dad and me, and yellow for Kas, remembering his favorite flavor.

"You know," my dad says, looking at me with mischief lacing his words, "Adohi is only thirty-eight." My eyes widen, but I try to collect my composure as I see Kas peer over at us from my periphery.

"Okay?" I ask, feigning ignorance.

"He's a good-looking man; maybe you should let me set you up sometime?" he asks, his broad smile making it difficult for me to deny him.

"I'm not really looking for anything right now, Dad, but I'll let you know," I tell him, glancing over at Kas. His cheeks are hollow from sucking them in, presumably holding his breath, but he releases a long one when my father nods.

We go back to working on the project, and once it's fully assembled, we stare back at it, standing a few feet away with our fists on our hips. "It looks great," I say.

My dad smiles, laughing as he scratches his head. "It looks"—he pauses—"*crooked*." At that, we all keel over laughing because it absolutely *does* look crooked.

My dad walks around the piece, taking it in at every angle, and bends forward, chuckling again. "There's a rock!" he says, leaning further forward to pluck it out from under the leg. The furniture shifts and nearly topples over onto him, but Kas darts out an arm, steadying it in time for Dad to stand and get out of the way.

We take it in again. "Now," I say, smiling with the accomplishment. "It looks perfect."

My dad nods, as does Kas, and he turns to him. "You free sometime before we leave on our holiday cruise? I could use your steady hands to help me finish with the carvings. You're better than anyone I've ever known at carving, even those who grew up doing it." Kas blushes as the compliment washes over him, laughing when Dad adds, "Besides me, of course."

"Of course," he chuckles, "I'm free in a couple of days. How's the twenty-second?"

Dad claps him on the back, heading inside. "Sounds like a plan."

We follow behind him, Kas's fingers grazing mine as his cell phone buzzes in his pocket. He pulls it out, reads it quickly, and sends a reply before tucking it back in his pocket and glancing over at me with a guilty expression.

My face twists in confusion, but I smooth the expression and take a seat at the kitchen table where Mom has molasses bars sitting for us. I pluck one up, bringing it to my lips, and sigh with the first bite, my eyes rolling in my head from the familiarity.

"I packed some for you to take home." She nods toward the tin sitting on the raw wooden entry table.

Dad coughs in between sentences, clearly having expended too much energy, overdoing it tonight till his lungs couldn't keep up.

We talk for the next hour until they send us home, wanting to make sure we get back safe with the rain.

As they walk us out, my dad cups Kas's cheeks, planting a kiss on his forehead, and Kas does the same, returning the sentiment. They whisper to each other before Kas opens my coat for me to walk into. I push my arms through the sleeves, and he zips it closed, pulling the hood over my head after I say goodbye to my parents.

When we get in the truck, I consider asking what my mom meant earlier but go silent as he stares back at the house he grew up in. A haunted look appears in his eyes before he puts the truck in reverse and turns us around in the driveway to pull straight out onto the gravel path to the road.

***

We drove all the way home in comfortable silence, my mind racing with unanswered questions, and Kas hummed along to the quiet music playing over the radio. When we pulled up to my building, he planted a kiss on my cheeks and asked me to text him when I got inside, not trying to weasel his way into my bed. It made me sick with worry, but I pushed it aside.

I texted him when I got in and again before bed, but he didn't answer until after I fell asleep.

I woke up the next morning with his goodnight text waiting for me.

Kas

Sleep tight my little viper <3

Chapter Thirty-Nine

Kassian

Wednesday, December 20, 2023

Coming to my game tonight?

Little Viper

You already know I am… You got my dad tickets to make sure I came. Asshole.

Asshole? I thought that was being sweet.

Little Viper

It's controlling, you dick.

Little Viper

You should be glad I was planning to go anyway.

I chuckle at that—of course she was.

***

You guys left before I got to say hi.

Little Viper

Sorry, dad wasn't feeling good. His cough got worse, probably from all this rain we've been having. The moisture sometimes makes it worse. He said he'll still see you on Friday though.

I'll keep you updated on how he's doing.

I'll also finish the carvings for him so he can get some rest. Even if the damn piece of furniture is for a guy he tried to set my future wife up with.

Little Viper

Thanks Kas.

Little Viper

Goodnight.

Goodnight my little viper <3

Chapter Forty

Aiyana

Thursday, December 21, 2023

Mom called me, worried they might have to cancel their cruise because of Dad's lungs. He promised her he'd go see his doctor and one of the healers before they leave on the twenty-third.

I head to bed, exhausted from lack of sleep this week. Every time I fall asleep, I have nightmares about my dad. Growing up being told your dreams are your ancestors' way of sending you messages only adds to the dread I'm already feeling.

Kas

Hey little viper, one of the guys is throwing a party for Ale's belated birthday on Saturday. Wanna go?

Kat already invited me.

Kas

You'll be there then?

Yes.

Kas

Woohoo! I can't wait to see you *insert kissy face emoji*

You're ridiculous.

Kas

Only for you ;)

Goodnight Kassian.

Kas

Goodnight my little viper <3

Chapter Forty-One

Kassian

Friday, December 22, 2023

I've been working on the intricate carvings with Aiyana's dad for the last four hours. My back and hands are killing me, but I'm acting as if I'm completely unbothered because I know the moment I stop, he'll try to help.

I've got maybe twenty more minutes of carving to do before I'm finished and can head home to ice my hands.

"Thanks for this, Kas." He smiles down at me, gripping my shoulder as I work.

"Anything for my favorite guy." I peer up at him, then continue working, my hands beginning to shake a bit.

"You still planning to marry my daughter?" He chuckles, and that has my attention. I set my tools down and turn to face him.

"That's always been the plan," I tell him, my voice steady and clear. This is a man with a heart bigger than anyone else I know, but he values respect and tradition. The way I broach this conversation will decide my fate.

He grips my shoulder more tightly, his eyes sharp as they bore into mine. He gives me a nod and releases me from his grip. "Better finish up in here. I'll grab you a drink for the road," he tells me as he heads back into the house.

My shoulders sag, and I drop my head into my hands. "Fuck," I grunt, shaking my head. That didn't sound promising.

I finish up, ensuring every detail is perfect before cleaning up and putting the tools away, dumping the shavings into the compost pile by the garage door before heading back in the house.

I wash up in the bathroom sink and grab the drink from the counter, chugging it down in just a few gulps.

Zuni leans against the kitchen counter with an easy smile across her ruby-red lips. "You know, we're both very proud of the man you've become. I don't think we tell you that enough," she tells me, making my heart swell in my chest.

"Thank you, *Etsi*. I appreciate everything you've both done for me. Truly."

"The pleasure is all ours, Kas. Now, tell me, what have you and my daughter got planned for the holidays since we'll be on our cruise?"

I chuckle. "She hasn't told you?" She shakes her head. "We're spending the holidays with Alessandro's family."

"Ah, so your sister finally pulled it together then, huh?"

I smile, loving how invested we all seem to be in their relationship. "Seems like it." I wink.

She pushes off the counter to envelop me in a hug, pulls away, patting my cheek, and says, "Maybe my daughter will do the same, hopefully soon, for your sake." She winks, turning on her heel to head out of the kitchen, leaving me stunned.

Did she really just say that? I won't deny that it's pretty validating to hear her voice the words I've been thinking for *years.* But I can't help but wonder how Aiyana would feel if she knew.

***

When I get back, I shower and send Aiyana a text to update her.

His cough is better. He saw the doctor today and he got the all clear to go on the cruise tomorrow.

Little Viper

Thank you Kas, it means a lot that you check on him like that.

Anything for you.

Goodnight my little viper <3

Little Viper

Goodnight Kas.

I crawl into bed and pass out within minutes, exhaustion from the day taking over.

Chapter Forty-Two

Kassian

Saturday, December 23, 2023

Aiyana's a little tipsy as she grinds her ass into me the moment Kat and Ale head upstairs as if we aren't all fully aware of what they're doing up there.

As much as it grosses me out, Aiyana's working overtime to distract me, and frankly, I'm just glad she's finally letting loose and allowing herself to have some fun.

I'm sporting a semi, trying my best not to bend her over and take her right here where all my teammates and their families can see me claim her.

I grip her hips tightly, running my lips over her ear. "Can I take my dirty girl to the bathroom and fuck you right now?" I ask, my voice coming out husky.

She turns in my arms, grabs my hand, and leads me up the stairs. I feel like we're in college again, and I kind of love it.

After the week I've had, I just want one carefree night with my girl, even if she doesn't realize she's mine yet.

We walk past a closet with the lights on and chuckle. A second later, the light turns off, and that sends Aiyana into a fit of giggles as she drags me into the bathroom. We both know Kat and Ale are in there, and while it makes me want to vomit knowing what's probably going on in there, I push the thought from my mind. She's an adult. A consenting adult, and it is *not* my business.

Aiyana shuts the door before peeking her head into the shower, looking behind the curtain. "You think someone's hiding in there?" I ask her playfully.

She rolls her eyes. "I've listened to way too many true crime podcasts to leave that shit up to fate alone. Good news though—we're all clear," she tells me, smiling broadly.

I pull her into my grasp and lift her ass onto the sink, working my fingers into her waistband and pulling them down her ass just past her thighs, then move her damp panties out of my way. She's biting her lip, eyes a little glassy. I stop, gripping her face. "You sure? You're not too drunk?" I ask, concern lacing my words.

She rolls her eyes again. "No, Kas, I've had a single beer. I'm a little less tightly wound than I was when we first got here, but I'm still able to consent," she tells me firmly and clearly as she pulls my hand back to the slick wetness between her thighs. "Now fuck me or get out so I can do it myself," she tells me with a laugh.

I groan into her neck, nipping the skin before sinking a finger into her, keeping a steady rhythm as she winds her legs around my waist. Her nails claw into my back, stinging in the most delicious way.

Her chest heaves as she gets closer to her release. Her lips fall open on a moan as I slip a second finger inside her, applying firm pressure to her clit with the pad of my thumb.

I watch as her body tightens, nearly falling apart for me, my name on her lips just as the door swings open. Kyle is standing in the doorway, eyes wide and apologetic. "Shit, sorry!" he says, slamming the door as Aiyana comes apart on my fingers, eyes wide and horrified but unable to stop her body's response.

When she finishes, she drops her head to my shoulder. "Oh my god, that's so embarrassing," she tells me.

I pull my fingers out of her, suck them into my mouth, and moan at her taste before fixing her clothes and helping her down from the counter. I smirk at her. "I think your orgasm was even stronger than it would've been had we not been caught," I tell her, chuckling. "Is my little viper into exhibitionism?" Quirking a brow at her, I laugh at the disdain on her face. She smacks my shoulder and stalks off, out of the bathroom and down the stairs, back into the throng of people down there.

She heads toward the kitchen, grabbing a beer from the cooler and popping the top, bringing it to her lips for a long pull, eyes locked on me the entire time. When she lowers the beer from her lips, I can't help but cage her in, back flush to the counter. My hands are on either side of her hips as I dip my head and swipe my tongue along her heavy upper lip, and again along that full lower one, the sour taste of her IPA zipping along my tastebuds.

She's staring at me, wide-eyed and shell-shocked, until her gaze finally averts, and she pushes me off of her. I look over my shoulder and see Kat and Ale heading down the stairs, their faces flushed and hair a mess.

I smirk, shaking my head in embarrassment as they approach us, their appearances ruffled.

When they're within earshot, Aiyana pushes herself off the counter and launches herself at Kat, winding her arm through hers as she pulls them away from Ale and me in the kitchen. He and I just shrug at each other and head back toward the guys playing beer pong like a bunch of frat boys.

***

"Come on, little one, let's get you upstairs," I tell Aiyana, hauling her over my shoulder as I drag her inside, thankful that no one seems to be in the lobby right now.

Kat and Ale shake their heads at her, laughing quietly because Kat doesn't drink and Ale was nursing the same beer the entire night. When we get upstairs, Kat opens their door for me but steps out. "I'm gonna stay at Ale's tonight. I'll head over early to help her pack though." She stands on her toes to press a kiss to my cheek. "You'll lock up for me?" she asks, and I nod.

"Love you, Kitty-Kat," I tell her.

"Love you." She smiles fondly, leaving me in the entryway with Aiyana's tiny limp body draped over me.

I bring her to her room, being careful only to turn on a lamp, not wanting to wake her. I lay her gently on her side of the bed before grabbing an oversized shirt from her dresser and sitting next to her. I leave her leggings on but work her arms out of the sleeve of her winter coat and then toss her skimpy top in a heap on the floor with it before sliding the shirt over her head. Then I work my fingers into her hair, undoing the tight bun at the top of her head, not wanting her to wake up with a migraine. Once it's undone, I do my best to braid it to the side and throw a blanket over her.

When I get back from the bathroom, she's snuggled her way into the center of the bed and turned the lights out, so I strip down to my briefs and curl in next to her, setting an alarm for five so I can get out of here before Kat gets back.

She wraps herself around me almost instinctively, sighing as her head hits my warm chest, and my arm wraps around her upper body, holding her tightly to me. I press a kiss to the crown of her head and whisper, "Goodnight, my little viper."

Chapter Forty-Three

Aiyana

Sunday, December 24, 2023

There's an unbelievably annoying rooster crowing sound blaring from somewhere near me. I smack my hand around, searching for the offending noise, but a large, warm, and calloused hand wraps around mine, bringing my fingers to his lips and pressing a kiss. His other hand must've silenced the noise because the horrendous screeching has stopped.

"Good morning, little viper," he whispers.

I finally pry my eyes open to be able to look up at Kas, lying bare-chested in my bed, looking snug as ever.

"Don't you ever sleep in your own bed?" I ask him, but there's no bite to my words.

"Not if I can help it." He shoots me a cocky smirk but works to unwind me from his body, standing and getting dressed in last night's clothes. "Kat said she'll be over early to help you pack for the next couple of days." My head is spinning, and I can't remember what it was I agreed to do today. He smirks again. "It's Christmas Eve, little viper. We're going to Alice's family home."

Realization floods my mind. "Oh shit, yes, I didn't forget." I sit up, feeling a little nauseous until I look down and see that Kas changed me into one of my sleep shirts, and one of the ugliest braids I've ever seen in my life is now hanging over my shoulder. My stomach swarms with butterflies. I push the thoughts away, shaking them from my mind quickly and sending a jolt of pain down the base of my skull. "I'm actually packed already. My bag's in the closet." I do my best to beam up at him.

"Bag or bags, plural?" he replies, a smirk plastered on his gorgeous face. "We both know you've never packed just a single bag for anything in your life."

I shrug. "Okay, bags," I tell him, drawing out the "s." "Asshole," I mutter half-heartedly.

He smiles, now fully dressed, and presses a kiss to the tip of my nose. "I've got to finish some stuff at my place. I'll be back to pick you guys up in a few hours."

***

I'm still a little bummed that we didn't get to spend the holidays with my family this year, but Ale's family has been so welcoming, and it's been really nice to get to hang out with Rose and her wife. Charlie is super sweet, while Rose is definitely a little socially awkward, though she holds herself with some serious confidence and blazes through life. Charlie is all about the banter. She's witty and boisterous—everything I love in a woman. Their love is timeless, and Ale's pursuit of Kat makes even more sense now that I've met his family. His parents, Gloria and Angelo, are madly in love, as are his siblings and their wives, Dante and Arielle and Rose and Charlie.

They give me the same warm feeling I get when I watch my own parents interact, but in the last few years, it's been different. Mom's always on high alert, waiting for the shoe to drop and Dad to wind up in the hospital, which he does pretty frequently.

I just hope this cruise helps cut through some of that tension they've been feeling.

When it's time for everyone to go to bed, Kat and Ale help the kids make a pillow fort and opt to sleep in the living room with them. Kas and I head up to the third floor of the brownstone home, where the guest rooms are located. The house isn't huge when you consider how many people grew up in it, but there are six bedrooms. They had the first-floor office converted into a room when Gloria's multiple sclerosis symptoms started becoming more cumbersome, so they're down there. The second floor consists of three rooms, and the top floor has the other two rooms where Kas and I will be staying. Separately.

At least, we're supposed to be.

The rooms are small, with a full-size bed in each and a small nightstand on the side closest to the door. The furniture is eclectic—random pieces acquired over time, likely from friends, family, garage sales, and the like.

The mattress in my room sits on an old metal frame with textured cream-colored paint. The metal bars wind together like grape vines on the headboard, and the bedspread is a deep eggplant purple with little gold beads embroidered into it.

The walls are covered in textured wallpaper, and there's residue on the legs of the nightstand where a child likely placed stickers that have since been scraped off. I smile at the thought of a young Alessandro running around this house with his siblings.

After unmaking the bed, I slip into the over-the-top Christmas pajamas Gloria left on everyone's beds. Apparently, that's a tradition for them too. *So many traditions.*

My family has tons of our own, but they're all embedded in our culture and rely heavily on what we're told is expected of us from our ancestors. I've never minded. Our traditions are what keep our culture alive in a world that was literally created to dismantle our entire society so many years ago.

I was so lost in my thoughts, I didn't hear Kas enter, his hands slipping around my waist as he hugs me tightly to his chest from behind, my back flush with his front.

He breathes me in. "You smell like snickerdoodle cookies." He laughs in my ear, his warm breath coasting over the skin, sending goosebumps down my arms.

I snort. "That's probably because I ate half a dozen of them."

His chest rumbles with repressed laughter, the sound gently shaking me from where our skin is connected. "I wonder if you taste like snickerdoodles now too..." He trails off, fingers winding in my hair as he adjusts the angle of my mouth for better purchase. His tongue swipes along my lower lip. "Mm, sweet like sugar," he says, and then his tongue dips into my mouth, his erection growing against my back. My head swims with need as an ache grows between my thighs.

He trails his hands down my waist, releasing my mouth as he slides his deft fingers toward where I need them. "Can I stay with you tonight?" he asks, and I nod, figuring no one will be coming up here anyway, not with Kat and Ale sleeping downstairs.

Spinning me around, he grips my ass, pressing me into his growing length, and a moan slips past my lips.

His hand shoots out to cover my mouth. Smirking, he tells me, "You'll have to be a good girl and come quietly tonight. Can you do that for me?"

I nod vigorously, and he chuckles again. "Suddenly so eager to do what I say. Who would've thought my cock would be the magic wand I needed to get you to agree to something?" He laughs before picking me up and hauling me against the wall with a gentle thud.

His hand comes between my legs, slipping the pajama pants down my thighs as he pulls my panties to the side. He pulls himself out of his pants, stroking the thick length of his swollen cock, squeezing the tip, and cum leaks out. I lick my lips, wanting to taste it.

Kas catches the motion and clamps his hand back down on my mouth before plunging into me.

My head snaps back to the wall, back arching my hips into him as he plows into me relentlessly. I wrap my arms around his neck, legs clamped around his waist, squeezing as I hold on for dear life. I bounce myself up and down his length, heat searing through me, and I know I won't last another minute. This man drives me fucking wild.

"Such a good girl," he groans into my ear, swapping his pace to slow down a bit, swirling his hips and hitting that spot that makes my eyes roll. The walls of my pussy are clamping down on him as he plunges in and out of me, taking him to the hilt and back all the way out again.

The pressure feels so good. I think I might implode with the sensations. My orgasm hits me out of nowhere, coming faster than I ever thought possible, his hand keeping my moans and screams to a minimum.[1] And when I finish, my pussy lips swollen and aching, he gives one last deep thrust into me. His jaw goes slack, eyes clenching shut as he turns rigid, pumping his hot cum into me.

We stand here for a while, our foreheads pressed together as we slow our breathing, and my tight core begins to relax. My gaze is cast downward at his chest; the viper tattoo seemingly stares at me, acting as a reminder of how much I really do mean to Kas, even if I'm just pretending it's only about sex.

A few more moments pass before he gently lifts me off of him and sets me on my feet, swatting my ass. "I'll go grab a washcloth and be right back," he says as he heads downstairs toward the bathroom. He returns a minute later with two washcloths, coming over to me and pressing the warm, wet one between my legs first, cleansing me, and then patting my sensitive skin dry with the second cloth. My cheeks flame at the sweet sentiment.

"Now get into bed because I'm fucking exhausted. Those kids wore my ass out today."

I release a long yawn and crawl under the sheets. Kas gets in behind me and drags me on top of his chest, pressing a kiss to my head. "Goodnight, my little viper, and Merry Christmas."

"Merry Christmas, Kas." I yawn, quickly falling asleep in his arms.

---

1. **Collide – Justine Skye (ft. Tyga)**

Chapter Forty-Four

Kassian

Monday, December 25, 2023

Aiyana and I woke up early, way before anyone else in the house, that is until we heard who I can only imagine was Dante muttering curses as he edged his wife for nearly an hour and a half. His room is the one directly below us, and it's separated by the bathroom and a hallway, so for his siblings' sake, I'm hoping none of them had to endure that shit.

Of course, the sounds turned Aiyana on, so she sucked my cock like a champ before climbing on top of my lap and riding me like my own personal cowgirl.

Best Christmas morning ever.

And man, this family likes to eat. I'm not complaining either. I was really into the brunch, followed by cookies, a midday nap, soccer with the kids in the yard, the massive early dinner everyone helped set up, all the desserts, and even that dumb elf thing.

All the kids were put to sleep upstairs, and Gloria and Angelo went to bed early, so we're all just sitting around the fireplace as Gianni plays the piano and serenades us all.

He and Dante clearly have a bit they do each year, which was honestly hysterical. They go back and forth in a duet that Kat and I always complained about as kids, but their version is incredible.

As the song comes to an end, Aiyana's eyes are wide and lit with excitement as she sits on the ground next to me. She's beaming up at Gianni as he plays the old piano he and his best friend, Alex, dragged out here. When the music stops, Aiyana claps her hands together like a crazed fan, laughter erupting out of her in a display of pure bliss I haven't seen since her dad's health took a turn for the worse.

It even drags a smile, a real, genuine toothy one, out of Gi, who is just about the most sullen guy I've ever known. He leans down between us, gently brushing a lock of hair out of Aiyana's face and behind her ear. A surge of jealousy rushes through me until his eyes turn to me, and he whispers to us so only we can hear, "If you thought that was good, wait till you guys hear our rendition of Dominick The Donkey, jing-a-di-jing, hee haw, hee haw." He chuckles and winks at me before straightening in his seat.

Aiyana releases a snort that makes Gi's shoulders shake a little with laughter, but he composes himself and pretends not to hear it.

I smile over at Aiyana and whisper in her ear. "Is that the kind of flirting you want me to do? Will that finally win you over?" I ask, cocking a brow at her, a wide grin spread across my face.

She snorts again, smacking my leg. "You're an idiot, and he wasn't flirting with me." She rolls her eyes and goes back to ignoring me.

A while later, we all say our goodnights, heading upstairs for bed while several of the parents stay downstairs with Kat and Ale.

I swat her butt as she walks ahead of me, and she climbs into bed, not bothering to ask if I'm sleeping with her tonight. We're so exhausted that sex isn't on either of our minds as we curl around each other. I press my lips to hers and then to the tip of her nose and mumble into her hair, "Goodnight, my little viper."

Chapter Forty-Five

Aiyana

Tuesday, December 26, 2023

Kas absolutely wrecked my body this weekend despite the thin walls of the De Laurentiis home. And I've never been more content.

Though I wouldn't admit that to Kas, of course. His ego is plenty big as is.

We've been texting all day as I've enjoyed relaxing on the couch, taking my extra holiday hours in stride.

Kas

What are we doing for New Year's Eve?

Nothing.

Kas

Oh stop it, NYE is your favorite holiday you asshole. Just because Kat has to work doesn't mean we can't do something.

He's not wrong. It *is* my favorite. I love the fireworks, the excited energy, and the feeling of newness that lights a spark under everyone to try something new. I'm not necessarily here for the "new year, new me" mentality because it's just cheesy, but I'm all about reinventing yourself in whatever capacity you choose to.

Fine. You plan it. Something with fireworks. Nothing cheesy.

And it's NOT a date Kas.

Kas

Sure it's not.

If you think it's a date, I'll back out. You know the rules.

Kas

Yes, I'm very familiar with your dumbass rules.

Kas

But okay. Not a date. And I have the perfect idea.

Kas's ideas usually make me nervous, and for good reason.

'Kay, goodnight Kas.

Kas

Goodnight my little viper <3

Chapter Forty-Six

Kassian

Wednesday, December 27, 2023

I know I just saw her, but I miss her already.

I shoot off a text to Aiyana and send up a prayer that she says yes to a lunch date tomorrow.

Any chance I could convince you to grab lunch with me tomorrow at Giovanni's?

Little Viper

Tomorrow is Thursday. I work.

Giovanni's is right across the street. I could meet you there on your lunch break?

Little Viper

Fine, but stop using my weakness for calamari against me.

Where's the fun in that? ;)

Goodnight my little viper <3

Little Viper

Goodnight giant pain in my ass </3

A broken heart? *How rude.*

Chapter Forty-Seven

Aiyana

Thursday, December 28, 2023

Kas

Still good for lunch at noon?

Yep.

Kas

See you soon!

I roll my eyes, push away from my desk, and grab my purse from under it. I stand and work my coat on, preparing for the short walk across the parking lot toward Giovanni's. I won't admit it to Kas, but I'm stoked for the calamari. I'm also starving, and my rumbling stomach acts as a reminder of that as I make my way through the office and out to the parking lot.

A short, older man holds the door for me as he leaves Giovanni's, and I thank him before heading in. Once inside, I search the room, and my eyes land on a sight that has my stomach in knots and bile climbing up my throat.

Giovanni's is a small Italian café with about ten round tables that comfortably seat two to four people. Each table has a small glass vase with dried wildflowers and maroon cloth napkins at each seat. The atmosphere is very relaxed, and quiet music plays in the background, usually creating a calming environment. *But not today.*

Today, I'm filled with nervous energy as I meet Kas for lunch because this suddenly feels like much more than I'd bargained for. Since when did we go from sleeping together to lunch dates in the middle of my work week?

My breath leaves my lungs, my body tight with regret because I'll *never* be able to just give in to our wants. Not while I'm tethered to my desire to fulfill family obligations and make my father proud, especially not now that he's sick.

They got back from their cruise yesterday, and my mom admitted that they'd had to see the on-board medical team a few times. Nothing serious, but the fear of losing him still welled in my stomach, churning bile.

My eyes meet Kas's, and his face lights up with a broad smile. He stands, heading straight toward me. His arms wrap around me in a hug that crushes my body to his, and some of my earlier anxieties begin to dissipate.

We can do this—*we* can be close friends and support each other without having to be *together* romantically, right?

He presses a chaste kiss to the top of my head, gently setting me back down on my feet. “How’s work?” he asks, pressing his hand into the base of my spine as he steers us toward our table.

I take a seat, grabbing the menu in front of me even though I already have it memorized. “It’s been good. I’ve been working on a project with Rose, and things are coming along incredibly well,” I say with a small smile. I feel really good about this project, and I know I’ve always had Kas’s support.

“That’s my little viper, kicking ass at work just like she does in every other part of her life.” He winks.

We spend the next hour talking about my parents’ cruise, and Kas surprises me when he shows me a ton of photos my dad sent him from their vacation. Mom sent me half as many as Kas received, so it was nice to see how much fun they had and that they got to relax a little, considering how much stress I felt when Mom told me his health was a little rocky while onboard.

Kas pays for our lunch and pulls me into his side, walking me back to work.

I come to a stop on the sidewalk, still several yards from the doors to my building, turning to face him. I place my hands on his cheeks and give into the emotions threatening to pull me under. My eyes well with tears as I press my lips to his full, warm ones, and before he can deepen the kiss, I pull away, stepping out of his grasp.

"I'll talk to you later," I tell him, calling over my shoulder as I hurry back through the doors of my office. *This is so unfair to both of us.* I want nothing more than to be with him every day between now and forever. But when I picture my dad's disapproval, my heart clenches as if he's reaching into my chest, taking my heart in his rough, scarred hands, and squeezing it hard until all the blood gushes out, leaving me empty.

My father adores Kas, *but that isn't enough.*

***

Tonight, when Kas texts me, I lie. My mind is too confused, and my body is too tightly wound to entertain a conversation with any semblance of normalcy. Just for tonight, I need to wallow in self-pity.

"Just tonight," I whisper aloud, promising myself.

Kas

You okay? You seemed upset when I left after lunch.

Yeah, just tired. Gonna head to bed early. Night Kas.

Kas

Goodnight my little viper <3

Chapter Forty-Eight

Kassian

Friday, December 29, 2023

I knew better than to ask her out to lunch. It was too much like a real date, and that's probably because I *wanted* it to be a real date.

She seemed fine with it, but when I walked her back to work, things seemed to shift as if she was second-guessing her decision to meet me.

How fucking stupid can I be?

Lacing my fingers through my hair, I tug and cup the back of my neck in anger. *I keep fucking up.*

No wonder she keeps finding excuses for us not to be together. I push her too far, too fast, and all because I'm just so desperate for any interaction with her that I can't seem to control myself. I shake the thoughts away and reach over to my nightstand, grabbing my phone and unlocking it. I pull up the number for Dr. Sanchez's office and speak with the front desk, scheduling a video call for this evening.

***

"And do you feel there's anything you could've done differently in that situation?" she asks me. There's no judgment in her tone, just a relatively open-ended question for me to consider.

"I think I need to just be more patient with her. I try to drag her along with me so she can catch up to where *me* and *my* feelings are, but it has the opposite effect. I end up just pushing her further away. She keeps saying my sister won't approve, and that's been her only reason why we can't be together."

I shake my head, letting the following words roll around in my mouth, feeling them before speaking them. "I genuinely don't think that's what's bothering her though. I don't know how exactly, but I can just tell that it isn't the real issue, but she won't open up to me about this *one thing*," I tell her, exhausted as we reach the thirty-minute mark in this conversation.

"You and I have discussed miscommunication and having time to sit with our emotions several times in the past. You know I'm never going to give you advice. That isn't what this is about, but maybe consider what you've learned up to this point and try to see things from a different perspective." She doesn't continue—just leaves me with that as I mull it over.

"So what you may or may not be saying"—I see her fight the urge to roll her eyes at me, but she remains professional—"is that she might just not be ready to discuss it, and I should give her the time to do so while acting as a safe space for the day that happens," I reply, feeling proud of myself for how far I've come.

She smiles, a real, genuine smile that she never gives me. "I'm glad you were able to come to that conclusion, Kas. How are you feeling now?"

I take another moment, fully considering before answering. "I feel better. A lot better than I did before this conversation. I know that my self-worth shouldn't be impacted by whether she wants to be in a relationship with me or not, and no matter how badly I want to change that, it isn't my responsibility to do so. Sometimes, people just need the opportunity to work things out for themselves. I'll always be a safe space for her, and I hope I can show her that with time and through my actions."[1] I feel like giving myself a pat on the back for that.

"I'm glad to hear you're feeling better, Kas. Do you maybe want to increase these meetings to weekly for a little while?"

"That might be a good idea, actually; let's plan to do that going forward. At least for a while."

“That sounds like a good plan. Call my office if you need anything in the interim. This was a good call, Kas. You really have come so far, and I hope you see that.”

I nod. “I do. I appreciate all of your help, Dr. Sanchez, really.”

She smiles at me before ending the meeting.

I set my tablet down and swap to my cell, sending Aiyana a text and hoping it reaches whatever part of her is hurting too badly to share with me.

> Goodnight my little viper <3 I'm always here for you, in any capacity you need me. Let me know if you need a safe space and I'll be that for you. Through anything and everything, always.

---

1. **Agora Hills – Doja Cat**

Chapter Forty-Nine

Aiyana

Friday, December 29, 2023

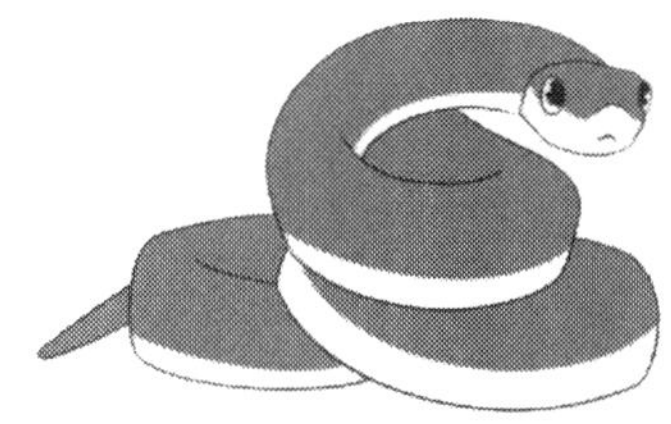

Kas's text has fucking ruined me.

My eyes are puffy, and my throat is raw from the tears I've shed the last half hour.

He *is* my safe space! He always has been, and I so desperately want him to know that, but I don't deserve to confide all of my sorrows in him, knowing that I'm the one causing this whole mess. I could just end things. Cut us both loose and give him a shot at being with someone else, but even the thought of that has my hair standing on end, nausea rippling through me. Selfishly, I don't think I could ever truly be happy for him if he found someone else.

Today, I decided that if I'm going to be a raging cunt about this whole thing and make it all about me, I might as well make him happy in the meantime. We can't have a relationship or get married, but I can still indulge him and do the things he wants us to, like go out on dates and do whatever the hell wild shit he's got planned for New Year's Eve.

I've thought about what he said all day, those words never fully leaving my mind as I ambled about my day, going through the motions on autopilot.

When I get home, I head to my room to shower and get changed, and then I plan to text Kas. I know I need to mentally prepare myself first, though, hence the long hot shower I'm about to take.

***

Thank you Kas, you're the best.

What are we doing NYE?

Kas

You think I'm the best?

Kas

Hah, I knew it.

I roll my eyes, knowing he's saying this shit despite probably holding his breath the last twenty-four hours, waiting for me to give him something, *anything*.

There's that ego again… So, our plans?

Kas

It's a surprise.

Ooh ooh ooh! I love surprises, tell me!

Kas

Then it wouldn't be a surprise, you fucking brat.

Would it surprise you if I told you I kind of like being called a brat?

Kas

Not at all lol. I'll pick you up at two on NYE. Dress comfortably.

Comfortable attire on NYE??? No sequins?????

Now I'm really lost!

Kas

Again… BRAT.

Kas

Call me?

My heart starts racing. I want to call him, I really do, but I can't be held accountable for the way my body responds to him. Even over the phone. And just like that, my phone is ringing with a video call.

I take a steely breath and answer; his hazel eyes and full lips light up the screen. He looks like he just got out of the shower; his dark hair is damp, and his jaw is covered in stubble from a few days of growth. I haven't seen him with this much facial hair in a while. I kind of love it.

He clears his throat, eyes glimmering with mischief. "You should take a picture—it lasts longer." He smiles as my face heats.

"I was just trying to work out why you have such a massive ego." I roll my eyes playfully. "Nothing I've seen so far is enough of a reason for you to drag that heavy thing around with you." I realize as soon as the words leave my mouth that I fucked up. He doesn't think I'm talking about his ego anymore.

"My dick is quite heavy, isn't it? Speaking of which, why hasn't it been inside that sweet cunt of yours since Christmas?" he asks, sending heat radiating straight to my core. I clench my thighs together, trying to regain my composure, but he can read my face so well.

"Put your headphones in, little viper."

I'm too turned on to deny him. I have no idea how this call took such a turn, but I open my side drawer, grabbing my wireless headphones and a vibrator. Then, rethinking it, I grab another... just in case.[1]

I pop the headphones in and get my phone synced, lying back on my pillows and working my shorts down my thighs, kicking them off. I grab the phone, facing Kas again so he can see the headphones in my ears, and I'm met with his hooded gaze. "Tell me, viper, have you missed my dick?" he asks me, his voice low and husky.

"Yes," I moan. "Grip your dick and pretend it's me clenching around you."

He pans the camera down so I can see that he's already doing just that. His large rough hand is dragging up and down the length of his swollen cock, the crown glistening with precum as he squeezes the head, making my mouth water with need.

"Flip your camera around, baby. I want to see you as you work those fingers inside your slick cunt."

Instead, I sit up, stacking several books on the office chair next to me, and lean the phone against it, using it as a makeshift tripod so he can see me, *all* of me.

"Goddamn baby, you're fucking gorgeous," he groans. "One second," he tells me as he sets up his own makeshift phone stand. The sight of him pumping his cock as his face contorts in pleasure, watching me slide my fingers through my wetness, is erotic as hell.

"Tell me what to do," I moan, swiping my fingers through my swollen pussy lips at an agonizingly slow pace.

His brow quirks, and he sits up, bending forward to squint at the phone screen. "God, are those toys next to you? You fucking filthy little slut." My whole body shudders, accepting his words as praise. "Press the smaller vibe to your clit, and show me how you'd pleasure yourself if you were all alone."

I grab the vibe, turn it on high, and rake it through my slit, settling it over my aching clit as my legs spasm, heat zipping through me as my pussy clenches. "Oh god, it feels so much better with you watching," I tell him, whimpering with need.

"You could be in my bed right now," he grumbles, then tells me, "but the sight of my girl coming undone for me like this is incredible too."

God, my girl?

"What next?" I moan, desperate to have something in me to clench myself around and fill the empty ache in my core.

"Pick up the other vibrator and slowly press it into your tight little pussy; angle yourself toward the camera so I can watch."

I turn my body as he told me to, letting my legs fall completely to either side, opening myself up for him to see as I pick up the thick vibrator. It's eight inches long, two inches wide, and has a loop at the end so I can slide my middle finger in it for a better grip.

I set the smaller bullet vibe that I'd been using on my clit to the side and use that hand to spread my pussy lips, holding them open as I press the thick tip of the larger vibe against my entrance.

"That's it, baby, nice and slow. Let me watch you stretch around it." Kas moans, my body on fire with need. Inserting the tip slowly, my body stretches around it. My lower back arches, and my head is thrown back.

"Now pump it in and out; pretend it's my cock spearing through that warm cunt of yours." A chill zips down my spine, my toes curling at his words as I watch him—outright stare at him as he pleasures himself. [2]"Because I'm definitely pretending my hand is your tight pussy. All that wetness," he groans, "it's all for me, isn't it? You're fucking soaked, and it's all for *me*."

There's no point trying to deny it. Every time I've ever been this wet, it's been because of him, whether in person or just in my imagination.

"God, yes!" I shout, the vibrator fully inserted, stretching me past the point of pleasure. I increase the speed of the vibrations and buck against it, my hips begging for more. "Fuck, Kas." I release a breathy moan, my hand snakes under my shirt, cupping my breast, and I pinch my peaked nipple, the pain mixing with my pleasure and creating pure fucking ecstasy.[3]

"Fuck that sweet pussy, little viper, and let me watch."[4] My eyes clamp shut as I shatter around the silicone, my limbs trembling, bright lights flashing behind my lids.

I hear Kas grunt out, "I'm coming. *Fuck*, your pussy looks so sweet."

When we're done, I pull the vibe out, and my own juices gush out around it, leaving a small pool of cum under me. My cheeks heat, but I right myself, pulling my shorts back on and running to the bathroom to get cleaned up. I grab a new blanket from the linen closet and toss the sullied comforter on the ground. I'll deal with that tomorrow.

Picking up the phone and bringing it back to my face, I see Kas lying down, his bulging bicep tucked under his head as a pillow. A small, lazy smile plays across his face, eyes hooded and bright. "That was really good practice for Sunday," he says, giving me a beaming smile.

I roll my eyes. "Goodnight, Kas." Exhaustion washes over me like a tidal wave.

"Goodnight, my little viper."

---

1. **Broken Clocks – SZA**
2. **Whore – In This Moment**
3. **So High – Doja Cat**
4. **Too Sweet – Hozier**

Chapter Fifty

Kassian

Saturday, December 30, 2023

I've got everything set up for tomorrow, and I'm stoked. I know this might not change anything between us, but seeing the pure joy on her face as we ring in the new year together is going to be fucking incredible. It might even be the highlight of my *entire* year.

Be ready by 2.

Little Viper

I will.

Little Viper

Always so bossy.

You like it…

Little Viper

Only when your cock is buried deep inside me. Otherwise, lower your goddamn voice when you speak to me -_-

You're a menace.

And I love it ;)

Little Viper

I am, and I know you do. Goodnight Kas.

Goodnight my little viper <3

Chapter Fifty-One

Kassian

Sunday, December 31, 2023

I'm shaking with excitement at the opportunity to see Aiyana, especially because she's going to lose her mind, in the best way possible, when she realizes what I have planned for us.

She loves adventurous, out-of-the-box plans, and I'm pretty sure I've come up with an outrageously perfect idea, but even if it's a total bust, at least I'll get to spend time with my favorite person.

It's a few minutes till two, so I'm a little early. I knock and wait, hearing Aiyana rushing around inside before the door finally pops open, and she's swinging it wide for me to hold as she grabs her coat. She slips the sleeves of her black coat on, holding it open as she does a twirl for me and asks, "Is this fine?"

"You look gorgeous." My heart stutters in my chest just looking at her, and my hands aren't even on her yet.

She rolls her eyes. "I wasn't looking for a compliment. I want to know if this outfit works for whatever you've got planned."

Realization dawns on me, and my cheeks heat. She's wearing long black leggings with a tight-fitting, long-sleeved burgundy shirt in an athletic spandex-type material, dark-red knit socks that come up over the ankle of her leggings, and black Reebok sneakers strapped to her tiny feet.

"Yep, you look perfect." The smile that curves her lips is too much for me to resist touching her any further. I settle my hands on her hips, dragging her small body into me and tugging her head under my chin. She fits against me so perfectly, it's like we're made for each other. Bending my head, I press a kiss to her crown, which is sporting her signature braid, and I take a deep breath, letting her scent fill my lungs.

In the summer, she smells floral like jasmine but warm like vanilla or cashmere, and there's always a hint of coconut or citrus. It's the perfect combination of intoxicating. But in the winter, she changes her scent, swapping out for something deeper, warmer, and more sensual, like amber and honey. Always sweet but not too sweet, just like her. *Perfection.*

She plants her hands on my chest, pushing away from me a bit to look up at my face. Her big brown eyes stare back at me as if they hold all the secrets of the world in them, and I could just stand here forever, staring into them. Her full upper lip puffs out as she decides we've been standing around too long, her smile turning playful as she pushes off of me more forcefully and turns out of my grasp to head into the hall.

"Come on, sweet ass, I'm starving." She stomps off toward the elevator and presses the down button, never one to wait on anyone, but *especially not me*. She's never had to wait for me though. She knows I'll always follow.

We make it down to my truck and pull off onto the main road, heading out of the city, and the moment she notices, she turns her whole body in her seat, staring me down with a quirked brow. "Where are we going? It's New Year's Eve; shouldn't we be staying in the city?"

I shake my head. "Nope, and you'll just have to wait and see."

She huffs at that but turns back to sit forward again, then leans across the center console to fidget with the radio station before opting to set up Bluetooth from my phone. I sneak glances at her, watching as she presses the buttons, figuring out my new stereo system herself, and I know better than to offer to help. She forms that little crease between her perfectly manicured, thin, dark brows, and the tip of her tongue sticks out of the side in complete concentration as she finally lands on the setting for Bluetooth. It took her a little longer because my radio is new and unnecessarily complicated.

"Phone, please," she says, holding her palm out to me. I grab it out of my pocket, slipping it into her hand, mine lingering for a beat, reveling in the warmth that radiates off of her despite the chill in the air. My hands return to the steering wheel, and she tries to open my phone, realizing she doesn't know the password.

"Does it have face ID? Can I just swipe it in front of your face?" I chuckle at her question.

"Just key in the code—the password is one-two-one-zero-nine-five." She does as I say but stops abruptly, looking up at me as we approach a red light, and her mouth hangs open slightly in shock when she realizes.

"Your password," she says, her voice almost a whisper, "is my birthday?"

I nod. "Best day of my life." I smile when her jaw drops even further, and she smacks my thigh just as the light turns green.

"You're such a kiss ass," she snarks, fully recovering, and it makes me snort out a laugh.

"Baby, I'll kiss your ass any day of the week," I retort, and I think I see her tawny skin flush from my periphery.

"Turn the radio on," I instruct her, giving her an opportunity to recover. She does, turning the station to an early two-thousands pop station. A familiar song starts playing, and without a second thought, I roll down the windows and start belting out the lyrics.

Aiyana's beautiful lips spread into a full smile before she grabs something from my floorboard and brings it up to her face. She starts bellowing into her makeshift microphone, using a shaker bottle I had rolling around from yesterday's practice.

One thing Aiyana and I have always had in common is our mutual love of karaoke and how incredibly *bad* we are at it.

We carry on like that the entire drive, singing at the top of our lungs as cars pass, honking and laughing at us.

But I couldn't care less because Aiyana has the most gorgeous smile, and I'm getting to see it in full force tonight.

Several minutes later, we pull up to a small diner in a nearby town. I chose the place because she and I used to spend every Sunday eating breakfast at a local diner when we were in undergrad, and this one reminded me of it. It's also pretty close to the place we're going to tonight, and I wanted to limit how much driving we did in the dark, especially on a holiday with a lot of drunk drivers out.

Chapter Fifty-Two

Aiyana

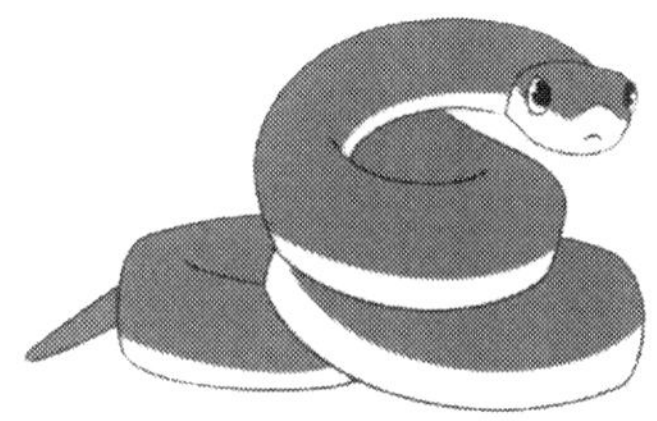

Kas pulls up to a diner in a small town that I'm not familiar with. We passed an emergency veterinary clinic a few minutes ago, but aside from that, there isn't much out here besides homes, well, and this diner, of course.

My stomach is rumbling and making some extremely unattractive sounds, so the moment Kas parks, I unbuckle my seatbelt and toss myself out of his truck, making a beeline for the door. He follows behind me, skipping ahead to pull the door open for me as if we're on some fancy date. Truthfully though, this is perfect.

I fucking *love* diners. There's nothing quite like fried eggs, white toast with butter and strawberry jam, and a freaking giant chocolate chip waffle. My mouth is watering just thinking about it.

The outside of the diner is pretty basic looking. It's a small white building with red windowpanes and a matching red roof, but when we get inside, it's clear this place is super retro, and I'm already obsessed. Black-and-white checkered tiles line the floors. An old-fashioned jukebox sits in the middle of an empty dance floor that I fully intend to take up residence on if given the opportunity. The walls are lined with mirrors and old-time photos of Lucille Ball from *I Love Lucy*, as well as some older pictures of items from their menu, including malted milkshakes I'd love nothing more than to nosedive into.

We step up to the hostess stand where an older woman with short, curled blonde hair stands, her light-blue eyes still glittering under her wrinkled lids, lips thickly lined with red liner crinkling at every angle. She smiles brightly at us, my eyes snagging on her outfit, which is composed of a thick knee-length pink skirt, a white collared button down tucked into it, with a black-and-white ruffled apron around the waist, and white flat sneakers.

My heart flutters around in my chest with excitement. I've always wanted to go to a place like this.

She greets us warmly and walks us over to a square, silver metal table with a red-and-cream top, setting down two menus. "Can I get you anything to drink?" she asks.

"Do you have vanilla cola?" I ask with a smile.

"Sure do," she says, writing it down on her notepad before turning to Kas.

"Just a water for me, please." He smiles brightly at her.

As soon as she walks away, I beam at Kas. "For the record, I fully intend to get a milkshake too; I'm just not sure which one yet. This place is *perfect,* Kas! I love it!"

He smiles broadly at me and places his large, warm hand on my knee, which sends a zing of heat through my body. "I'm glad you like it, little viper. Now are we ordering one of everything on the menu?" he asks me, his serious expression telling me he's absolutely prepared to do just that.

I snort. "There are about two hundred items on this menu, Kas. Even the two of us couldn't finish all that."

"Hey now, I'm up for the challenge. You good just splitting a bunch of stuff?" he asks, but he knows that's my favorite way to eat out.

I nod enthusiastically, and when the woman I'd assumed was the hostess comes back with our drinks and pulls out a pad and pen, she asks, "You two ready to order?"

Kas looks over at me, and just as I'm about to order my usual, he rattles off our order. "She'd like the two eggs platter with white toast and strawberry jam, two chocolate chip waffles with syrup on the side, extra butter, and whipped cream." He pauses, confirming with me, and I nod, my chest clenching at the realization that after all these years, he still remembers my exact order. He continues, "We'll also take a cheeseburger done well with a side of fries and honey mustard. Could we also get an eggs benedict, a side of fruit, and a root beer float, please? Oh"—he turns to me—"what shake do you want?" he asks knowingly.

My gaze sweeps back over the menu before landing on a malted chocolate, cookies and cream shake, so that's what I order. The waitress smiles, not even remotely fazed by the size of our order, and heads back to the kitchen.

"You remembered my order," I tell him, leaning into him and pressing a chaste kiss to his cheek. He shudders under my touch, and I pull back, knowing I shouldn't be entertaining this but wanting to so badly.

"How could I forget?" He laughs. "We went to that diner nearly every Sunday for four years, and you always ordered the same thing, though I added the second waffle on for me."

The memories flood my system, my heart aching again, and I shake my head, pushing the thoughts out.

I steer my gaze over to the dance floor where the jukebox stands untouched. "I wonder if it works," I say absentmindedly.

I hear Kas's chair skid across the floor, making a loud noise, and he reaches down to me with his arm extended. "Let's find out."

Taking his hand in mine, he pulls me to a standing position and drags me along toward the shiny box. As he takes out coins from his pocket, my brows shoot up my forehead. "You carry coins with you now?" I ask.

He flicks me gently between the brows, rolling his eyes at me dramatically. "I planned ahead for this exact moment, obviously," he says, shaking his head with a small smile as he inserts a quarter and pushes me toward it with a firm hand on my lower back. I sort through all of the music, finally landing on a familiar song that's bound to shatter my heart in two, but I don't even care because I'm just trying to live in this one perfect moment with Kas.

I press K8, and the machine makes a noise before the music starts trickling through the speakers. The people at the tables around us snap their attention toward us, looking quizzically as Kas pulls me into his arms. We sway to the sounds of Elvis Presley's velvet baritone as he sings "Can't Help Falling In Love."[1] My body presses tightly to Kas's, his arms bare in his tight-fitting black T-shirt, revealing the tattoos that wind up his hands, onto his forearms, disappearing under the shoulders and peeking back out around his neck. I wind my arms around his neck, letting the music envelop us in this moment, one I know my heart won't ever recover from, but I did this to myself.

Kas pulls me in more tightly as two older couples make their way down here, swaying slowly together, and a tear falls down my cheek, knowing Kas and I will never be like that. Old and gray and so madly in love with our spouse that we do cringey things like dance to old songs in the middle of a diner on New Year's Eve.

Kas catches the tear with the pad of his thumb, wiping it away and pressing a kiss to my mouth. His lips are soft as he peppers mine with tender kisses, and when the song ends, he pulls me even closer and holds me until we see our waitress heading toward our table, balancing our monstrous order in her arms.

He hooks my arm through his, and we shuffle back to the table, but I'm a little unsteady on my feet, my heart heavy and mood down as a result.

We take a seat as she unloads everything, and I look up to catch what her name is. Her name tag reads, "Lucy," and that gets a small chuckle out of me. *How fitting?*

Kas eyes me curiously, and when she's done, she looks between us and asks, "Anything else you need, sweethearts?"

We shake our heads. "Thank you, Lucy," I say, and she gives me a gentle smile before leaving us to eat our food.

My stomach grumbles on cue, so loudly that Kas peers over at me, holding in a laugh, and tells me, "Dig in."

He doesn't have to tell me twice! I unfold the red paper napkin and lay it across my lap, pulling the plate of eggs toward me. Just like the diner we used to go to, when you order two eggs, they give you three.

I start with a piece of toast, slathering a thick layer of strawberry jam on the toast point, and nearly moan when the buttery carby goodness hits my tongue. "There's just something so damn good about white toast with butter," I groan, speaking around mouthfuls, and Kas smirks at me, his hazel eyes crinkling at the corners.

He shakes his head, smiling down at his plate as he cuts the burger in half, placing one side on my plate. I grin up at him and take the top bun off, placing a fried egg on top and returning the bun. I bring the burger to my mouth, and this time, I release a low groan that has my eyes twitching. It's that good.

You'd honestly think I haven't eaten in years with the way I'm eating right now. Kas leans into me, whispering in my ear, "If you keep making those sounds, this whole restaurant is going to find out what it sounds like when you come around my cock in a diner bathroom."

A jolt of pleasure zings through me, straight to my core, and my inner walls clench. He leans back in his seat, taking a bite of a fry, but he does it slowly, eyes locked on me, and it feels so sensual, I'm starting to get hot. I shift in my seat, putting the burger down and wrapping my hand around the pretty light-green glass that's overflowing with the chocolatey shake and topped with so much whipped cream it defies the laws of gravity that it ever made it to this table at all.

I pluck the maraschino cherry off and keep my eyes locked on Kas as I put the sweet but sorry excuse for a fruit into my mouth, chewing slowly. After I swallow, I lower my lids seductively, pop the stem of the cherry in my mouth, and tie it into a knot. When I'm done, I flick my tongue out, showing him the tied knot sitting on the end of it.

When he leans in to take it from my mouth with his, I smile into the kiss, the tension from earlier gone and replaced with a new one, something lighter and more flirtatious that crawls under my skin and makes me dizzy with lust.

He sweeps his tongue through my mouth and tugs my hand into his lap from under the table, placing it on his hard erection. I squeeze as he steals the knotted stem from me before pulling away and setting it on a discarded plate that once held the eggs benedict he devoured.

I smirk at him, grazing my hand down his length and returning my hand to my fork to continue eating. He lets out a long, shaky breath and mutters, "You're gonna be the death of me, woman."

I chuckle at that and dive back into my food, glad that a more familiar air of lightness is surrounding us.

A while later, we're full. I'm slurping up the last drops of my milkshake, making a loud noise that has Kas chuckling into the crook of his elbow.

Lucy heads over to us. "Could I interest you in some dessert?" she asks, and while I'd love to say yes, I'm absolutely stuffed.

"I'm so full, I think I'd explode if I ate anything else, but thank you so much," I tell her and Kas. They both laugh, and he declines as well. She brings the check back, and he hands her his card before I can even offer to pay.

"You're such a guy. Next time, I'm paying," I say, rolling my eyes.

His hand grips my thigh, squeezing as he leans in. "You can try," he says in a low, gravelly tone.

When she returns, he fills out the check, leaves her a large tip in cash, and scoots out of his chair, holding his hand out for me. I stand, work my way into my coat, and loop my arm through Kas's when he offers it to me.

Tonight, I'm letting myself off the hook from all the guilt I know will still be there tomorrow. I might as well give myself the night off from some of it.

Kas opens the truck door for me and helps hoist me up. I know I'm short, but I can get up into the truck myself. I swat at his hands, and he chuckles softly behind me, finally letting me grapple for purchase on the side rails, pulling myself the rest of the way in.

He rounds the side of the new, shiny red truck and climbs in behind the steering wheel. I also notice the twine necklace I made him the year everything went to hell with his parents, but what I don't recognize is the small, wooden tribal emblem hanging like a pendant through it. He has them hanging over his rearview mirror.

"Where'd you get this?" I ask as I reach forward, rubbing my thumb over the smooth carved wood.

"Your dad carved it for me and gave it to me for our graduation from high school. I found it the other day and figured I'd put it somewhere I can see it."

That has those butterflies taking flight in my stomach again. I give him an awkward smile and change the subject. "So where are we going now?" I ask, trying to sound eager. But truthfully, I'm so damn full, I'm not sure I can do anything right now.

"Well, I planned around your massive appetite, so I figured we'd go park at this place I came across a while ago and watch the sunset before heading over to the real event of the night."

"Sounds like a plan," I tell him, skin warming from the truck's heater.

We sit in silence as he drives us toward the national park, which ends up only being a seven-minute drive. He reverses in, parking so the back of the truck is facing the massive rock side on our left that meets with the brush and dips in the middle like a valley where the sun is starting to set. It's gorgeous.

He leans behind the seat, grabs a duffle bag, and tells me, "Wait right here; I'll grab you in a second." I nod, suspicious but unwilling to ruin his fun.

A few minutes later, he's helping me out of the truck, bringing me along the other side of the vehicle until we're standing in front of the truck bed, which he has popped open with an air mattress he must've had back there already blown up. There's a mountain of tan-and-green blankets, fuzzy cream pillows, and a string of twinkling battery-operated lights. He grips my hips and seats me on the edge of the mattress, then climbs in after me.

My heart is swelling, and I feel like the fucking Grinch, except my heart grows three sizes every time I'm with Kas, and it's starting to become a problem.

I can't help the way my eyes well with tears, but I brush them away quickly, and when he lies down, resting his head on a pile of pillows with his arm behind his head, his bulging biceps and monstrous thighs catch my eye, and a new feeling starts to overwhelm me.

I smirk at him, gripping onto this new feeling, though *holding on for dear life* is more like it.

Scooting down toward him, I lay my body across his, my hands framing his face, and he doesn't miss a beat. Arms wrapping around me, he pulls me on top of him and devours my mouth in a searing kiss that sends shivers down my spine. He pulls back, looking so deeply into my eyes that I'm afraid he's seeing my soul splayed out and raw. Rubbing the rough pad of his thumb over my cheekbone, he says, "Come here," and pats the bed next to him. "Watch the sunset with me," he murmurs so quietly I almost miss it.

I shift in his lap, rolling over onto the side he was patting, and rest my head on his shoulder, slinging my arm across his taut abdomen. We watch as the sun slowly sets along the horizon, and as the chill starts to set in, he wraps me in his warm embrace and covers me in a soft blanket.

The sunset is gorgeous, one of the most beautiful I've ever seen. The colors are the most vibrant shades of purple, pink, and orange, the sky lighting up like it's the universe's canvas and it's decided to paint with watercolors tonight.

Kas clutches me to his body, and when the sun has finally set, I look up to see that his beautiful face is blotchy, and a single tear has fallen down his cheek. He sees me and gives me a small smile, but I kneel over him and kiss the tear away, brushing the salty wetness with my lips before pressing a series of kisses across his face and finally landing on his lips.

I know how special sunsets are to Kas. When he was little, his mom and grandma, whom he called Lola, would take him and Kat to the shore or really anywhere with a nice view for holidays and birthdays. They'd have a picnic and talk about what the new day would bring them, saying the sun was setting to wash away the bleakness of the day before, and that with the new day, beauty would rise with it.

When his mom was shot, she was never the same, constantly agitated when he or Kat would go to see her, and eventually, her caretakers asked them to stop. Then, a few years later, Lola passed away too. During both of those times, Kas shut down, and even though he wouldn't talk to anyone but me for such a long time, I'd still see him watching the sunset from wherever he was. He'd sometimes sit out on the back patio for hours in silence, just thinking. I always thought it was where he felt most connected to his mom and Lola.

He wraps his arms around my waist, crushing me to him, and leaning in, he presses a kiss to the divot between my shoulder and collarbone. "Thank you, little viper," he whispers.

---

1. **Can't Help Falling in Love – Haley Reinhart**

Chapter Fifty-Three

Aiyana

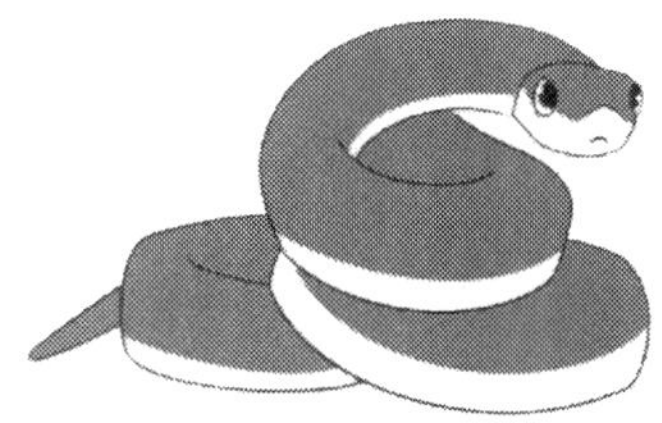

"Alright, are you ready?" he asks me, his excitement bubbling over. That mother fucker blindfolded me when we got in the truck, saying it was a five-minute drive away and he didn't want to ruin the surprise. As annoyed as I acted, I actually really love surprises, so I'm stoked.

"Yes!" I shout. "I wanna know!" I tell him, and as I do, he cups the back of my head, bringing me in for a kiss that has me clenching my thighs with need. "Stop stalling. If your surprise sucks, I'm sure we'll still enjoy it." I laugh, joking with him.

"My surprise *does not* suck!" he chides adamantly as he pulls the blindfold away and reveals a wide-open field with a single white plane with silver lettering across the side. A stout man with a reddish beard and bald head stands by the plane, waving at us with a massive grin on his face. There's a small runway that the plane is seated on, and beside the man are three backpacks. My eyes swing from Kas to the man and back.

"Kas," I say apprehensively. "Are we..." I trail off, trying to wrap my mind around it.

"We are!" he says, gripping my hips and twirling me around. My hands shoot to his shoulders, holding on tight, and the laugh that bubbles out of me is one of pure, reckless abandon.

"I love it!" I gush, cheeks twitching from the huge smile I have plastered on my face. "This is perfect," I tell Kas before I leave him to run straight ahead toward the man still waving at us.

"Hey there, I'm Greg, and up there"—he points to the dark-haired man with the deepest shade of smooth brown skin I've ever seen, sitting in the pilot's seat—"is Aaron. He'll be your pilot, and I'll be jumping with you and Kas." He leans in, lowering his voice an octave so Kas can't hear from where he's standing, still several feet away, as he introduces himself to the pilot. "I don't know if Kas told you or not, but he's come three times a week to finish up his solo dive requirements so he could be the one holding you for your dive today." He smiles at me, all of his yellowed teeth on display in a full, genuine smile.

I shake my head, fighting the grin that's making its way onto my face. "I'm a lost cause," I mutter under my breath, begging myself to come up with another way to make this work, but I've been over it a hundred times. There is nothing I can do to explain the situation to Kas so he doesn't think this is unrequited on my end while also maintaining his relationship with my father.

I do my best to push the thoughts out of the forefront of my mind as he heads toward me, slinking an arm over my shoulder. "Ready to go?" he asks Greg, and when he nods, Kas turns to me. "You ready, little viper?"

I beam up at him, pushing all of my reservations about this out of the way.

I nod vigorously, then run toward the plane and up the step. I'm glad I had the running start because there aren't normal stairs like on a larger plane or a private one.

When Kas gets in, he's carrying both of our bags. "You forgot this," he says, smiling and shaking his head in a mock look of disapproval, but he looks younger and more vibrant in this moment than I've seen him in years.[1]

Leaning across me, he grabs the seat belts and buckles me in, then reaches into his coat pocket and pulls out a beanie that he places on my head, tugging it down over my ears. Greg passes a pair of headphones to Kas, who places them on my head over the beanie, and once we're all secured with our equipment, we take off down the runway.

Most people would probably feel a little anxious doing something like this, especially not having had the chance to mentally prepare, but not me. I'm fucking *thrilled.*

My blood is practically singing with the adrenaline coursing through me, and the widest smile is spread across my face. I live for moments like this. Skydiving has been on my bucket list for so long that I've even taken the beginner's course for when I finally got the opportunity. But every time I've tried to go, either no one would go with me, or the one time I actually decided to go on my own, the weather conditions were too dangerous on the day I picked. Not today though. *Today is perfect.*

Aaron said the visibility is perfect, and the weather is a little warmer than it has been around this time in recent years. There's a little wind, but it's only three miles per hour, which is apparently low.

I'm practically vibrating with the thrill of finally getting to do this and with one of my favorite people on the planet.

Kas's hand reaches out to take mine, wrapping it in the warmth that I feel through our gloves. I squeeze his hand, grinning over at him, and his face lights up like the most magnificent fireworks display.

I can't help but tell him, so the next words gush out of my mouth in a loud shout. "You're beautiful!"

His brow quirks in confusion. "What?" he yells back at me, leaning closer, so I yell it again, louder this time, and his cheeks turn bright red as he averts his gaze toward our joined hands. He lifts them and presses a sweet kiss to my knuckles.

Greg interrupts to tell us we're almost at altitude, and I've never been more exhilarated in my entire life than I am at this moment, waiting to plunge back down to earth in Kas's warm embrace.

Greg makes his way to us, holding onto the bars overhead to steady himself. He helps us buckle in, double and triple-checking everything. Kas does his own checks over and over, ensuring we're safe before clipping me to him with the first carabiner. He sits on the edge of the plane with the door open, and Greg helps me balance as I make my way to him so we can finish connecting ourselves. When we're ready, I'm sitting in Kas's lap, my face frozen, a chill running through me despite the heat of his body pressed against my back. My hands are shaking from the cold but also from the endorphins.

I'm staring out over the clouds, the deep, dark abyss in front of me, city lights illuminating the ground below us, and the field we're meant to land in is in the distance. My heart is pounding out of my chest as Kas clutches me so tightly to him that I can barely breathe, and the smile spreading my cheeks is so wide that I'm afraid my gums will dry out from the lack of saliva.

When Greg tells us we're all clear to jump, Kas's arms sweep over my own before winding back around my waist, holding me impossibly close, and before we jump, he says into my ear, "Fall with me, Aiyana."[2]

And I do.

Our bodies fall forward, wind whipping around us as we careen closer and closer to the ground. We're screaming with complete, unadulterated fucking joy. My heart feels like it's been whipped around, rushing to my toes and back up to my throat, my head dizzy with glee.

I turn my head toward him, and his lips swipe along mine in the most dizzying kiss before breaking free and pointing ahead of us. "Look over there, baby." More chills skate down my spine at his words. "It's all for you," he says, pressing another kiss to the side of my neck. Suddenly, I'm falling, hard and fast and with no end in sight because Kassian Aurelio Narvaez is the sweetest man alive, and I am so madly in love with him that when the fireworks go off in an incredible display of color, I'm ruined. No one will ever be enough. No one besides Kas.

I reach my hands behind me, clasping them behind his neck as he laughs, no, fucking *giggles* into my ear, hundreds of fireworks lighting up the night sky. Every shade of red, orange, yellow, green, blue, purple, gold, silver, and everything beyond and between is displayed in front of us. As if skydiving weren't enough of a thrill, I get my own personal fireworks display as I fall. I fall so hard, deeply, madly in love with this man, and not for the first time.

My heart cracks wide open, and the contents feel like they're spilling out as my body shakes with all of the emotions. And when it ends and he takes my hand in his, we pull the parachute together. In this moment, it feels like calling a truce. Like pulling this parachute is our agreement to be a safety net for the other, whenever needed.

I may not be a lot. I may not be able to give Kas what he wants and desperately deserves, but I can give him this. I can be the safe haven he's always been for me until someone else comes along to do a better job than I ever could.

---

1. **Moment – Victoria Monét**

2. **SLOW DANCING IN THE DARK – Joji**

Chapter Fifty-Four

Kassian

Monday, January 1, 2024

Aside from the headache, Aiyana seemed fine after we landed. Hell, better than fine. She was positively fucking glowing from the adrenaline rush.

When we got back to my apartment, we sprawled out on the couch with desserts we picked up on the way home and watched the ball drop on TV before I dragged her to bed and made love to her like I'd never done before.

It was sweet and sensual, not at all rushed. I got to take my time, coaxing every moan and tremble out of her sweet little body for hours.

I look down at her in my arms, her hair a tangled mess, her face relaxed, and it's the most beautiful thing I've ever seen. I want to wake up every day to this woman wrapped in my arms, head on my chest as I kiss her senseless.

One day.

Chapter Fifty-Five

Aiyana

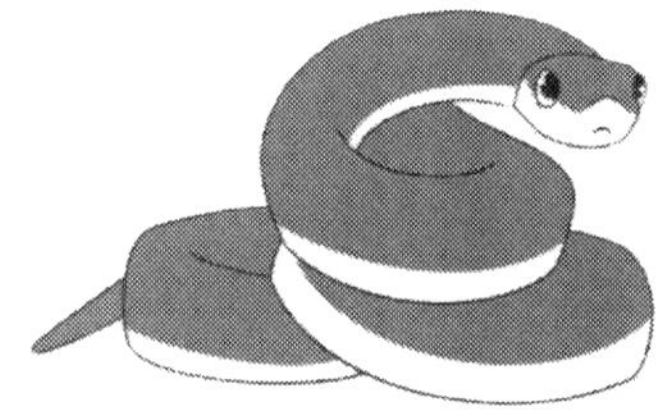

The bed's still warm, but I'm alone in it, my body a puddle in Kas's red satin sheets, a heavy duvet tossed over me, keeping me warm and comfortable. I smile to myself, my heart full from last night.

I've never had more fun in my life than I did jumping out of that plane with Kas. Pushing myself to a seated position, I muster up the energy to get out of bed, my body aching from the comedown of the adrenaline and the long hours that Kas drove into me, slow and steady as he made me come over and over and over again.

God, that man is perfect.

I shift to the edge of the bed and slide out, literally. These satin sheets are like butter. I slide around in them, but the good news is Kas will never have any real wrinkles, judging by how smooth his pillowcases are.

I stand on unsteady feet and make my way to the bathroom, brushing my teeth and using the toilet before following my nose down the stairs and into the kitchen.

Kas is standing over the stove, gray sweatpants hanging low on his hips as he cooks.

I whistle at him, causing him to spin around toward me, a smirk lighting his face as he peers at me over his shoulder. "You were supposed to stay put; I was bringing you breakfast in bed," he tells me.

"When have you ever known me to do as I'm told?" I ask, my voice taunting as I approach him, winding my arms around his abdomen, hugging him from behind, and pressing a kiss to the center of his spine.

He rumbles with laughter, and I feel it in every corner and crevice of my body. "Literally never," he admits.

His arms stretch overhead as he reaches for a plate out of the cupboard and begins piling food on it. He's made scrambled eggs with cheese and crispy bacon on the side. My stomach growls, and he chuckles. "Just one more minute, and you'll be eating."

I release him so he can continue what he's doing without risking burning either of us.

We sit at the dining room table and dig into our food, enjoying the comfortable silence until he clears his throat and looks up at me with an inscrutable expression.

I set my coffee down and lean back in my chair, folding my hands in my lap and steeling myself for the conversation ahead.

"I've got a string of away games soon that run into next week," he tells me, eyes sad. "Can we plan to do something when I get back? It's gonna be a longer stretch than usual."

At his words, my lungs simultaneously deflate, releasing the worry at the same time that my heart clenches, hearing the sadness in his voice.

"Of course, Kas. When do you get back?" I ask, picking my coffee back up and relaxing a bit into the leather chair.

"We fly out tomorrow night for a game in Vancouver, then onto Washington state, and we're back for a night on the sixth before leaving again on the seventh for a couple more days. So we'll officially be back on the tenth, and then we have a home game on the eleventh," he explains.

I nod slowly, thinking it over and organizing the dates in my head. "Okay, I've got book club with Kat and Alessandro's family on the sixth, but maybe I can stay over on the eleventh after your game?"

He smiles broadly at me. "Sounds like a plan," he says before his voice turns cheeky and his lips quirk with interest. "What book are you guys reading?"

I release a full-bellied laugh at that, shaking my head. "I'm not really sure of the name. Gloria invited Kat, though, and apparently, they got me my own copy of the book, which I should really start reading."

"Mhmm," he says, assessing me. "Is there any sex in it?"

"Oh yes, definitely," I tell him, pretty sure that was one of the selling points Rose's wife, Charlie, gave me to sell the book club idea to me in the first place.

“Alice’s mom is really something else.” He laughs. “She’s so sweet, but that woman has some seriously interesting hobbies.”

“Hey, we’ve all gotta find what we love, right? And for Gloria De Laurentiis, it’s smut.” I snort.

He laughs at that and continues digging into his food.

We finish eating, and I head upstairs to shower, except the shower leads to other things...

Chapter Fifty-Six

Kassian

Aiyana heads up the stairs toward the bathroom, and I can't help the pull I feel toward her. My legs carry, no, they fucking drag me across the floor toward her, and I take the steps two at a time to meet her in the bathroom just as she's stripping out of the T-shirt she took out of my dresser this morning.

I gather her in my arms, pressing open-mouth kisses to her jaw, neck, and shoulders as my hands reach for the hem of the shirt, lifting it up and over the smooth curve of her abdomen. She lifts her arms over her head, and I tug the shirt off, tossing it behind me.

She grinds her naked ass into my groin, my dick perking up and trying to drive itself between her cheeks. My hands come around her and cup her breasts. Her head falls back onto my shoulder as I squeeze them, tugging on her nipples and swirling my thumbs over the sensitive buds.

Her arms come up, hands skating along my jaw as she shifts, tugging my hair and groaning as I drive my dick deeper, spreading her ass cheeks and nestling the head of my dick against her tight little asshole.

"You want me to fuck your ass?" I ask, voice low and husky.

"God, no." She laughs, but it comes out as an awkward mix between a laugh and a groan. "Put your cock in my pussy and stretch me out, Kas," she moans, her voice light and breathy.

I chuckle against her and spin us around so we're facing the mirror, leaning her over onto her forearms so she can watch as I take her from behind. She shifts, gripping the dark granite countertop and angling herself back toward me. My hands skate down her spine, leaving a trail of goosebumps in their wake, and I reach between us, sliding a finger through her slick heat as I grip my cock in the other hand.

My legs are practically shaking from how tightly wound I feel. Heat is licking up the base of my spine, and my dick is fucking throbbing.

"You want me to take you from behind?" I ask, taunting her. "Just like this?" I slide the crown of my cock, absolutely dripping in precum, through her swollen pussy lips, adjusting so the tip is sitting right against her entrance.

"Yes," she moans, thrusting back to meet me, but I don't let her take control as I meet that sneaky little thrust with my own and plow straight into her. "Fuck, Kas!" She screams my name, and my cock twitches inside her.

"Yes, baby?"

"Fucking choke me, Kas," she says, and the ripple of pleasure that slices through me is unlike anything I've ever felt. I wrap my hand around her throat, her neck so slender and thin that my hand makes a nice little necklace at the base, and I groan at the sight.

Her mouth hangs slightly open, taking short gasps for air as I press down more firmly and slide my cock all the way out before plunging back in. I hold her steady with one hand on her hip and the other remaining on her throat.

I gauge my next words and figure, *what the hell, she can slap me for this later,* before they leave my mouth. "Does my dirty little slut like it when I choke her and use her dripping, needy pussy as a fuck toy for my dick?"

Her eyes widen slightly at that, but then her lids droop, hanging low and heady, as she releases a strained groan. "Yes." Then another moan and, "Fuck, that shouldn't be so hot." She sounds almost pained at the admittance, her voice strained and needy.

I glide in and out of her, praising her. "Such a good girl," I say as she clenches down around my length. "So tight and wet for me."

I watch in the mirror as her full breasts bounce, and her light-brown nipples beg to be sucked on, but I clear my thoughts, trying not to get distracted.

"Can you slip your hand into your wet cunt and rub that needy clit of yours?" I ask, not sure if she's able to hold herself up with just one arm.

She nods, and I release my grip on her throat ever so slightly as she reaches down, swiping a finger through herself, swirling her juices around her clit, driving her closer to her orgasm.

As her body milks me, taking me deep inside her, I feel my balls tighten. My body goes stiff as she shatters, falling off the edge like a plane taking a nosedive, and she shakes and trembles around my cock as I meet my release, filling her with my cum.

When she's sated and slumped against the sink, her hair stuck to her sweaty forehead, tan skin now flushed, I pull out of her slowly and deliberately, watching as our combined cum pools out of her, sliding down her thighs, and my dick twitches to life again.

She rights herself and wraps her arms around me, pressing a kiss to my jaw and gives me a lazy smile, eyes hooded. I lift her up and carry her into the shower.

Chapter Fifty-Seven

Aiyana

Tuesday, January 2, 2024

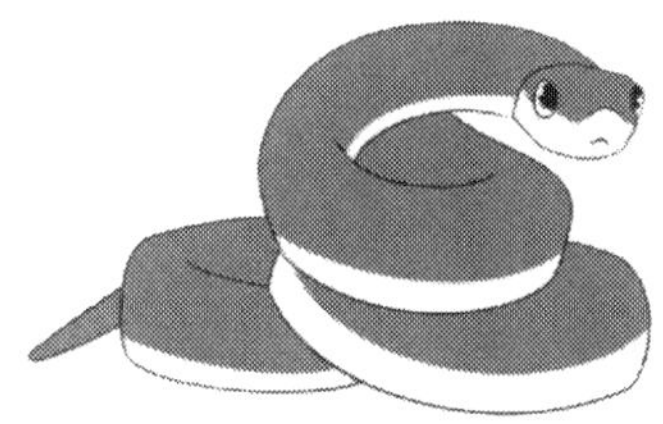

Kas leaves tonight for a long string of away games, and I can't say I'm not bummed. I know I'll miss him, but I think the time apart could be good for us. We've gotten so wrapped up in being in each other's company that it's made it difficult to separate what we are and what we wish we could be.

I unlock the door, hang my bag on the hook in the entryway, and slip out of my coat, hanging it in the hallway closet before slipping my shoes off and kicking them in too.

Kat should be home soon, so I make my way into the kitchen, open the fridge, and groan at the lack of food. We need to go grocery shopping, but she was working all weekend, and I was off having the most incredible night of my life with Kas.

When I got home yesterday afternoon, I was so sore between my legs that I didn't leave the house. I managed to change my bed linens, do the laundry, and vacuum the apartment, but not much else. When Kat got home, she was exhausted, so she took a bath, and we binge-watched trash TV with Alessandro.

I'm so glad they found each other, and I'm even more glad he loves the same TV shows that we do. It makes it so much easier to balance hanging out with him if it doesn't mean having to watch some horrible action movie.

Chapter Fifty-Eight

Kassian

Wednesday, January 3, 2024

The air is fucking frigid, and with my body fat percentage being so damn low this late into the hockey season, I don't have much insulation to work with, so despite my winter coat, which honestly resembles more of a parka, I'm still freezing my ass off.

Vancouver is a beast this time of year, and as much as I enjoy the nightlife, I'd much rather be back home in Philly, preferably with Aiyana in my bed.

Before I can travel too far down that train of thought, Kyle smacks me on the back, grinning at me when I turn my attention to him. "City boy freezing out here, huh?"

I shake my head, smirking. "Kyle, you're from fucking Chicago. We are *both* city boys, dumbass." I chuckle.

Matt, JJ, and Ale all catch up to us; evidently, Kyle and I were both hauling ass from the parking lot to the hotel. "Fuck, that feels good," Matt says with a groan as we enter the warm lobby of the hotel we'll be staying at for the next couple of days.

The hotel is a weirder one, definitely not representative of Vancouver itself. It's smaller than the places the team is used to staying in, and it has a quirky vibe that's reminiscent of a log cabin but more of a cushy, log cabin kind of feel. There's a small reception desk that looks much more like a home bar than anything else, but it's well decorated, and the real draw is that we were able to rent out the entire place, so we can relax without the prying eyes of the public. It just gets exhausting having to wear a mask of confidence in public in case people are watching. Sometimes, it makes my head spin.

After checking in, we head down the long corridor that's painted a muted green with paintings of the outdoors, and unfortunately, a few taxidermied pieces greet us at the end of the hall. I cringe internally. I've never understood why anyone would want a dead animal on their wall.

At the end, the hall forks off with a hallway of dark, wooden doors with gold metal placards indicating the door numbers. We all split off, me following JJ as we got paired together tonight. Coach Allister prefers to assign rooms for really no good reason, but honestly, the team gets along so well that none of us have ever had a reason to complain.

We unlock the door, and JJ heads in, with me trailing closely behind. We both stop abruptly in the entryway, wide eyes, and jaws slack. "What the fuck?" we both say, eyes snapping to each other and back to the bed. Not *beds*. One queen-size bed sits in the center of the room, a green, red, and blue comforter that looks like the original owner's grandmother must've quilted it herself lies on top. A cherrywood nightstand on either side and nothing else.

I'm not the tallest guy on the team by any means, but at six two, and two hundred twenty pounds, I'm still a big guy. And frankly, JJ is massive. Absolutely not a fucking chance we will fit on that together, and there isn't a pull-out in the room. "I call the window side," JJ grumbles, realizing there isn't another option and resigning to the situation.

I hang my head, tugging on the hair at the nape of my neck, and release a long groan.

"You think we'll break that thing if we both lie on it?" I ask him, only partially kidding.

JJ chortles. "Hah, only one way to find out," he says, flopping down on his side of the bed, landing with a thump that threatens to take the legs out from under it.

I drop my duffle bag on the ground next to the closet and climb in next to him. Our elbows touch if we lie on our backs, but I think we should fit if we both sleep on our sides. "If we're spooning tonight, I call little spoon," I tell him.

"Deal, but why little spoon? This reminds me of these things called 'tropes' that Veronica always tells me about. She said one of her favorites is the 'one-bed' trope where the couple isn't together yet, and they're forced to share a bed." He laughs.

"I don't plan to fuck you tonight, JJ; sorry to disappoint. I just like to be held sometimes," I reply, my voice taking on a whimsical quality as we banter.

He rolls over, throwing an arm around my waist and tugging me to him. It startles me so much that when I realize what he's doing, I laugh so hard my cheeks are aching, and our bodies are trembling so hard we're shaking the damn bed. Not that that would take much with how flimsy it is.

Before we can compose ourselves, my cell dings in my pocket, so JJ unlatches himself, getting up to use the bathroom. "Here's to hoping the toilet is bigger than the bed." He laughs as he walks away.

My eyes roam over my phone, and thankfully, it's a text from Aiyana.

Little Viper

You arrive safely, eh?

Sure did, don't ya know?

Freezing my ass off over here though.

Little Viper

I wish I were there to warm you up.

Little Viper

Also, do people in Canada really talk like that?

I don't think so. LOL

Ah, so we're being playful tonight and not grouchy. This bodes well for me. I smile, staring down at my phone and contemplate my next reply, but before I can send anything, JJ saunters back into the room, his massive frame taking up half the space. He stares at me with a small smirk curving his lips, and his dark-brown eyes pierce me with his gaze. He chuckles. "That Aiyana again?" he asks knowingly.

"Of course." I smile back at him. He takes a seat on the edge of the bed and leans over, staring at the screen.

"What are you planning to say?" he asks, quirking a dark brow at me.

I roll my eyes at him. "If I knew, I'd have typed it out and sent it already."

"Here, let me help," he tells me as he tries to snatch my phone away.

"Not a fucking chance," I tell him, holding firmly onto the phone, and he gives up easily.

"Okay, well, try to keep it down if you two have phone sex. I'm gonna take a nap before we have to head out for the game tonight," he says, rolling over onto his side to face the window.

I don't respond to that, knowing he's just being a pain.

I stare back down at my phone, contemplating what to type.

Little Viper

Kassian, are you really going to leave me on read?

Oh shit.

Truthfully?

I couldn't come up with a worthy reply and just stared at my phone the last five minutes.

Little Viper

That was almost sweet.

Almost?

Little Viper

Yes, until I realized you thought any of your replies are worthy of my greatness. ;)

Oh never little viper, but I can always try.

Miss me yet?

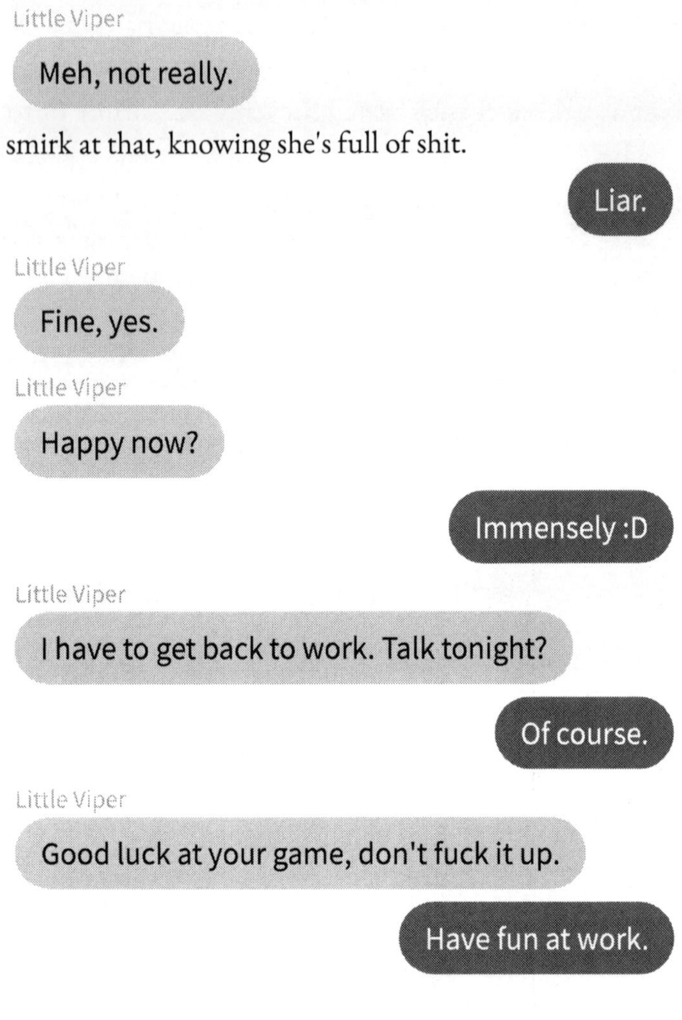

Little Viper
Meh, not really.
Liar.
Little Viper
Fine, yes.
Little Viper
Happy now?
Immensely :D
Little Viper
I have to get back to work. Talk tonight?
Of course.
Little Viper
Good luck at your game, don't fuck it up.
Have fun at work.

I smirk at that, knowing she's full of shit.

***

Coach Allister isn't one for giving pep talks, so he has our assistant coach do it. Once he's done, we finish suiting up and head out onto the ice to warm up.

I'm doing a few laps around the ice to start my warmup, though I swear to god it's so much colder out here than at our rink. It's got to be how cold it is outside that's affecting us so much.

We've started out pretty strong, but I'm exhausted. My muscles are starting to get fatigued already, and I have to use extra energy to warm up my body compared to when we're in warmer climates, but I'm still sweating like a whore in church out here.

I watch the puck, bouncing my gaze back and forth between the men on the ice and the black rubber zinging around. My skates slice through the ice beneath me, my heart pounding in my chest, and the adrenaline rush keeps me pushing my body to its limits.

I've taken several hard hits tonight, but I've also dished them out, so I can't say I'm upset about it. Alice has scored twice, and JJ and I are kicking ass tonight, literally. We're having to be a little more aggressive than usual, though our usual is pretty aggressive anyway since we play defense.

We win by one point, and the high that leaves me with is nothing short of exhilarating.[1] *This* is why I love hockey. Among other reasons, but this feeling, like I'm on top of the world, fucking flying, it's unbeatable. The only other time I feel like this is when I'm with Aiyana. Having the two together? Hockey and her? It could be an addictive drug—something I package up and store away for myself despite the killing I'd make if I sold it. Figuratively, of course.

***

When we get back to the hotel, JJ and I collapse into our shared bed, elbowing each other in the sides and finally agree to face in opposite directions.

I check my phone, and thankfully, Aiyana texted me. Though she's being sassy, which, luckily for her, happens to be something I love.

Little Viper

Lookin' a little sluggish out there hot shot…You feeling okay?

Fucking freezing here, colder than usual. We still won though. Aren't you gonna congratulate me?

Little Viper

Sure, tell Alessandro I said congrats on the win… you know, since he did most of the work ;)

Now I *know* you're just being a smart ass.

Little Viper

Congratulations Kas, I'm glad you didn't fuck it up.

Little Viper

Heading to bed.

Little Viper

Goodnight.

Goodnight my little viper <3

---

1. **Mad at Me. – Kiana Ledé**

Chapter Fifty-Nine

Aiyana

Thursday, January 4, 2024

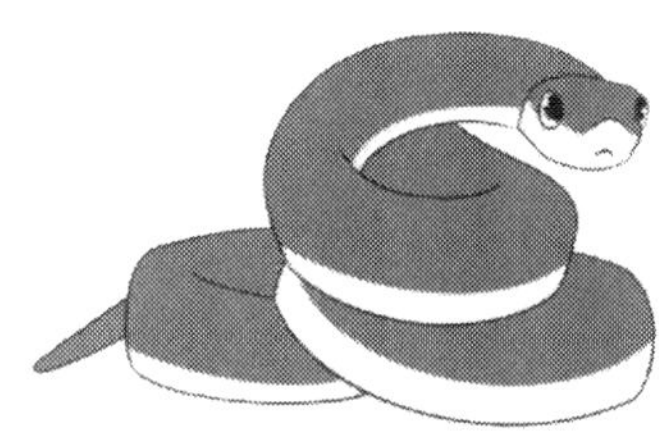

I'm really excited for tonight. Kat told me this morning that this new bar I'd been dying to go to just opened. She usually isn't huge into the bar scene, but they have a really extensive mocktail menu that she's excited to check out.

I toss on a short red dress with lipstick to match and a pair of strappy black heels. Before meeting Kat in the living room, I take one last look in the mirror, and my reflection almost shocks me. I haven't been genuinely happy in a long time. Not since my dad's diagnosis, and after that, having to leave Kas? It's been horrible, but for the first time in so long, I *look* happy.

My inky-black hair is done in loose waves, falling just above my hips.[1] My deep brown eyes aren't framed with dark circles, but rather, full lashes, and my cheeks are a light rose color that isn't from blush. I smile at my reflection, raking my hands down my frame, smoothing the dress.

I feel good, but I refuse to dig too deeply into the reasoning. A reason I'm fairly certain I already know but would rather avoid acknowledging.

***

"Oh my gosh! This place is freaking gorgeous!" Kat says excitedly.

"Even the bar is made from pink salt!" I point at the bar, the entire thing a large block of salt with a light embedded into it, lighting it from within. I imagine the top is coated in something so spilled drinks don't dissolve it.

The hostess walks us to our table. We hop up onto the high-top stools and immediately reach for our menus.

Kat scans it quickly, and I watch as her eyes light up. "They have a lavender martini mocktail!" Her obsession with anything lavender is unmatched, and frankly, she's onto something. Kat's the reason I crave that honey lavender ice cream so often.

She settles her hands in front of her, resting them on the table, fingers interlaced with one another. Her wavy hair is hanging around her face as she looks over the rest of the menu.

"Okay, so a charcuterie board to share and the grilled shrimp with mushroom and spinach rice pilaf for me, and the same but with grilled sea bass for you, right?" I ask, wanting to clarify before our waiter arrives.

***

As it grows later in the night, there are more and more people flooding the dance floor. We weave our way through the throng of sweaty bodies and sidle up next to a wall made entirely out of salt, lit from within just like the bar.

The live band starts playing an upbeat song that Kat and I both know.[2] We toss our arms around one another, swaying in rhythm to the beat of the song, moving our shoulders and nodding our heads to the tempo. I can't help but laugh at all the childhood memories of Kat dancing flooding in. She was the absolute worst, and frankly, she still is, but it's nice to see her let loose.

As the band shifts between songs, accepting suggestions from those in the crowd, our movements change, matching them. *I feel good*. I needed a girls' night.

My mind is getting hazy from the two drinks I've had and the exhaustion of the week that's starting to settle in. The anxious feelings I was battling earlier seem to have drifted away. Kat smiles at me brightly, and her eyes spark with excitement as an idea pops into her head.

She drops her arms from my waist and pulls her cell out of the black cross-body bag she has draped over her shoulders. Wrapping a delicate arm around my waist, she pulls me closely into her side and takes a series of photos of us before fiddling with the phone for a minute, locking it, and placing it back in her bag.

***

I drag my aching body back into the apartment, dropping my bag at the entryway and sliding out of my heels, kicking them off. I groan as my sore feet pad across the floor and into my bedroom.

"Tata, love you, bye," Kat says, sounding every bit as exhausted as I feel.

"Tata, love you, bye, you gorgeous, gorgeous girl," I call over my shoulder at her. I strip out of the red dress, the silky material pooling at my feet as I unclasp my bra, tossing it in the hamper alongside my panties, and head into the bathroom for a much-needed shower.

My beachy waves are now in knots, and my cheeks are flushed, but a lazy grin spreads across my lips as I take in my reflection for the second time tonight. I'm content. Things are turning around for me. Maybe I *can* have the things I want... someday.

---

1. **Feeling Myself – Nicki Minaj (ft. Beyoncé)**
2. **Laffy Taffy – D4L**

Chapter Sixty

Kassian

Friday, January 5, 2024

I'm exhausted, and it's late. I *should* be going to bed now, resting up for the day ahead, but my cell phone keeps going off, and I can't help but think about Aiyana.

We hadn't spoken today. Maybe it's her.

I see Kat's name flash across my screen, and the words "image downloading" ping every few seconds. I hastily unlock my phone, go to the messenger app, and open our thread.

What awaits me brings a huge grin tugging across my lips.

Aiyana and Kat are pressed side by side, staring into the camera as they laugh, their heads thrown back and mouths wide, white teeth gleaming across the screen. I scroll to the next photo, and it's one of Aiyana kissing Kat on the cheek, but half of Kat's face is cropped out of the image. There are several more, all increasingly more chaotic, their dark hair in tangles around their faces, a sheen of sweat glistening across their foreheads. Aiyana's fucking award-winning smile is spread across the screen in every one of them.

I feel like I've won the damn lottery. There is *nothing* better than having my own private collection of photos of the woman I'm desperately in love with. Even if she never picks me, I'll *always* pick her. It may seem a tad stalkerish, but I've been taking candid photos of her since we were in middle school. I even had those old ass photos downloaded and quality-adjusted a few years ago.

I smile down at the pictures for a period of time that I'm thankful no one had to witness because I'd never live it down, then send Kat a text thanking her and telling her I hope she had a fun night. By the looks of it, they both did. Kat doesn't usually go out much, but it's nice to see my sister enjoying a night out with her best friend.

I swap over to my message thread with Aiyana and shoot her a text that I hope she's awake to see. I missed her all damn day, and unfortunately, a few photos don't even begin to put a dent in the need I feel for this woman.

I saw you and Kat had a good night ;)

A minute goes by without a response, and I'm convinced she's probably in bed, but before I can lock my phone, three little dots move across the screen, indicating she's typing.

Little Viper

How do you know we went out?

Little Viper

Are you stalking me again Kassian???

I send her the slew of pictures from Kat in lieu of a response and wait for her reply.

Little Viper

Oh my god! She's a traitor!!!

Little Viper

I look horrible in those photos!

Stop it.

I'm gritting my teeth, rage searing through me at her words. How could she possibly think she's anything less than the most gorgeous person on the entire fucking planet?

You're fucking STUNNING, little viper. Keep talking down about yourself and I'll make you pay for it...

Little Viper

...

Little Viper

How?

Oh fuck, now my dick's getting hard.

I'll show you when I get back in town...

Little Viper

Sounds like a plan ;) Nighty night Kas.

She's not even fighting me on this? I'm not sure what I did to deserve this simply fucking incredible series of events tonight, but I'm not questioning my luck.

Goodnight my little viper <3

I give her another minute, waiting to see if she'll reply despite her having already said goodnight. When she doesn't, I put my cell on the nightstand and knock out for the night, dreaming of her gorgeous smile.

Chapter Sixty-One

Aiyana

Saturday, January 6, 2024

"Okay, okay, so maybe I didn't *actually* finish reading the book!" I finally admit, dropping my head into my hands as I laugh, getting pelted with pillows as Alessandro's family shouts at me in outrage. I feel a pillow whack me over the head and register that it had to be Kat.

I turn to her, my eyes wide, mouth agape. "Oh my god! You too?!" I cackle at her, our heads falling backward onto the worn-out floral couch in Gloria De Laurentiis's living room.

Everyone settles down, lightly chuckling at me as I toss the pillows back at each of the women sitting in the living room for book club. Gloria had invited Kat and me to attend. I wasn't able to make it to their last one. They said they normally text each other throughout the month about the book and have an in-person book club at the end of the month. But with everyone having some time off around the holidays, they all finished the book before I even had a chance to get halfway. It was really good, though, if not a bit close to home. I kind of felt called out by the main tropes, considering it was a "best friend's brother, idiots in love, hockey romance" book. I'd say I'll finish it in my own time, but they've already got next month's book picked out!

"Alright, we'll let it slide this one time," Charlie tells me, rolling her eyes playfully as she lounges back against the chaise, Rose's legs draped over her lap as she rubs small circles up and down her calves.

"How far *did* you get into the book?" Rose asks, eyeing me curiously.

"About halfway. Honestly, I read the smutty scenes a few times." I grin, and Gloria smacks a hand down on my thigh, laughing a full-bellied chortle that wrings another smile out of me.

"That's my girl!" she says from my right. This older woman has the heart of a saint, but she's a damn tyrant. *I adore her.*

"Okay, well then, we can definitely talk about the smut, at least! And frankly, that's the most important part anyway, right?" Arielle asks, waggling her auburn eyebrows suggestively.

I lean over, reaching for my wine glass that's sitting on the coffee table before taking a sip and tucking my legs up in front of me, resting my elbows on my thighs, a lazy grin settled across my face.

"You start then since you didn't finish it and all," Rose says, smirking at me, her pink hair tossed up in a messy bun and mischief playing across her soft features.

"The first scene is obviously the best," I tell them, fully confident in my words. "That first scene was full of passion and longing, and the way he took control of her? Instant tingles."

"I agree wholeheartedly, though I'm a sucker for a mutual masturbation scene, and that one was pretty spicy. I mean, *come on*, toys, *and* it was over a video call?" Arielle giggles, fanning herself dramatically. Her eyes swing over to Kat.

Kat's cheeks flush with embarrassment, and her hand settles against her chest as she tugs on the gold pendant hanging from her neck, a telltale sign that she's uncomfortable. I don't exactly blame her. She's kind of shy until she gets comfortable enough to be herself entirely, but it doesn't help that her boyfriend's mom is sitting four feet away, expecting her to spill her guts about her erotic, bookish fantasies.

"I thought the book was really sweet," she starts. "It honestly reminded me a lot of Kas and Aiyana's relationship." She looks at me, a smirk growing as I choke on the sip of wine I just took. I'm sputtering, coughing up the stringent liquid as my eyes bug out of my head, but she continues. "And for that reason, I refuse to talk about the sexy scenes." She laughs and adds, "I have no desire to think about my brother's sex life, so I'm out." She shakes her head as she eyes me.

I finally recover from my near-death experience long enough to get a few words out. "This book is nothing like Kas and me." I roll my eyes, hoping to put extra emphasis on the words I'm speaking, and a weight settles in the pit of my stomach. *Okay, it's exactly like us.*

"Oh, come on. You mean to tell us you've never thought about shacking up with Kat's brother?" The question comes from Rose, almost startling me with her bluntness, but thankfully, Arielle and Charlie chime in and rescue me from the awkward situation. Somewhat anyway.

"If I were into dick, I'd be all over that," Charlie says, her voice alight with laughter as Rose smacks her shoulder.

Arielle interrupts. "Oh, I agree wholeheartedly. He's got this suave, achingly sweet but dangerous vibe about him." Her brows shoot up her forehead as she turns to Gloria. "Just like Dante, but obviously, your son is the absolute best," she rushes out, making Gloria laugh some more.

"Oh, shut it, Red. I *know* you only have eyes for Dante. Don't think I didn't hear the shit you were doing up there"—she motions toward the floor above us—"on Christmas Eve, ya nasties." She shakes her head, laughing at Arielle's discomfort.

At that, everyone bursts out laughing. "I *knew* that's what I heard!" I laugh, recalling the distinct sound of the headboard banging against the wall, though I almost feel bad knowing she's likely taking the blame for not only herself but for Kas and me too.

A flush travels through my body at the reminder of that weekend.

I hear the door unlock, and the guys all trail in; Angelo, their dad, leads the rest of them inside. Dante, Luca, and Gianni enter the living room, Angelo standing behind Gloria as he presses a kiss to the crown of her head, bending down to whisper something into her ear that makes her smile broadly.

"Well, well, well, dirty birds, what are we reading this month?" Luca asks, chuckling as he snatches the book from the table behind Kat, flipping through the pages.

"Can you even read?" Dante taunts, smacking him over the head and grabbing the book back from him, handing it over to Kat. She smiles up at Dante, and he gives her a wry grin before taking a seat on the floor beside Arielle. He wraps his tattooed arms around Arielle and hoists her into his lap, making her squeal as he plants kisses along her jaw, holding her tightly to his chest.

Luca heads into the kitchen, and Gianni pulls up a chair, takes a seat, and nods at me in acknowledgment. I swear he gives me a small smile, but I can't be too sure since he speaks very few words and smiles even less.

Kat leans into me. "We should head out soon. I told Ale I'd call him before bed."

I nod at her. "Sure, we can leave whenever you want." I'm honestly itching to text Kas, and I can't do that with his sister right next to me.

"What are we reading next month?" I ask Gloria. She leans down, grabs up a tote bag filled with books, and hauls it into her lap.

"Are we feeling another hockey romance?" She waggles her brows around the room, and the guys all groan in unison.

"Isn't it a little weird that you read so much hockey smut? You know, considering most of your kids play hockey?" Luca calls from the kitchen.

Dante chuckles at that, shaking his head, and Arielle hollers back at him, "No one's thinking of your ugly mug, Luca!"

That's a blatant lie, and she knows it. Luca is gorgeous—dark hair, a strong jaw, and heterochromia with one icy-blue eye and one sage-green one. No one corrects her, though, opting to chuckle awkwardly as several of us say the same thing.

"That's not what your best friends have all been saying," Luca says smugly as he reenters the living room, a mug in hand that he places in Gloria's palms, not releasing it until her grip is firmly wrapped around it. She smiles up at him, thanking him as he gives her a small, warm smile, then returns to his usual smug demeanor when he looks back at the group.

Arielle rolls her eyes, shaking her head at him, but a small smirk dances across her lips.

Rose speaks up. “For the record, *I'm* her best friend, and I have never once had an interest in you, Luca.”

Arielle rolls her eyes. “We know, Rose,” she chides softly.

Gloria takes a sip of the liquid before placing the mug on the table beside her and rummaging around in her bag of books. She takes a moment, sifting through them, and when she finds what she's looking for, she pulls it out and throws her hand up, clutching a book with a green cover and a red sports car on the front. There's also a couple leaning on the hood and what I'm pretty sure are a bunch of dogs, but I can't make it out from my seat on the couch.

"This one's a soccer romance!" she exclaims. Everyone turns silent for a moment, eyes darting to Gianni, the air thick and then bursting like an overfilled balloon as the room erupts in laughter, and Gianni groans loudly.

"Oh, I've been waiting for that one, actually!" Kat says excitedly. "The MMC has some seriously hot, sad-boy vibes, and I *love* soccer romances!" I can attest to that. She's read practically every soccer romance available.

Rose pulls her phone out from her back pocket, looking down at the screen as she types. "What's the name? I'll buy a few copies and overnight them," she says with finality.

"*Quake,*" Gloria says, and Rose nods, never looking up from her phone.

After a moment, she tells us with a grin, "Okay, ordered."

I extend my legs, stretching them out in front of me, making my way to a standing position. "This was really fun, but Kat's dick whipped," I say. "Sorry, Gloria." My eyes swing to hers, and she bubbles with laughter despite my crudeness. "So we've gotta head out so Kat doesn't miss her call with Alessandro."

I lean down to hug Gloria, pressing a kiss to each of her cheeks as she does the same to me, and thank her for her hospitality.

We spend several minutes saying our goodbyes and finally head home. I know I blamed Kat for us leaving, but I'm exhausted.

***

Kas

I hear book club with the De Laurentiis family got a little wild, huh?

Wild by whose standards? Your sister's?

I know he must be referencing Kat's take on how the night went, likely overhearing some of her conversation with Ale.

Kas

So there wasn't discussion of Dante and Arielle getting freaky on Christmas Eve?

Kas

I feel kind of bad honestly… Half the blame is ours.

I plead the fifth.

Kas

Ah, well, I hope you enjoyed your night.

Kas

I miss you.

My heart cracks open a little wider every time he says it. This time, I finally give in. I'll blame it on the wine.

I miss you too Kas.

Kas

I should get to bed…

I'm exhausted, so same here. I'll watch your game tomorrow so don't tell me what happened! I recorded it tonight.

Kas

I would never…

Kas

Goodnight my little viper <3

Goodnight Kas.

Chapter Sixty-Two

Kassian

Sunday, January 7, 2024

I have to fight the urge to set one of those countdown clocks on my phone, telling me *exactly* how long it'll be before I see Aiyana again. It feels like when I was a kid, and Kat and I went on our yearly family cruise, or, at least, we tried to until Dad started using the money for alcohol. We'd mark up the calendar, counting down the days the entire summer until we finally got to go.

Except now, I'm just excited to have Aiyana's soft, sweet little body wrapped in my arms.

How was your day?

Little Viper

Relaxing!

Little Viper

I watched your game…

Little Viper

You need to let off some steam? Looked like you were taking out a lot of frustrations on the other team.

The only frustrations I have are with not having you in my arms, and my dick buried deep in that sweet pussy of yours…

We rarely text like this, but I'm hoping she'll play along. Maybe get her worked up for when she sleeps over in a few days.

Little Viper

That's a pretty good reason to be frustrated.

Little Viper

I hear my pussy is incredible. *Chef's Kiss*

Who the hell else are you 'hearing' this from???

Little Viper

Just you…

Little Viper

For now anyway.

Little Viper

KIDDING!

You'll pay for that, woman…

Little Viper

Looking forward to it ;)

You're such a goddamn tyrant.

Little Viper

Sure am.

Little Viper

I've gotta head to bed, I have a project processing early tomorrow and need to leave a couple hours early.

Sleep well.

Goodnight my little viper <3

Little Viper

Goodnight Kas.

I'll have to make a mental note to send her breakfast and coffee in the morning. There's no way she'll wake up early enough to grab coffee, let alone feed herself.

Chapter Sixty-Three

Aiyana

Monday, January 8, 2024

I can't believe I forgot to allow time to make myself a damn coffee this morning. Normally, I'd just slip out and grab one, but the whole point of me being here this early is to finish a really time-sensitive process, so I can't right now.

If I see Rose anytime soon, I'll ask her to grab me a coffee and a scone or something real quick.

My stomach rumbles in protest at the thought, but I can't step away from this. It's too important.

***

"Hi, are you Aiyana Kaan?"

I jolt out of my seat, nearly knocking my chair over in surprise. Clutching my chest and righting myself, I look up at the startled man wearing a familiar take-out uniform.

"Uh, yes, but I didn't order anything," I tell him, though I might just take whatever he's got anyway, I'm so damn hungry.

He looks at the bag in his hand and back at me. "No offense, but your name isn't exactly common. So if you're Aiyana Kaan, I'd really appreciate it if you'd just take the food so I can get back to work." Clearly, this guy won't be winning any congeniality awards.

I resist the urge to roll my eyes at him. Instead, I give him a blinding smile and gladly accept the food and drink he hands me, thanking him as he turns and jogs away.

I take a long swig of the coffee, the caffeinated goodness buzzing around on my tongue. *Fuck, that's good.* White chocolate mocha—my favorite.

Pulling the bag into my lap and peeling the sticker with the receipt off, I tear into it like a wild animal, hunger surging me forward. There's a sandwich wrapped in very familiar paper from my favorite bagel place, and I'm immediately giddy with excitement.

I fucking *love* bagels. I unwrap the sandwich, and I'm greeted with a smell that makes me moan in pleasure; inside the folded white paper is a giant Asiago everything bagel with smoked salmon, cream cheese, red onion, cucumber, tomato, and extra capers. Shaking my head, I smile down at the sandwich and take a massive bite, my eyes rolling to the back of my head. I chew, savoring the delicious flavors, and once I swallow, I can't help but lean forward and do a little seated dance with my feet, making a "tippy tap" sound on the linoleum flooring beneath me.

I text Kat to thank her for the breakfast and go on with my day. She must've known I'd need the pick-me-up, and it's already looking much brighter.

***

My Wifey For Lifey

Hey, I hope your day's been good so far! But that wasn't me. Sorry, I'm just not that thoughtful haha.

Really? Who the hell else could it be?

I almost send the text, like an idiot, before realizing exactly who it must've been that sent it.

I delete the message to Kat and send something else instead.

Huh, so weird, hey, if it's free, it's for ME!

I hope your day is amazing! See you tonight, love you!

She doesn't respond, probably seeing patients and being the badass physician assistant I know and love.

Thank you for the breakfast!

It was much needed!

Kas

Any time. Don't need my little viper striking on some unsuspecting soul at work ;) We both know how hangry you get.

Ah, I see.

So this was an act of kindness for my coworkers, got it.

Kas

Exactly ;)

I shake my head and the resulting smile off my face. He needs to stop being so damn perfect, or I'll never get over him. I'm already convinced I'll never move on, but he doesn't make it any easier. Not that he's trying.

Chapter Sixty-Four

Kassian

Thursday, January 11, 2024

Little Viper

Mind if I stop over before your game and leave some clothes? I got out of work a little early today so I should be able to make it over in time.

No problem, but you could always just forgo clothing entirely…

Little Viper

Ha ha.

Little Viper

I'll be there in twenty.

Can't wait.

I haven't been home in almost two weeks, and I'm thanking my past self for deciding to clean up the place before the long trip away. Otherwise, I'd be running around like a madman trying to get it in order before Aiyana gets here.

God, I've missed her.

I don't know what the hell I'll do if she ever decides to completely cut me loose. Shaking the thought out of my head, I make myself busy for the next nineteen minutes, making tea and folding laundry.

***

I hear a light knock on my door and slide across the floor in my socks, nearly using the door to stop my body from barreling through it. Righting myself, I run my clammy hands down my torso, smoothing my shirt and trying to act calm before opening the door. Even after all this time, she still has me acting like a crazed teen with a crush.

Gripping the door handle, I twist and open it. A whoosh leaves my lungs when I see her, relief flooding my system, and in an instant, my body feels like it's on fire.

She's wearing my jersey.

She gives me a sly smile, placing a hand on her hip before popping it out. "You gonna let me in or what?" Her brow is raised in question, but her tone is teasing.

I roll my eyes at her, feigning annoyance as I open the door wide for her to pass through. "Don't be a brat," I tell her, and when she passes me, I let the door slam shut as I swat her ass.

She whips around to face me, mouth popped open in surprise and eyes alight.

"Me? I'm not a brat!" she tells me adamantly, but her tone tells me she knows damn well that she's a fucking tyrant.[1]

I ignore her words, grabbing the bag she's got slung over her shoulder. I don't expect the weight of it, but I carry it easily up the stairs with her trailing behind me. "What the hell do you have in here? It weighs half as much as you do."

"Just some clothes and maybe a few other fun things," she teases, and my brows shoot up my forehead, dick twitching in my sweats.

We get up the stairs, and I immediately drop the bag to the floor, turning to grip her hips and haul her body against mine. She's so light that I have no problem hoisting her up, her legs instantly wrapping around my waist. She squeals in delight, tossing her head back, a huge smile on her face as laughter rings through her.

I nuzzle into her neck, gripping her ass and pressing her more firmly into me. Running my nose along the length of her slender neck, I take a deep inhale, and I'm flooded with her rich scent. I can't help myself; I nip the side of her neck, then suck on the sensitive skin, and she melts into me, running her fingers through my hair and gripping the roots.

My dick is hard already, and she can feel it. She bounces up and down the length, seeking pressure where she wants it most, but still latched to my front like a monkey climbing a tree.

"Someone's eager," I hum into her neck, holding her tightly to me, not wanting to loosen my grip on her yet.

"Just," she breathes, her voice sounding breathless, "fuck me, please, Kas. I know we're low on time, but *please* just fuck me."

Her words light a spark in me that sends me over the fucking edge.[2] I haul her onto the bed, sliding my body down hers to grip the waistband of her leggings and tug the material down, taking her panties with them.

She squirms up the bed, trying to sit up or position herself better, but I'm a man on a mission.

I kick out of my own pants and climb up the bed, positioning the head of my dick at her entrance. "You know you never have to beg," I tell her, my voice low as I swipe the head of my swollen tip through her slickness.

"Oh god," she moans, tossing her head back, hands reaching out to her sides to grip the black duvet as I piston my hips forward, sinking deep inside her. I let out a groan as she pulsates around me.

I reposition myself, angling so my face is closer to hers as I lean forward, pressing my lips to her full bottom one and sucking it between my teeth. She cries out, wrapping her arms around my neck and pulling me closer.

"You feel so damn good," I praise, her lips parting and chest heaving as I rock in and out of her. "You miss this, little viper? You miss how my dick feels inside you?"

Her eyes blink open, fire lighting behind her chocolatey irises as they refocus on me. "As much as I like my vibrators..." She pants, dragging in a deep breath as I rock into her relentlessly, speeding my movements to pull her closer to her release. "I fucking *love* your dick." She manages to smirk at me.

I groan, burying my head into her neck and running my hands down her thighs, bringing them up and around my waist, then planting my hands on either side of her head as I pull away from her delicious scent. I want to watch her face as she shatters around me.

"Kas, I'm close," she tells me, but I already knew that. She's so wet, coating my shaft and pulsating around me, sending electricity down my spine and straight to my cock.

"I know, baby," I tell her, looking her in the eyes. "Come for me, little viper."

And she does.

"Kas," she shouts, her body jolting under me, and the sight of her in my jersey, writhing beneath me, is my fucking undoing.

I lose myself in her, coming so hard I see stars.

***

It took everything in me to get to this game tonight, and it fucking blows.

And to think, I could be at home in bed with Aiyana right now, if I had just faked a sudden illness—maybe said I'm six feet under and need to go to the emergency room or some shit. *Anything* to get out of this utter hell.

But no.

Instead, I started this game bored out of my damn mind. The other team wasn't even fucking trying. We're up four to zero and might as well call it quits now, but the other team decided to bring out a rookie player they've had on probation for a while, and for good reason.

I'm taking hit after hit after hit, dealing with a shitty team and their aggressive rookie who's going after Ale for some unknown reason. I don't know if he's just trying to prove himself by taking out our starting center, but this shit needs to stop, and the refs aren't calling any fucking penalties.

The longer this game goes on, the more likely it is that someone will get seriously injured, and that should never happen. Fights happen in hockey all the time. Not usually against our team as we're pretty straight shooters, but other teams? Sure. All the time. It's normal when the pent-up frustrations of the game come flowing over, but the refs break it up before anyone can get really hurt. There are *rules* for our fights to protect us against just that!

So the fact that this guy is just blatantly going after my teammates and clearly targeting Alessandro is not okay.

My body is shaking with adrenaline; the need to toss my gloves to the side and fight his ugly ass wells up inside me. I'm not even watching the puck anymore, deviating from my spot near the crease and opting to follow the rookie around, eyeing him closely as he approaches Ale. I see him jut the blade of his stick out, aiming to trip Ale, but I push forward, sliding between them and spraying the rookie with ice as I pass.

Ale saw me coming and moved out of the way, dodging the stick and avoiding getting himself hurt by some dumbass with something to prove.

Coach Allister shouts at me, and I make my way over to the boards. "What the fuck was that? Watch the damn puck, Narvaez!" he shouts when I'm close, and I shake it off, zipping around the players and getting myself back in position.

I'm watching the puck and simultaneously defending it, preventing the other team from getting near Kyle as he swiftly drives it home toward the goal, and suddenly, time stops.

The buzzer sounds, indicating we made the goal, but as I whip my head around, a huge smile on my face, excitement rears through me until I see it in slow motion. The rookie leans forward with all his weight, giving himself every ounce of momentum he can muster as he pushes himself into Ale, catapulting him head-first into the boards.

He lands with a thud so loud I think his helmet might've broken the ice.

Once the moment of shock has washed away, I make a run for him, but then I see Kat.

She's throwing her small body over the boards, her face in anguish as she makes her way to him, yelling his name and collapsing at his side. I know she's got him. I also know there's nothing I can do for him that she or our trainers can't, so I turn my attention elsewhere.

Rage overtakes me; everyone on the ice is either standing in shock, dumbstruck and unmoving, or shouting at the refs, the other team, and most of all, the rookie.

I take off toward him, not giving a single fuck about our team's clean record.

When I get close enough to him, I tear my helmet off and toss it to the side, letting my stick drop with it before pulling my gloves off.

He's been looking for a fight—that much is clear. He swivels his head to me, grinning before doing just as I had, and when the gloves are off, I literally circle him like prey.

I see his brows draw together as he sizes me up, probably realizing now that I'm stronger than he is. My body is a well-oiled machine made from years of contact sports and a routine that an Olympian would be jealous of.

He shrugs and runs at me, but before he can make contact, I rear back, giving my fist the start it needs to fly right at his face. The satisfying crunch of cartilage hits my ears, moisture from his blood and saliva marring the skin of my knuckles and spraying across my face.

He falls backward, but before he can hit the ice, my hands spring out, gripping his jersey in my fists and bringing him into me. "You wanted a fight, now you're gonna get a fucking fight," I grit out, then push him just out of my reach. He brings his fists up in front of his face and swings one out. It connects with my side, and I barely flinch, the anger rushing through my blood and dulling any pain I might feel from it later.

I give him a twisted grin that doesn't feel right on my face, laughing at his efforts and connecting my fist with the underside of his jaw. His teeth clank together, but he manages to stand upright.

Out of the periphery of my vision, I see the medics rushing Ale across the ice on a yellow stretcher with Kat in tow, and that one second of distraction is all it takes for the little fucker in front of me to take his shot, busting my lip wide open. Hot blood pools in my mouth and drips down my chin, but no pain follows. I'm numb to pain right now. Because of this slimy little fucker, my sister is probably on the verge of a panic attack.

My heart clenches in my chest at the thought of her in pain, and the storm blowing through my thoughts overtakes me again.

The crowd's shouts drown out around me again as I focus my sight back on the coward before me. He looks smug, having gotten a decent shot in.

I send my body rocketing into his, pushing him down on the ice where he lands with a thud, his skull cracking off the ice, but he doesn't lose consciousness, so I don't back down. My knuckles meet his face repeatedly until they are split and bloody, both of ours mingling together. The only thing that stops my onslaught isn't the refs trying to pull me from him nor my teammates shouting at me to stop, but one simple word breathed from her lips that makes me obey in an instant.

"Stop."

My hands fall to my sides, and I rock back on my heels, succumbing to the exhaustion my body's been fighting with nothing but adrenaline. I look up to see her standing there, eyes locked on mine, brows furrowed. Her lips are pursed, and her arms are crossed over her chest as she shakes from the cold of being on the ice.

I snap out of it immediately, moving quickly to stand and skate the short distance to her as she tries not to slip on the ice, wearing her sneakers. Again, I'm stunned at how gorgeous she is. That's a simple fact that I'll never fully get used to.

Tossing my arms around her and pulling her to me, I rest my chin on top of her head, and she lets out a single sob, her body shaking with suppressed cries. "I'm so sorry," I whisper against her hair, but pull my face back when I remember my lip is split open and bleeding.

"Just take me home, Kas. Let's just go home," she whispers, her voice shaky.

I nod, but she can't see me, so I drag her along, ignoring my coach's calls for me to talk to him. I leave her sitting in the bleachers and rush to the locker rooms to change with lightning speed, not wanting her to have to wait for me any longer.

I don't even shower, figuring I'll do it when I get home. I just need to make sure she's okay and find out what's going on with Ale and Kat.

A few of my teammates try to speak to me when they see me but quickly back off, realizing this is not the time for this conversation. I'm in absolutely no frame of mind to speak to anyone right now.

As soon as I have my things together, I rush back to Aiyana and find her waiting for me in the tunnel, ready to go. I wait until we're outside and nearly at my truck before hauling her into my body, pressing kisses to her forehead, and apologizing over and over again.

I know I scared her. I know she hates violence, but I also know she was afraid to see me like that, completely out of fucking control.

She presses her cheek to my chest, tears streaming down her face as she cries quietly in my arms.

When she's done, she sniffles one last time and pushes away from me, walking to her door and tugging on the handle. She looks at me, her eyes hard as she pins me with an unrelenting stare that chills me to my core until she juts out that hip and smirks at me. "Open the damn door, Kas. It's freezing, and I shouldn't have to wait on your slow ass." She rolls her eyes at me as I recover from the absolute whiplash she just gave me, fumbling with my keys and unlocking the door. She pulls it open the moment it unlocks, but before she can try to toss her petite body in the seat, I grip her hips and set her in the seat myself. Grabbing her seatbelt and leaning across her, I buckle it, making sure she's secure before pressing a chaste kiss to the tip of her nose. It's cold, and that sends bile crashing through my stomach.

She should never have to be uncomfortable. Not while I'm around, and yet, I've made her upset more than once tonight, and now she's fucking cold.

I know I'm not thinking rationally. We live in the Northeast; of course she's going to be cold in the middle of January, but that rationale doesn't settle me any. I make my way around to my side of the truck, and as soon as I'm inside, I blast the heat and turn the music on to one of her favorite stations. Heavy metal music thrums through the speakers, and she relaxes against the door, resting her head on the window and letting out a small, contented sigh that weasels its way into my heart, soothing the restless beast that's taken hold.[3]

---

1. **TYRANT – Beyoncé (ft. Dolly Parton)**
2. **Let Me Love You – Ariana Grande (ft. Lil Wayne)**
3. **Living Dead Girl – Rob Zombie**

Chapter Sixty-Five

Aiyana

My mind is whirling with the absolutely horrible turn of events that took place today. Here I thought I could have an easy day at work, get out early, have mind-blowing sex with Kas, watch a good game, and end the night with a few more orgasms, but no.

Instead, I had to watch my best friend's boyfriend get his skull smacked across the ice, and then her brother attack the guy who did it.

Kat called to let us know that Alessandro seems stable for now; they have to do a lot of imaging to rule out anything more serious, but right now, it just looks like a bad concussion. They didn't see any bleeding on his first brain scans, but they don't want to miss anything, so they'll be repeating them soon.

Kat said she'll call us when she gets more updates, but I wouldn't be surprised if she forgets. She has a lot on her plate right now, and I know she's struggling to hold it all together. Kas and I asked if we could stay with her, but Alessandro's whole family should be there soon, so she asked us to give them space.

I look over at Kas; he's sitting on the edge of the black leather couch, his head in his marred hands, still covered in crusted blood. Scooching across the couch cushions, I position myself next to him and tentatively place a hand on his back. When he doesn't flinch, I rub small circles along his spine and watch as his body slowly starts to loosen.

Several minutes go by, just like this. A heavy silence descends upon us, and my heart aches for him.

He's not a violent person by any means. He loves hockey, and he's an incredible defenseman, but he isn't overly aggressive in his plays and only puts the necessary amount of force into his movements.

"What happened out there?" I breathe, waiting for his eyes to meet mine as he slowly pulls his hands from his face to meet my gaze with his hazel ones. "That wasn't you, Kas. You were reacting to a situation. A blip in time. A horrible moment, but *that wasn't you*." I stress my last words, emphasizing them so he knows what I'm referring to.

This isn't the first time I've had to drag him out of these awful feelings that come swirling through his beautiful mind. When his father shot their mother in front of him before ending his own life, it wrecked him. He blamed himself, and for the longest time, he truly believed it was his fault. He was just a child for all intents and purposes, a teenager who heard a noise and went to find out what was happening. It took him *years* of therapy and self-reflection to find the truth: that his father was mentally ill, and he was destined to shoot his mother whether he came out of that room or not. But for so long, Kas thought he made him do it—believed by leaving that room and confronting his father, he pulled the trigger in haste, then shot himself when he realized what he'd done.

But none of that was true.

His father was struggling. Struggling with his own demons and losing a battle that ultimately ended in *his poor decisions* hurting the people he should've been protecting.

I see it now. Kas's mind is playing tricks on him, spiraling him into the false belief that he had something to do with what happened to Alessandro and with how his sister is suffering. I'd bet my father's life that right now, he's considering his actions out there as a sign that he's just like his father under certain circumstances.

Kas continues staring into my eyes, his jaw tight, eyes glassy with unshed tears as he digests my words, but I can tell he doesn't believe them; they aren't sinking in.

I move closer to him, pressing my thighs to his and holding his cheeks in the palms of my hands, making him look me in the eyes and praying he'll hear me *and believe me*.

"Kas, you are not your father." I say the words slow and steady, allowing their meaning to hang between us, but he tries to pull back from me, his eyes clenching shut as if to block out my insinuation. "Kassian Narvaez, you listen to me," I continue when his eyes pop open at my sternness. "You aren't violent. You aren't a bearer of bad circumstances. You aren't a bad person, Kas. You're an incredible person with a heart of fucking *gold,* and you're the only one who doesn't see that." He tries to open his mouth to speak, but I continue, cutting him off with my next words. "What happened tonight was horrible." His eyes widen in horror, clearly thinking I'm talking about *his* behavior when that couldn't be further from the truth. "But absolutely none of it was your fault, Kas. You didn't do anything wrong. That guy had something to prove, and Alessandro was his target, but you? You did nothing besides defend your friend."

His chin trembles as he breaks down in front of me, his body crumpling as he lays his head in my lap and releases a long sob. "I could've fucking *killed* him, Aiyana, if you..." He pauses, sucking in a strained breath. "If you hadn't been there, I don't know if anyone could've gotten me off of him. I was blinded by my emotions and couldn't think straight."

Running my hands through his silky waves, trying to soothe him, I tell him, "Kas, you're the best person I know. You would've stopped." I don't say anything else. I don't need to. I don't care how many times he needs me to repeat the words; I'll say them over and over again until they sink into that thick skull of his.

"How do you know?" he asks, his voice smaller than I've ever heard it, and it chills me to my core. I remember the years after the incident that changed everything for him. He didn't speak to anyone for months. Anyone besides me, that is.

I never told Kat. I've carried a lot of guilt for that fact alone, knowing I could've eased her worry if only she'd known he was speaking to someone, even if it wasn't her. He just felt so much shame, and he begged me not to say anything. He wasn't ready to speak to anyone else, and I didn't want to push him.

"Because I *know you,* Kas. You. Would. Have. Stopped." I enunciate every word.

"I would've stopped," he whispers, his voice almost imperceivably quiet as he repeats my words.

I nod my head, knowing he can't see me. "You would have stopped, Kas."

We continue this several times, him quietly repeating my words until it finally seems to settle in as the truth.

We stay here for what feels like hours with his head in my lap as he presses kisses to the inside of my thigh, running his fingers over my calves as he mindlessly repeats my words until, eventually, he goes silent. Kas's taut muscles start to relax, his body finally giving in to his exhaustion, breaths becoming shallow as his chest rises and falls rhythmically. I can't bring myself to wake him, though I want to clean his wounds. I'll do it in the morning.

I manage to wiggle out from under him so I can get ready for bed, turn out the lights, and bring a blanket to join him on the couch.

When I'm ready, I curl around him, my head against his chest, and can't help the audible sigh that leaves my lungs as he curls his arms around my waist, pulling me closer to him. Even in his sleep, he can't seem to get close enough to me.

Chapter Sixty-Six

Aiyana

Friday, January 12, 2024

My eyes start to flutter open, the light from the massive windows peering in and illuminating the open living space.

Lifting my head off of Kas's chest, I look down to see that he's already awake and smiling, his eyes crinkling at the corners as he gazes up at me, trailing my features and stopping at my lips.

Heat pools in my core as a smirk starts to curl his lips—the split bottom one has crusted shut now, and bruises have blossomed along his jaw. He cups my cheek, pulling me into him and pressing a soft, warm kiss to my lips.

It feels too intimate, especially given last night's circumstances and the fact that I'm literally not supposed to be letting things with him get too emotionally involved. Though I know I'm an idiot for even trying to believe that lie.

"How're you feeling?" I ask, my voice a little rough in my just-waking state.

Kas blinks up at me as if the memories of last night are suddenly flooding back in, and a pained look takes over his previously relaxed features.

He shakes the darkness from his thoughts and does his best to give me a smile. "I'm sore and in desperate need of a shower, but okay. We should get up though. I'll need to bring Kat her meds. She doesn't need to be without those *and* dealing with everything else."

I nod my agreement and pull myself off of him, standing by the couch and extending my hand out. I know he doesn't need my help getting up, but he takes my hand in his, getting swiftly to his feet.

His dark waves are a mess, his knuckles bruised and crusted with his dried blood, and his shirt rumpled.

"Shower with me?" he asks, and I give him a small nod, following him up the stairs to his room.

Once we're stripped and the water is warm, we each step into the shower, letting the water wash away the pain that yesterday brought. I motion for Kas to take a seat on the waterfall ledge he has in this enormous shower of his, and he does, quirking a brow at me in question. I grab the bottle of shampoo, squeezing a sizable amount out into my hands and lathering it up before running the suds through his hair, massaging his scalp as I go.

Kas releases a low groan, hands darting out in front of him to grip my hips. When I'm done, I wordlessly motion for him to tilt his head back, letting the stream from the waterfall fountain wash the sandalwood-scented shampoo away before repeating the process with his conditioner.

When I'm done, he places me in the seat he was previously occupying and does the same for me. My heart swells at his tender touch, and I fight a moan from escaping my lips as he works his fingers through my scalp, massaging as he does.

He finishes, and I stand, taking his hands in mine and inspecting them. The scabs and blood have been cleared from his skin, leaving behind irritated red wounds and bruises. We take turns lathering each other in bodywash and rinsing off, and when we're done, we dry ourselves, change, and head back downstairs before we head out.

***

We dropped by the apartment to let out Alessandro's dog, Tank, though his dog walker left a note saying she'd be back in a couple of hours. Luckily, Gianni had already contacted her, making sure Tank would be taken care of in Ale's absence.

When we got in, there were a few reporters camped outside, waiting to ask us questions, but we ignored them. By the time we left, there were at least a dozen more.

After retrieving Kat's meds and bringing them to her at the hospital, I'm relieved to hear that Ale seems to be doing well. Unfortunately, I still have to head into work, so Kas insists on bringing me.

When we arrive, he puts his truck in park and grabs my hands, bringing each of them to his lips to press a tender kiss along my knuckles. "Thank you," he whispers as he does this, "for not leaving me and for believing in the good in me."

My heart cracks. How can he still think he isn't the incredible, kind, and generous person that he is? "*All* of you is good Kas. Thanks for taking me to work," I tell him, leaning forward to press a quick kiss to his cheek before turning and pushing the door open, climbing out as he chuckles at me. This truck is too damn high up for me.

I huff when I get to the bottom and wave before making a beeline for my building.

Chapter Sixty-Seven

Kassian

Saturday, January 13, 2024

I called Kat last night to see how she was doing but couldn't get much of a response. It seems she's overwhelmed, and with her anxiety, I can absolutely understand that. She isn't used to the constant media coverage, and having her life on display for the world to see is something she hasn't gotten used to yet.

I'm confident that she will, though, one day. She and Alessandro are endgame, plain and simple.

I grab my phone, staring at the screen and hoping that'll magically make a text from Aiyana appear, but it doesn't. We haven't spoken much since I dropped her off at work. I texted her to see how Kat was *really* doing, and she gave me the condensed version that eased my worry a bit.

How're you guys doing this morning?

Little Viper

Kas, open your search engine and type in your sister's name.

Her words send a boulder sinking straight to the pit of my stomach. I frantically swipe our message thread away, finding the search bar and typing in "Katarina Narvaez." What I see makes me fucking nauseous—the media spinning tales for their own gain. Nothing new, but terrible all the same, especially when it's about my sister.

Has Kat seen yet?

Little Viper

I don't know. She hasn't left her room yet.

Little Viper

I'm calling Alessandro now.

I'll be over soon.

***

The rest of the day doesn't get much better.

Chapter Sixty-Eight

Aiyana

Sunday, January 14, 2024

When I was a kid, I thought I wanted to be famous, like one of the Cheetah girls. I'd stand on my dad's old trailer as if it were my own personal stage, and I'd sing my heart out, belting the lyrics to every pop song I knew. Hell, I thought I'd be the first Cherokee woman to win *American Idol*.

But now? Now, I'm so fucking glad I went into STEM instead.

In the last couple of days, I can't even count how many reporters I've flipped off. I'm sure they're absolutely loving the stories they can make out of that, but I don't give a damn. If it takes the attention off of Kat and Alessandro, I'll be happy. Plus, frankly, they don't deserve any answers besides the one I've given them. To fuck all the way off.

Chapter Sixty-Nine

Kassian

Monday, January 15, 2024

Coach Allister called a meeting prior to our game, explaining that we needed to be on our best behavior and that we were having a press conference after the game to clear some things up. Hearing about Alessandro's diagnosis of multiple sclerosis the way we had didn't feel good, especially as one of his best friends, but I can't say I'd be forthcoming with that kind of information if I were him either.

From the sounds of it, he was receiving treatments and taking care of his symptoms, and his athletic trainer had been made aware, so he was always under her watchful eye. That said, it was still a bit of a slap in the face, and the press was eating it up.

After Coach told us all to clear out for warm-ups, he pulled me aside to discuss my behavior at the game the other day. But instead of the lashing I was expecting to receive, he gave me a slap on the shoulder and a look of approval I hadn't known I needed until I got it.

***

A few of us are gathered in the conference hall, watching as everyone involved prepares for the onslaught of questions they'll need to dodge and strategically answer to avoid creating an even worse situation.

I wait anxiously, my hands getting clammy, and beads of sweat start gathering along my spine, this charcoal-gray suit suddenly feeling too heavy and tight.

The press asks questions, and Matt Bowman, our captain, answers several of them, with Ale following his lead, as I'm sure he was directed to by our PR manager.

The meeting drags on, and the more questions asked, the more my heart stutters, thinking of how my sister is probably taking it all. She hasn't been answering my messages today, so I know she isn't doing well with all of this.

A reporter I recognize for all the wrong reasons stands, and her line of questioning digs deeper into topics that have absolutely nothing to do with hockey.[1] She throws around accusations she knows nothing about, and as she does, my fists clench tighter and tighter until my knuckles are white.

Then she does the unthinkable.

The words fall from her lips, a web of lies and truths carefully intermingled in just the way she needs to spin the perfect story that'll get her on the map, and with each word, blackness seeps further and further into my mind, dragging me back to that day.

"... Is it also a coincidence that she and her brother have some very sticky history?"

I can barely hear Alessandro's reply. His words don't make it past the darkness looming in my mind. My "sticky history," as she refers to it, is mottled with a deep emotional trauma that I've never fully recovered from.

And now it's about to be put on display for the whole world to hear.

"Wow, true love must be real if you're willing to deal with all *that* baggage." Her words cut me like a knife, digging straight into my heart, driving it deeper and deeper with every sharp-tongued word she speaks. "I mean, what child hides in a closet while their brother witnesses their own father shoot their mother in the head before turning the gun on himself? Stuff like that makes for really fucked-up adults, but I'm sure true love endures and all that." She looks so smug as she says it. And she's not wrong.

"Stuff" like that really *does* make for a fucked-up adult.

---

1. **STRINGS – MAX (ft. JVKE & Bazzi)**

Chapter Seventy

Aiyana

I'm staring at the TV screen in front of me in abject horror, so many thoughts swirling through my mind.

What the fuck just happened?

How did she find out about any of that?

And has Kat seen it?

But the thought that replays over and over like a broken record is about Kas. How will he recover from having these wounds torn open all over again?

I scramble across the couch, checking the time and realizing Kat's shift is almost over. I try calling her, but she doesn't answer, sending me straight to voicemail. I try her again, but the same thing happens. I call Kas, and his phone must be off because I get his voicemail too.

I rush to my room, changing hastily and preparing myself to run to the hospital to get Kat, but I hear the front door slam shut and know she's seen it. I hastily change back into my pajamas, tossing my bedroom door open. My heart crashes to my toes as I take in the dark room.

My feet pad quietly across the floor as I pass the living room and kitchen, making my way to Kat's room on the other side of the apartment. I knock lightly on her door, waiting a beat before barging in. I make out the small lump in the center of the bed, sobs wracking her body hidden under the green duvet.

Without hesitation, I climb in behind her, wrapping my arms around her and holding her until she falls asleep.

Chapter Seventy-One

Aiyana

Tuesday, January 16, 2024

I wake up to the sound of Kat crying in the bathroom, but at least she's up and making an effort to take care of herself. I know it hasn't truly set in for her though. When it does, I just hope she'll let Alessandro in.

I climb out of bed and make my way to my room, grabbing my phone off the nightstand, and as I swipe to my texts, my heart sinks as I see one name on my screen with three simple words that break my heart in two and send me into overdrive.

Kas

I need you.

Some people would think what I'm about to do is fucked up, but given the choice between Kas and Kat, I seem to choose Kas more often than not. Kat has people who love her and want to protect her and help her dig herself out of her thoughts when they're too much to bear. And while Kas has people who love him too, he's lacking in the trust department. As in, he doesn't trust anyone. Anyone but me, that is. It's a simple fact I've never gotten over and not something I take lightly. I'm not even sure he'd trust Kat with this because he's so damn worried about keeping her sheltered from his raw and sometimes overpowering emotions that he doesn't let her take care of him.

So, without hesitation, *I choose him.*

I'm on my way.

Chapter Seventy-Two

Kassian

I got in from New York late last night, feeling utterly numb as we flew into Philly. I'm unsure of how I even got myself home, but as soon as I did, I crashed.

My body gave out on me, collapsing to my knees the moment I entered the door.

I spent the night like that. Lying in a heap on the floor, unable to get up as the nightmares I lived through flashed through my mind at warped speed. It didn't help that I had gotten an email from Mom's nursing home yesterday morning. I requested regular updates, which they were happy to send. Kat doesn't know about them, which is for the best, but I like to know how she's doing, even if it breaks my heart a little more every time.

A stiff, aching pain radiates through my entire body, but my mind is still numb, trying to catch up to the inevitable pain I'll be in when it fully sinks in.

I stretch, my limbs sore from being crumpled on the floor all night, and the nightmares I endured sit heavily on my chest, threatening to suffocate me. Sitting up is more difficult than it should be, so once I'm in a seated position, I let my head hang heavily in front of my chest, hands planted on the ground, both literally and figuratively trying to ground myself.

My head snaps up at the sound of the elevator doors opening, and a moment later, I hear someone entering the door code before it softly snicks open.

Aiyana's standing in the doorway, her hair in a messy bun on top of her head, dark circles under her crazed eyes. They travel over the room, taking it in and finally landing on me, a mess on the floor. She slams the door shut, dropping her bag and running toward me, falling to the ground in front of me. My arms shoot out to grab her and haul her into my lap before she can hurt herself, and the moment she's in my arms, I fall apart.

She clutches me tightly to her small frame, holding my head to her chest as I release a guttural sob, my whole body convulsing with the weight of the emotions crashing down around me.

This is it. *This* is the moment it settles in. Every detail of my past coming back to fucking haunt me, crushing me beneath it. The heaviness of it threatens to kill me as my heart pounds erratically against my chest, begging to break free of the prison that is my body.

Memories flood me. My father's booming voice as he belittled my mother, telling her how worthless she was, how much of a mistake their marriage was, and how she could never make anyone happy. My mother's sobs as she begged him not to shoot her, pleaded with him to put the gun down and just let her leave. His crazed responses and the look in his eyes when he turned to see me standing there with a horror-stricken expression across my face before moving jerkily, aiming the gun at my mother's face and pulling the trigger before turning it on himself. I can hear my own sobs as I held my mother, sticking my fingers in her wound to stop the bleeding. The way her body went limp in my lap as I lost her pulse, waiting for someone, *anyone,* to come help her. Performing CPR on my own mother will go down in history as the worst day of my life.

Memories of Kat's cries when I finally went to find her, covered in our mother's blood but refusing to leave her alone any longer after the paramedics had taken her and someone removed my father's body. Kat looked at me like I was a monster but clung to me as if I were her savior. Though I was neither. I was just a broken boy who had pieces of his future stolen from him.

And then the darkness swept in like a wave crashing along the shore, dragging me off to sea as I drowned in its current.

I wouldn't eat, barely got my schoolwork done, and never ever spoke to anyone, anyone besides Aiyana that is.

Her soothing voice murmurs in my ear, pulling me back to reality and out of the throws of my traumatic past.[1] I can't make out what she's saying, but it doesn't matter. She's here, and that's all that matters.

***

"Shh, shh, it's okay, you're okay," she coos in my ear, still clutching my head to her chest, gently rocking us back and forth as she stays seated in my lap, my fingers digging into her soft skin as I hold her tightly to me.[2]

There's no way to know how long we've been sitting here, as I lose myself in my misery, but she never left.

I draw in a long, shaky breath as I loosen my grip on her, pulling my head back from her chest to look up into her gorgeous chocolate eyes. Her eyes are glassy, red, and swollen as they search my face, assessing me and peeling back all my layers in a way no one else ever has.

Aiyana untangles herself from me, working her way into a standing position and extending her hand out, helping me up from the hard floor. I groan from the soreness but can't help turning to her and clutching her cheeks in my palms as I gaze down at her. She looks up at me, meeting my eyes, and my lips come crashing down on hers.

She lets out a startled gasp but quickly recovers, wrapping her arms around my neck and drawing me in closer. Her tongue sweeps across the seam of my lips, begging for entry, and I oblige, more than happy to let her fall into the numbing pleasure I'm silently asking for.[3]

Sliding my hands down her face and around to her backside, I grip her firm ass tightly, hauling her up my body and walking her backward up the stairs.

Once at the top, she slides down my body, landing softly on her feet, and I get to work undressing myself. She takes several steps back, undressing and standing in front of the bed, entirely too far from me. Just as I'm about to walk toward her, she says, "Tell me what you need, and I'll do it—anything—just say the words."

Her soft bottom lip juts out, eyes filled with desire, and suddenly, I'm filled with a need to let her absolutely consume me in every sense of the word.

I harden my gaze, gripping my cock and stroking myself as I look her in the eyes and say, "Get on your fucking knees and crawl to me."

Her eyes widen slightly, but Aiyana falls to her knees, keeping her gaze locked on mine as she crawls toward me, never breaking eye contact. When she's finally in front of me, she reaches up to grip the base of my cock, squeezing until a drop of precum beads at the top, and she licks it off. A groan wracks my body, my fingers tangling in the roots of her hair, pressing those soft, warm lips around my length as I make her choke on me.

She sucks deeply, letting me fuck her throat, her body an analgesic to my mind but lighting my body on fire. Sparks of pleasure climb up my spine as she takes every inch of me to the back of her throat, her head bobbing as I urge her on, my balls tightening as my release drives closer. And just as I'm about to come, she grips my ass with her small hands. My cum spurts down her throat, a moan climbing from her lips as she sucks me dry. "You're so damn beautiful when you suck my cock like that, little viper."

Aiyana pulls back, wiping the side of her lips with the back of her hand after my cock bobs out of her mouth, still erect but less so.

"Use me any way you need to, Kas," she tells me, honesty lacing her words, and a pang of guilt seeps into my stomach. Something about the idea of making her feel used in any capacity, even if she's asking for it, makes me feel ill. I brush the thought away, choosing not to dwell on yet another thing that makes me feel like an absolute waste of space.

I lift her off the ground, pulling her body close to mine, and back her onto the bed, my dick hardening against her soft skin. I bury my head in her neck, not even checking if she's ready because I know she is. Gripping the base of my hard cock, I swipe the tip through her wet folds, causing her head to arch back as she lets out a soft cry of pleasure. "You want me buried deep in this pussy, don't you, little viper?" I ask her, my face still buried in her neck, breathing in her rich signature scent, the one I literally fucking dream about being wrapped in on nights when the nightmares threaten to take hold of me.

"God, yes, Kas," she responds, her fingers digging into my hair, holding my face tight to her. I enter her, my body going still with the feeling of her tight pussy clenching down around me. I nip at the skin of her neck and shoulder as I drag my cock through her fucking heavenly cunt. I pull out of her, sliding down her body to bury my face between her legs.

I grip her thighs, tossing them over my shoulders as I rake my nose through her slick heat, pressing the tip against her clit. She cries out, gripping my hair tightly, and as her body coils under me, her fingers pulling tightly on the strands of my hair, I get lost in the taste of her.

I nip on her pussy lips before sucking on her clit. My tongue darts inside her, sweeping inside to draw out a long moan from her.

“Kas, please. It’s too much. Just fuck me,” she screams.

Slithering up her body, I press kisses along her stomach, making my way up to tug on her nipples before burying myself back inside her.

She bucks against me as I enter, her nails clawing at my back. The feeling of being inside her is intoxicating. It’s dulling all the anger and heartache I’ve been drenched in recently, and when her cunt spasms around me, her head falling back on a loud moan, we come undone together. The release is so strong that I lose myself in it.

The numbness I had felt for just a few moments is being replaced by an agony that clenches down around my heart in an unbearable way, making me never want to feel *anything* again if it means not having to feel *this* again. A single tear slips down my cheek, wetting Aiyana's shoulder as the shame I felt for so long threatens to take hold of me.

Aiyana feels the wetness on her shoulder and pulls my head up to look at her. "Kas, you *saved* her. You're so damn busy saving everyone else that you never stop to save *yourself*, so someone else has to make you, and it's gonna be me."

I shake my head at her. "Did I save her, Aiya? Did I really? Or did I just selfishly keep her around for her to live out the rest of her life as half the woman she once was?" Anger seeps into my voice, but not at her questioning; it's at myself.

I pull out of her, climbing off the bed to pull on a pair of sweats, and she crawls around, stopping when she finds one of my oversized shirts that hits her below the knees like a dress.

She climbs back in the bed, scooting to the middle and patting the space beside her. I've never been able to deny her anything, so my feet move me toward the bed as if under her spell.

I climb in, lying down against the pillows stacked against the headboard, just how I left them yesterday morning since I never actually made it to bed last night.

Aiyana rolls onto her side, resting a leg over my thighs and perching on her bent elbow to look at me.

"Kas, what you did wasn't selfish. You weren't thinking about what would happen if you had no parents. You were acting on a moment in time, something so many people, let alone teenagers, wouldn't have been able to do in that moment. And she's living a content life in a wonderful facility with a man she loves dearly." She squeezes my hand tightly in hers, and I know what she's saying is true. Kat stopped asking for updates on our mother's care when we were told she had a boyfriend, and the staff sat us down to tell us that the only time she'd get agitated was when we would visit. So we stopped. Kat must've told her all of that, though, because I never wanted to bother her with it.

"Hey, Kas," she says, peering up at me through thick lashes. "Where'd you go?" She references the place my mind had just taken me. When I don't answer, she asks, "When was the last time you had a meeting with your therapist?"

I'm slightly taken aback by her question, my mind reeling, embarrassment starting to sink in as I realize what a fucking wreck I must look like to her. No wonder she won't commit to me. I'm not the man she needs, especially with everything going on with her father. But I love her more than words could possibly explain, and for that reason alone, I know I need to do better. *Be better* for her.

And for myself.

I clear the shock from my face and try for a softer expression, aiming to ease her mind and hopefully keep her from seeing that I'm broken, missing integral pieces of myself that it seems only she's able to find.

I clear my throat, sucking back the emotions I've been feeling, reeling them in a bit before I start. "I know what you're saying is true, and what my mind is doing is twisting reality, but it's not easy to see past that." I sigh, and she burrows herself closer to me, holding me as she listens. I know I need to include her in this, need her to feel like the important missing piece in my life that she so clearly is. *Clearly, to me anyway*. "Will you stay with me for a call with Dr. Sanchez?"

She doesn't hesitate. "I'd love nothing more." She presses a kiss to my chest, sitting up to look at me. "Plus, I took the day off from work for you, so you're buying me breakfast." She winks at me with a small smile, clearly trying to lighten the mood, and it works instantly. The tension begins to unwind, loosening the strain I've been feeling from the emotions I've had coiling around me like chains, choking me.

This woman is both my undoing and my salvation; even a simple smile from her acts as a balm to the wounds I just had torn back open after years of trying to mend them.

---

1. **Hello – Aqyila**
2. **Show My Love for You – Demise**
3. **Every Kind Of Way – H.E.R.**

Chapter Seventy-Three

Kassian

Wednesday, January 17, 2024

Aiyana stayed with me the entire day, and I tried like hell not to worry about Kat. It was difficult, but after speaking with Dr. Sanchez, it became very clear that I need to start prioritizing myself more.

We discussed that I can't take care of others if I don't take care of myself first, which is a simple enough notion, but it's not easy to put into practice.

Dr. Sanchez was thrilled to have Aiyana join our meeting, and in a way, I think it furthered my understanding of why I need to care for myself first. I felt a tremendous amount of relief by the end of our conversation, recognizing the dark abyss I almost let myself get dragged into, and while I can't say my mood is spectacular, having my little viper nearby helped tremendously.

Aiyana's lying against my chest, soft breaths puttering from her mouth as it hangs open ever so slightly. Her cheek is smashed against my bare abdomen as I run my fingers through her soft hair.

I dip my head, pressing a kiss to the crown of it. "Baby," I mumble into her hair, her body stirring with the sound. "You've gotta wake up, little viper," I whisper, her eyes fluttering open.

Her soft lips curl into a small smile as her eyes meet mine. "Morning, Kas."

"Good morning, little viper," I reply, unable to help the massive smile grazing my lips at the sight of her, smiling, happy and content in my arms, in my *bed*.

"What time is it?" she asks, her eyes scanning the room for her phone, which is likely somewhere downstairs, left with the pile of discarded clothes from last night.

"It's 6:30 a.m." Her eyes widen with panic, so I rush to assuage her. "Don't worry, I ordered food and coffee. It'll be here soon. Get up and showered, and I'll drive you to work."

She rolls her eyes as she sits up, moving to get out of the massive bed. "I've got my truck downstairs, Kas. I can drive myself."

"I know you can, but I want you to stay here tonight, and if you drive yourself, you won't come back," I tell her, allowing myself to be vulnerable.

Her eyes soften. "Kas, I've got to go home, at least for tonight. I don't have any more clothes here that I can show up to work in—" I cut her off.

"Then I'll buy you a whole wardrobe worth of clothing, anything you want," I tell her in a rush of desperation.

Shaking her head at me, she heads to the bathroom, bare-ass naked, long hair swinging just above her tanned, round ass. "I need to make sure Kat's okay. I haven't heard from her much, and I'm worried."

She has a good point, so I resign, nodding my agreement despite her back being turned away from me. I head after her, fully intending to wash that gorgeous hair and eat that beautiful pussy for breakfast before she leaves for work.

Chapter Seventy-Four

Aiyana

Friday, February 2, 2024

A broad smile spreads across my cheeks, my heart racing with excitement as my fingers curl around the keys of my beat-up old pickup truck. When I get to it, I haul myself inside and hurry to turn it on, the bite of winter chilling my bones, but not even that can dampen my mood.

Things went exactly as Gloria and I had hoped, better even. We had put together a plan to get back at the reporter who caused so much damage. The plan went off perfectly, and the media blew up with praise for Kat and Alessandro. Some news stations even outwardly shamed the reporter who started this whole mess, Carol Strobof. We even found out that she was fired, so she hasn't made any statements since that day.

Kat and Ale have mended things and then some, falling gracefully back into each other's arms, and I'm shaking with excitement for the night ahead.

I *love* game nights! It's also the first time I've gotten to see Kas in a couple of days, and as much as seeing him *shouldn't* excite me, it does. Immensely so.

Heading toward the penthouse, I turn the knob on the radio, finding a station playing upbeat pop to match my current mood.

As soon as I see the huge building in front of me, I hurriedly park, not bothering with the complimentary valet as I grab my purse and haul ass toward the lobby.

Impatiently, I wait for the elevator, and as soon as it lets me off with a *ding*, I bound toward our door, entering the code, and letting myself in. I hurry to change, tossing my shoes in the coat closet as I head to my bedroom door, looking over my shoulder at the stove to check the time. I let out a quick breath—I've got five minutes before Kat gets home and probably fifteen before the guys get here.

My hand wraps around the doorknob, turning it and pushing the door open. I search for the light switch and flick it on. A loud screech leaves my throat, my hand clutching my chest, eyes wide with fear as my heart pounds. Lying in the center of my bed is Kas, clothed in dark-wash jeans and a black T-shirt that hugs his bulging muscles, showing off the dark tattoos winding down his forearms.

"What the fuck, Kas?" I shout at him as he laughs, the sound booming throughout the room, his head thrown back against the mattress as it shakes with his movements.

"I figured you'd miss me, so I wanted to surprise you," he finally answers, a wide grin spread across his face.

Shaking my head at him in annoyance, I point at the living room. "Get out!"

He throws his long legs over the side of the bed, working to stand and head over to me. As he approaches, my fist clenches, darting out to jab his abdomen, and I have to fight the string of curses trying to make their way across my lips. His abs are hard as stone, and my tiny fists are not made for fighting.

He notices the pain stricken across my face despite my best efforts, and he reaches out to pull my hands into his as he brings them up to his mouth, pressing a kiss to the knuckles of each one. "I'm sorry I made you hurt your little fists of fury." He chuckles, but there's sincerity in his tone.

I do my best to stay upset at him, but I've never been that good at denying this man anything, even when I know I have to.

Lowering my hands back to my sides, Kas trails his calloused hands up my forearms to my shoulders, my neck, and finally, my face, cupping my cheeks tenderly in his grasp. He bends down, our immense height difference making it difficult for him to angle himself the way he wants, but he manages, pressing his forehead against mine. Closing his eyes, he breathes me in before greeting me with those murky green irises. His lips descend upon mine in a soft, achingly slow kiss that leaves me breathless, and just as he pulls away, we hear the front door burst open, sending my body jolting away from his, eyes darting to the open door, ensuring Kat hasn't seen us.

"Aiya!" she calls to me. "You home yet?"

"Hey, babe, I'm in here. Kas just got here too," I tell her, padding out into the living room to meet her.

Kat's dark waves are gathered into a slicked-back ponytail, her dark-purple scrubs indicating the end of the week. She always reserves her purple scrubs for Fridays.

Kas follows behind me, rushing over to his sister and wrapping her up in a bone-crushing hug as he twirls her around in the entryway. The smile that's overtaken her face makes my heart clench inside my chest. She was miserable for what felt like ages but was really less than two weeks, and I find myself taking note of every smile that has graced her lips since then.

"Hey, Kitty-Kat, how was work?" Kas asks her, placing her back on her feet before heading into the living room to plop down on the couch, his long legs draped over the side.

"It was good—actually a little slow, but that's good. It means fewer people in need of urgent care, so I can't complain," she tells him, heading to her room. "I'll be out in just a minute. I'm gonna get changed."

Kas turns his attention back on me as soon as she's closed the door behind her. "What do you want for dinner, little viper?"

"Chinese," I answer immediately, having thought about it all day. I'd also kill for some sushi and wings, but I know Chinese food will be the cheapest option and the easiest to order for the four of us.

He gives me a smirk. "Uh-huh, and what else?"

I shake my head at him. "Just Chinese," I say, hiding the surprise in my voice that he knew I'd want multiple types of cuisine.

"Yeah, right. I've never known you to be satisfied by just one type of food. Remember when you used to make me take you to the buffet that had hibachi, sushi, which was extremely questionable by the way, Chinese, seafood, tacos, and pizza?" He chuckles. "Until we got fucking food poisoning, and Kat and I finally convinced you to stop dragging us there."

My smirk twists with the memory. He's right; that buffet was disgusting, but the *food* was delicious, *and* they had an ice cream bar. Though I haven't gone to a buffet in years; some things you just can't overlook once you've learned about them.

"Fine." I huff at his knowing gaze. "Chinese, sushi, and wings."

His lips curl up into a smirk, eyes crinkling at the sides as he says, "That's my girl." His voice takes on a sultry quality that doesn't match the current conversation.

His words send sparks of heat zapping their way down my spine, my thighs clenching together to soothe the ache in my core as dampness floods me. As soon as he takes in my reaction to his words, heat sparks in his gaze, and he makes a move to stand just as Kat's door bursts open. She steps out, now wearing an oversized sweater and leggings, and her hair hanging down her back in loose, wet waves.

"Hey, what should I order for dinner?" she asks us, but Kas is quicker to answer than I am, still in a daze from the remnants of lust swirling around inside me.

"I'm already on it." He smiles up at her, relaxing back against the couch cushions and throwing his legs up again as he pulls out his phone, turning his attention toward the screen in search of dinner.

***

"Aiyana, we're at a point where I'd genuinely consider you one of my best friends, but this shit has *got* to stop!"

I glare up at Alessandro's hulking form, sizing him up from his place seated beside Kat on the other end of the velvet couch. "What *shit* do you speak of?" The thing is, I know exactly what he's talking about, but this is half the fun of the game. The arguing.

Kat and Kas roll their eyes at me in unison. "You know what you're doing," Kas tells me with a smirk.

"Mhmm," Kat agrees. "She sure does."

My glare falls, laughter bubbling out of me. "Okay, *fine*," I concede, tossing my cards down on the ottoman. "You better watch it, Ale. I used to be able to get away with this before you came around."

"You've gotten away with murder your whole life. It's time for a change," Kas pipes in with a smirk that makes my heart flutter.

"I don't like getting teamed up on. You're gonna make me cry," I whine.

"You're a brat." Kat chuckles, leaning into Ale. I watch as he smiles down at her, adoration clear in his gaze as he pulls her more tightly to his side and presses a kiss to the top of her head.

"I won't deny that simple fact, but what I said still stands. House rules! Pick up twenty cards or kiss the person to your left." I sit back, feeling smug.

"You're insufferable. You know damn well I'm not picking up twenty cards."

"Then kiss." My brow lifts, antagonizing him.

Ale lets out a huff of air, running his fingers through his dark waves before placing both palms on the tops of his thighs. He directs his attention to his left. "Do I have your consent to kiss you?" he asks.

"Whatever."

Looking to his right toward Kat, she smirks and gives him a nod, answering his silent question.

Alessandro leans forward, both hands reaching out to cup Kas's cheeks before he plants the world's most chaste kiss right on Kas's lips. Simultaneously, Kat and I drop to the cushions, barreling over in laughter.

I fight to suck air into my lungs, Ale's disgruntled expression sending me into another tizzy of laughter.

Kas sits comfortably on the edge of the ottoman, a wide smile spread across his freshly kissed lips as he chuckles. "God, you're a fucking idiot," he says, shoulders still shaking with laughter.

Ale's eyes widen, swinging between the three of us. Kat is still lying on her side, seemingly unable to get enough air in her lungs. "What am I missing?" he asks.

"Man, you could've just kissed my damn cheek or even my hand. She never specified a body location," Kas clarifies.

Ale groans. "Good fucking lord, woman. If Kat doesn't do it first, *you* will be the death of me."

"Oh, come on. You mean to tell me you've never wanted to plant one on those full, kissable lips of his?"

From the way his brow quirks and the sly grin that spreads across his lips, I know I've fucked up.

"Can't say I have, Aiya, but it sure seems *you've* given it some thought."

Rolling my eyes, I deflect. "I was just joking; don't be gross."

"I don't know, his lips *were* pretty soft. Maybe you should give it a go." He winks at me, and I feel my cheeks heating. I *never* blush, but this asshole just called me out.

"You better watch it, *Alice*, or it'll be thirty cards and something *much* more interesting on the next round."

***

Alessandro's arm is slung around Kat's waist, some part of him always touching her as if by breaking that physical connection, he'll somehow lose the emotional one. Though I imagine he just likes being near her; it's how I feel about Kas, though our situation is so wildly different from theirs.

When they first met, they couldn't date due to a provider-patient relationship rule, but that was easily fixed by having Alessandro swap providers. The same can't be said about Kas and me. Nothing is going to change the fact that my father explicitly told me not to marry outside of our culture, and as much as it pains me to hurt Kas, going against my father's wishes is something I'm just not prepared to do.

Ale leans in, pressing a kiss to Kat's shoulder as she yawns. "You wanna head to bed, *gattina*?" he asks her, indicating to me that she'll be spending the night at his place instead.

She nods her agreement, a sleepy smile grazing her lips as she looks up into his eyes. He smiles lovingly down at her before turning his attention back to me. Kas exits the bathroom and heads back toward us as Kat and Ale stand. "I think we're gonna head out," Ale says to us, walking over to me, arms out for a hug that I reciprocate, letting his muscular arms wrap around me briefly before he hurries back to Kat's side. She hugs Kas and heads toward the door, Kas making no real effort to leave with them.

I eye him quizzically as Kat and Ale make their way to the door, and Kat turns back to Kas. "You heading home soon?"

"Yep, just figured I'd help Aiyana clean up a bit before I go." He smiles at her, though we didn't exactly make a mess. There are a couple of dishes in the sink, and I'm working on putting the game we were playing back in the box.

Kat gives him a small, knowing smile as she turns, giving us a "goodnight" over her shoulder and heading across the hall.

The door snicks shut behind them, and the moment it does, I turn, my eyes meeting Kas's. His hands are in the sink, covered in soap suds, as he watches me. Taking several steps backward toward my bedroom, I watch as his eyes widen when my fingers reach the hem of my shirt, pulling it over my head. Kas turns the faucet on, hastily rinsing his hands before drying them on a dishcloth and running toward me.

I turn on my heel, making a beeline for my bed, loving the thrill of having him chase me, literally.

As expected, I'm much slower than the pro athlete with a foot and a half on me in height. I feel his arms wrap around my waist from behind, pulling me into his chest. He nips my earlobe, dragging it through his teeth slowly. "Thought you could outrun me, huh?" He breathes into my neck, his voice low as it reverberates around me.

I chuckle, trying to lighten the mood as an out-of-sorts darkness seems to have descended upon us. "Was that a line from *Twilight*?" I ask mockingly.

"Stop trying to deflect; me chasing you turns you on, and I know it," he grumbles, and a chill travels through me, my legs trembling with the desire suddenly pulsing through my body.

How does he know?

His calloused fingers run up and down my bare forearms, leaving goosebumps in their wake. "While I was in your room, I was snooping," he tells me, and I immediately know what he's getting at. "My *nasty* fucking girl listens to audio erotica, huh? You want a stalker, someone who only wants you, my little viper?" His words cause my stomach to twist in the most delicious way. "I knew you liked it rough, but it turns out you like it *really* rough, don't you?" he asks, and for the first time in what feels like my entire life, I feel myself slipping into a role of complete submission. I'd never trust anyone else to dominate me, which is why I listen to those recordings in the first place, but Kas? He'd never intentionally go too far, which is why I find myself answering his next question the way I do.

"Can I fulfill a couple of those fantasies for you tonight?"

"Please," I whisper.

A hand slides up my abdomen, snaking up to my throat as his other arm keeps me pinned to his chest. His hand squeezes tightly, so tightly my eyes are burning with unshed tears. "Please, what?" he grits out.

"Please, Professor," I cry out. He groans as he lifts me into his arms, carrying me over his shoulder and back into the living room. He lands a firm smack to my ass, and I tense up, heat coursing through my core. He stops in front of the wall of windows, dropping me to the ground in front of him. My knees smack on the hard flooring, and I hide the wince of pain, not wanting him to stop the illusion for fear of really injuring me.

He steps backward until his legs make contact with the ottoman, unzipping his jeans. He fists his engorged cock, his eyes never leaving mine. Kas takes a seat, his legs spread wide as he leans back on one arm, stroking himself.

"Strip for me, and let the class watch as you do," he says, eyes darting behind me to make a point of the show I'm about to give anyone out on their balconies tonight.

I stand on shaky legs, reaching behind me to unclasp my black lace bra, letting it slide down my arms and onto the floor.

There's a look in Kas's eyes that I don't fully recognize. He's turned on, but something tells me he's also a little shaken at my willingness to be dominated by him.

My hands make their way to my waist, inching my sweats down my thighs, dragging my panties with them. Once I'm standing straight, completely bare to him, his head falls back, eyes closed as he grips himself so tightly that a bead of precum spills out. I fight the urge to crawl to him and lick it off.

As if sensing my exact thoughts, his eyes fly open, crinkling at the sides as he takes me in. "Look at you, standing there naked for me, your cunt fucking dripping while you wait for me to fuck you up against that glass for everyone to see," he taunts, shaking his head slowly. "What a nasty little slut my favorite student is."

Oh, for fucks sake, why is this turning me on so much? My thighs clench together, desperate for friction.

He stands, prowling over to me. "You're fucking salivating for my cock, aren't you? You want me to let you suck me off? We can call it extra credit."

I nod, but that doesn't appease him, his hand snapping out to weave into my hair. He uses the leverage to push me to the ground once more, this time with less force.

"Use your words, little viper. Do you want me to fill your throat while you gag around me?" he asks, his voice rough and firm.

"Yes," I beg.

"Yes, what?" he grits out again.

"Yes, Professor," I moan.

"Good girl." He snickers, tsking at me as he lines the head of his swollen cock up with my mouth, swiping his cum on my lips. His hand moves to my mouth, and slipping two fingers inside, he curls them into my throat, causing me to gag, sputtering as I gasp for air, my clit aching to be touched.

Removing his fingers from my throat as drool pools in my mouth, he realigns his cock against my lips and mutters, "I can't wait to watch you slobber all over my cock like the little whore you are." Immediately after the words leave his lips, he plunges into my mouth, fucking my throat with his cock as my own arousal drips down my thighs.

His motions are relentless. I'm gripping the back of his thighs to support myself, heaving as he uses my body, and I couldn't be more turned on than I am in this moment.

Abruptly, he pulls out of me, gripping my chin as my hands slip down his thighs, landing on the floor beneath me while I fight for oxygen to flood my lungs. "Get up," he grunts.

I work myself into a standing position, and his hands grip my hips as he spins me to face the wall of windows. He walks us forward, my body plastered to the glass, and my cheek squished against it. Kas's warm breath skates across my flesh. "Touch yourself while I fuck you from behind and make everyone watch."

Instinctively, my hand reaches for my clit, the pressure jolting me as my legs quiver. Kas's hands glide down my thighs as he pulls them apart, spreading me wide for him. "I'm gonna fill this tight little cunt with my cock, stretching you out as you come undone for me, but you can't come until I fucking tell you to."

"Yes, Professor," I moan.

Without warning, he plunges into me, fucking me roughly against the window. A new fear of this glass fucking cracking beneath his brutal pounding fills me in more ways than one.

I'm teetering on the edge, my eyes clenching closed as I work my clit, chasing the high that I so desperately need. Kas is degrading me, then praising me in the next breath, his massive cock stretching me relentlessly as he does.

He's grunting behind me. "Fuck, little viper, you take me so well," he says like it's a curse, one hand reaching forward to grip my face as his fingers dig punishingly into my cheeks. "I plan to fill you with my cum, and when I'm done, I'll let you finish, but if you come with me, I'll pull out and finish myself."

An unfamiliar whimper leaves my lips, my body humming with need. His hips slam into me once more, stilling as he fills me. My own orgasm fights to take hold of me, but I refuse to let it. When he finishes, he rips my hand away, pulls my clit between the pads of his fingers and says, "Come for me, little viper." Those same fingers clamp down on my clit, pinching it so hard my body skyrockets to another dimension, waves of euphoria crashing through me as I quake against the glass.

Several moments pass as we just stand there, allowing the filthy, depraved feelings that had come over us to float away, dissipating.

Kas loosens his grip on me, spinning me back around to face him as his eyes search mine. "Was that okay?" he asks me softly, and my heart cracks infinitesimally.

"I promise it was," I assure him, and a glimmer of something lights his hazel eyes, his mood shifting back to the normal teasing I'm so familiar with.

His full lips pull into a smirk; gripping my waist, he heaves me up, my legs and arms wrapping around him as he carries me to bed and drops me on the mattress. "Stay right there," he says, heading into the bathroom and returning a few moments later with a warm, wet washcloth and a dry one. "Spread your legs." I do as I'm told, and he takes his time, wiping away the mess he made and patting me dry with the dry cloth. When he's satisfied, he returns to the bathroom and reappears in nothing but his tight black briefs.

His eyes search the room and land on my dresser. Kas pulls out a sleep shirt and heads back to me, kneeling on the bed. "Arms up," he instructs. He slips the shirt over my head and arms, then pulls the covers up and nods for me to crawl in.

As soon as I'm under, he turns out the lamp and starts walking toward the door. My heart suddenly races with the thought that he's leaving me after that, but I know I can't say anything. We aren't together, and we never will be. It's my rule, not his, so I'll be damned if I make him feel like shit for doing exactly what I've asked him to. Though as I wait for the telltale sign that he's gone, it never comes. The door doesn't slam shut; instead, he reappears with his arms full of our clothing from earlier. He slides the closet door open and dumps the clothing in my laundry basket before closing the bedroom door and climbing back into bed with me.

His arms wrap around me, and his chin rests on the top of my head. A few quiet moments pass before he speaks again. "You know those windows are one way, right? I'd never actually let anyone see you like that."[1]

A small smile lights my face. "I do know that, Kas."

"Good," he says, pressing a kiss to the top of my head. "Goodnight, my little viper," he whispers, and another crack fissures my heart.

Someday, it'll be broken beyond repair. I should probably come to terms with that before it happens.

"Goodnight, Kas."

---

1. **Wicked Games – Kiana Ledé**

Chapter Seventy-Five

Aiyana

Saturday, February 3, 2024

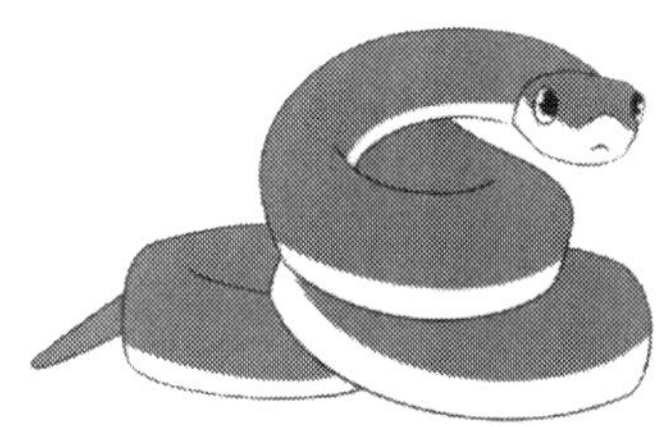

My eyes snap open, a familiar ringtone filtering through the room. Kas's weight presses me into the mattress as my heart starts to calm down, realizing it must be later than I thought if Mom is calling me.

"Kas, get off of me," I groan to him, trying to reach for my nightstand as the screen of my cellphone illuminates with the incoming call. I answer it just in time, Kas grumbling behind me.

"Good morning, *Etsi*," I tell her, trying not to sound as exhausted as I am.

"*Usdi*," *baby*. My heart stutters in my chest, alarm bells ringing all around me. A cold chill rushes through me at the sound of my mother's broken voice.

"What is it? What's wrong?" I ask frantically, begging for details that are bound to paint a perfect picture of the nightmare that I have unfolding in my mind.

Kas jolts up, worry painted across his face as his eyes bore holes into my skin. I look away, unable to hold myself together when he looks at me like that.

"*Usdi*," her voice breaks as she tries again. "It's your father. *Please* hurry. Come now before it's too late." If my mind wasn't already reeling with the worst-case scenarios, she just filled in all the blanks, leaving me cold and frantic.

I feel Kas's warm fingertips graze my skin as he pries the phone from my hand, bringing it to his ear. "We'll be there shortly, Zuni." I hear my mother's muffled voice but can't make out what she says, but Kas responds quickly, his voice hushed. "Don't worry, *Etsi*. I'll bring our girl to you safely, I promise."

He ends the call, sliding out of the bed and taking my phone with him. "Get dressed," he states firmly, his voice the only sound that makes its way through the low buzz that's flooded my brain. "Aiyana," he says, trying to reach me, my eyes slowly making their way up to his face, a numbness settling within me. "Baby, you need to get up and get dressed. I'll be right back. I'm gonna get Kat."

I nod as best I can, climbing from the bed and letting my legs drag me to my dresser.

Chapter Seventy-Six

Kassian

My heart is lodged in my throat as I leave my beautiful girl to dress herself, knowing she needs me to get Kat more than she needs me to dress her. The quicker we act, the faster I can get her to her father. The man who's been more of a father to me than my own ever had.

I grab my phone, dialing Kat's number as I get dressed, praying she'll answer the fucking phone. When the call eventually goes to voicemail, I try Ale's phone with the same result.

I pry my shoes on my feet and run across the hall, pounding my fist against Ale's door. "Open up! Kat!" I'm banging on the door so long that my hand is red and bruising with the force.

The door swings open, and Ale stands in the doorway, his eyes wild and hair tousled. Kat comes running up from behind him, her arms wrapped around her waist, hugging herself. "What the fuck?" Ale shouts at me, but I push past him, ignoring his anger.

I run to my sister, my hands gripping her shoulders as I look her in the eye, preparing to deliver a blow that sends a chill down my spine.

"Kas." Her lip trembles, tears filling her eyes. "What's wrong?" she asks me, and her cracking voice breaks my fucking heart.

"Kitty-Kat, it's Aiyana's dad. He's in the hospital, and we need to go *now,*" I urge, silently pleading with her not to make me elaborate right now.

She nods. "Go get Aiyana. We'll be ready in two minutes." She rushes, hurrying back to Alessandro's room. Without a second thought, I run back across the hall, unlock the door, and sprint back to Aiyana's room. I find her in a heap on the floor, half-dressed, as her tiny frame lays crumpled, her hands gripping her head as sobs wrack her body.

I fall to my knees beside her, gripping her hands in mine and pulling them away as she curls into my lap. "Baby, we need to go, please. I need you to get up." She nods in between sobs, and I work to get us both up off the ground. She stands on shaking legs, and I grip the waistband of her leggings, pulling them up her thighs before moving to put socks and shoes on her feet.

Once she's dressed, I all but drag her out into the hall, where Kat and Ale meet us seconds later.

Kat rushes to Aiyana, wrapping her arms tightly around her in a fierce hug. She whispers something to Aiya that makes her nod her head before she straightens, standing tall now with her head high as she marches toward the elevator with Kat in succession.

My girl's putting on a brave face for now, but I'll be there when it becomes too much to bear.

Chapter Seventy-Seven

Aiyana

Kas's tires shriek to a grinding halt as he pulls into the parking space outside of the hospital. My heart is pounding out of my chest, my body cold as exhaustion settles in, the initial shock of my mom's call fading away. The moment the car is in park, I'm flying out of the passenger seat, door flinging open. My feet hit the pavement, and I'm off, running full speed ahead toward the sliding doors, which, thankfully, open quickly on my arrival.

I nearly knock into an older woman in a wheelchair as she's exiting the hospital with her caretaker, yelling, "Sorry!" over my shoulder as I make my way to the receptionist. My hands smack down in front of me, steadying myself on the counter as I pant heavily. The bewildered receptionist looks up at me, her eyes wide with shock.

"Can I help you?" she asks me hesitantly.

"My father, his name is Qaletaqa Kaan. What room is he in?" I rush out. She nods, looking down at her computer screen to find his name.

A firm, warm hand makes contact with my lower back, and I turn my head slightly to see Kas leaning in to whisper in my ear. "Just take a deep breath, please; we'll get it sorted out," he tells me.

Shaking my head, lips pursed, I let out a long breath as new tears fill my eyes. My voice cracks as I whisper back, "You can't know that, Kas."

Just as the words leave my mouth, the receptionist says, "He's in room four-seventy-four."

And just like that, I'm bolting toward the elevators, but this time, Kas has a firm grip on my hand as he lets me drag him behind me. I frantically press the elevator button and am rewarded with the distinct *ding* as the doors open. Kat and Ale follow behind us as we cram into the small space, and Kas presses the button for the fourth floor.

Moments later, we arrive, the doors open, and my eyes immediately zone in on my mother across the hall. She's pacing, with her slender hands resting on her hips, her lip between her teeth as she anxiously bites the thin skin.

"*Etsi*!" I shout, rushing toward her, Kas in tow. Her head snaps up, and her arms open wide for me to step into her embrace. Kas releases his grip on my hand, allowing me to take my mother's small frame into my arms, crushing her to my body.

"*Usdi*," she mutters into my hair.

"Where is he?" I ask her in the same breath.

"They took him downstairs for some imaging; he seems to be stable now. For a while there, we didn't know how things were going to go."

I feel my heart rate begin to slow the smallest amount as the meaning of her words seep in.

"So, he might be okay?" I ask hesitantly.

"It's not good, but they think they can make him comfortable, and we're trying to see if he qualifies to be pushed to the top of the transplant list," she tells me, her tone solemn.

Pulling gently out of her grasp, I look into her dark-brown eyes, her worried expression mirroring mine. "I guess we'll just wait for the doctors. Is there anyone I can call?"

She shakes her head in response. "No, not now. In a few hours, when people are awake, we'll call the community and get the healers here. The hospitalist on his case approved us having them cleanse his room, so we'll just wait for that. Hopefully, your father will be back any minute," she tells me, her voice hopeful.

I nod, holding her hand as we take a seat in the cold room, the white walls adding to the chill.

Kas takes a seat on the floor beside me, and I cock my head to the side, giving him a quizzical look.

"I'm staying by your side," he tells me firmly. I don't have the energy to argue or tell him why that's not a good idea, especially not now.

Kat squeezes my shoulder. "I'll go grab the nurse and see if we can get some more chairs in here."

As she turns to leave, Ale stops in front of me, crouching down so we're at eye level. He places his hands on my knees, squeezing them reassuringly. "Do you need coffee or something to eat?" he asks me, then looks to my mom.

She gives him a gentle smile, shaking her head. "No, thank you, Alessandro."

His gaze turns back to me, my hands moving to sit on top of his for a moment. "I'm okay, but thanks."

He nods, standing and heading out after Kat.

Several minutes pass by before Kas moves, resting his head on my lap as if I forget where I'm at or *who* I'm seated beside. My fingers absently make their way into his hair, trailing through the soft strands mindlessly.

My mom clears her throat beside me, giving me a sidelong glance but saying nothing.

***

"*Edoda*, should I call the healers now?" I ask my dad expectantly.

"Yes, *Usdi*, but just Adohi, please. I don't want to worry the whole community until we have answers."

I nod at him, his frail body lying in the hospital bed as he struggles to breathe despite the high-flow oxygen.

Just as I'm leaving the room, the doctor walks in, his tall frame towering over me. It seems he realizes the height difference, so he looks around the room, pulling over a chair and taking a seat. "I'm Dr. Achebe, the pulmonary transplant surgeon. Unfortunately, it appears that your scans have significantly worsened since you were last admitted a year ago. I've gone ahead and informed UNOS of your condition, and we're hopeful you'll be able to receive a lung transplant in the next month or so. However, I have to be clear that you might not make it another month. There are a lot of factors that play into this, and transplants are few and far between, but like I said, we're hopeful." His voice is kind, reassuring, but firm, ensuring we're all clear on the state of my father's health.

My heart clenches at the reality of the situation.

I could lose him.

"I understand that your family is Cherokee. Would your healer be able to inform me of any rituals or special religious practices you'd like us to acknowledge during the surgery? This kind of planning will help us if the time comes for the transplant and will avoid delays."

"Yes, we were just about to give him a call. I'll go do that now," I say, standing, but Kas stops me, grabbing my hand.

"You stay. I'll call him." He nods for me to hand him my phone. I don't hesitate, just hand it over. He knows the healers as well as I do, so there's no point in wasting an opportunity for a few extra minutes with my dad.

"Thank you, Kas," I say as he heads out through the doors.

We continue speaking with the doctor for several more minutes, Kas returning to inform us that Adohi will be here within the hour.

When the doctor leaves, Kat and Ale head home to get changed and bring some clothes back for me since I refuse to leave my dad tonight.

Chapter Seventy-Eight

Kassian

Monday, February 5, 2024

I approach the door to Qaletaqa's room with clammy hands, my heart racing with worry. Every moment I've spent away from him has filled me with a sense of dread. He seemed to be doing a lot better yesterday, but anything could happen, and the fear of him dying suddenly has me plagued with worry.

As I open the door, my heart rate calms when I see Aiya sprawled out in a recliner, lying squished beside her mom. Her dad is safely in bed with a small smile on his face.

"Kas," he says, beaming at my entrance. "That was quite the game last night!"

I chuckle lightly at him. "Always so worried about hockey. Don't you know you're in the hospital and should be focusing on getting better?" I joke.

"Don't *you know* it's good to keep your mind busy when you're in a crappy hospital bed?" he chides, laughing at me.

"Touché," I reply. "I come bearing gifts though."

"Is it food?" Aiyana questions, her eyes wide with excitement.

"I wouldn't dream of coming without," I tell her.

"Then you can stay," her mom jokes.

"You two are the most food-motivated people on the planet—you know that?"

"They've got to keep their energy up for all the time they spend ragging on us!" Qaletaqa jokes, abruptly coughing into a napkin.

"Hey now, if you two weren't such pains, we wouldn't have to keep you in line!" Zuni tells her husband, a broad smile stretched across her ruby lips.

"Alright, put out or shut up. What's in the bag, Kas?" Rolling my eyes, I walk over to Aiyana, pulling over a chair and handing her the bag.

Her eyes light up, the first genuine smile I've seen from her in days boasting beautifully across her face.

She tears the bag open and pulls out the sushi and donuts, making cute little noises of excitement. "Thank god! I needed sugar, and the sushi doesn't hurt." She winks at me.

Her dad puts his hand out expectantly, and she places a blueberry cake donut in it. Taking a huge bite, he mumbles around it, "Did I ever tell you that you're my favorite man?" he jokes. I know those donuts are his favorite, which is why I drove nearly forty minutes to get them and had to beg the owner to make a fresh batch when she told me she didn't have any of the blueberry available.

"Not enough." I laugh and see Aiyana roll her eyes at me.

"No one needs to add to that big head of yours," she deadpans.

Throughout the entire interaction, her mom is eyeing us, taking note of every word we say. I'm not sure if this is something she's always done or if I'm just now noticing it because of my slip-up the other day when I put my head in Aiya's lap. At any rate, I hope she's at least happy about the development in our relationship, or at least, what I hope will become one.

***

"It is now 8:00 p.m. and visiting hours have ended. Please make your way quietly to the exits. We at Philadelphia Medicine appreciate your compliance," we hear over the intercom.

Gripping the armrest, I push myself into a standing position. "I guess that's our cue. Want me to walk you out?" I ask Aiyana.

She nods, standing and gathering her things. I give her mom a hug and a kiss on the cheek before moving over to her dad, doing the same. He grips me tightly before reluctantly releasing me.

Turning toward Aiyana, I reach for her things, holding them for her so she can tell her parents goodnight before we head out.

"I love you so much, *Edoda*," she murmurs to her father, clutching him close to her.

"Come back tomorrow and watch Kas's game with me?" he asks her, hopeful.

She smiles down at him. "Wouldn't miss it."

"Goodnight, *Etsi*," she tells her mom and heads back toward me, reaching for her things. I give her a firm head shake and lead her to the elevator before walking her to her truck.

Once her belongings are inside, I pull her into a bone-crushing hug, and thankfully, she doesn't resist. Her body melts into mine, her arms wrapping tightly around me with her face buried in my chest.

Sobs begin to wrack her body, sending a chill of sadness through me. I don't say anything, knowing that's not what she needs right now.

I just hold her.

I hold her until her body goes still and her breathing slows, then she pulls out of my touch. Running my thumb under her eyes, I wipe away the tears that have mottled her clear, tawny skin.

"Goodnight, Kas," she mutters and walks around to the driver's side of the truck, hoisting herself inside.

"Goodnight, my little viper," I whisper as she slams the door shut and backs out of the parking space.

Chapter Seventy-Nine

Aiyana

Friday, February 9, 2024

"Alright, you two, I'm heading home for a few hours to shower and get a few things done around the house. I'll be back later," Mom tells us as she heads out.

Grabbing the remote, I set the TV up for Kas's hockey game. "Scooch over," I instruct my father.

He does his best to move all the way to the side of the bed as I lower one arm rail to allow me a little more room. It helps that I'm petite; otherwise, there's no way we'd be able to make this work.

We watch the game, screaming and hollering so much that the nurses have to keep coming into the room to tell us to keep it down. The most recent time, the nurse threatened to send me home because it was after visiting hours anyway, and I'm not really supposed to be here. Dad started getting worn out anyway, coughing much more frequently, and quieted down as a result.

"That boy is really a force to be reckoned with." He beams.

"I'd say so. He's one of the best defensemen in the league right now."

"Not just right now," he says.

We continue watching, and when the game is over, my dad lays back with a huge grin. "That's my boy," he says proudly.

His words send an odd mix of warmth and nerves fluttering through me. If only he fit into my father's wishes of me marrying "within my culture." He'd be even more of a son to him than he already sees him as.

"Yeah, Dad, Kas is great," I reply noncommittally, pushing the bile working its way up my throat back down.

"He's helped me out so much over the last few years. He's even gotten really good at carving, maybe better than me at this point," he tells me.

My brows pull taut. "Helped you out?" I ask, confusion lacing my words.

"Kas comes over at least once a week, and sometimes, two or three times, when he isn't on the ice. He makes sure things are done around the house and helps me finish projects. You didn't know that?" he asks me, clearly surprised.

My heart begins to race as it clenches painfully in my chest. *Even when I wasn't around, he was still taking care of me, and I didn't even know it.*

"I had no idea, but I'm glad he was around while I wasn't." I give him a tight smile, guilt seeping in. When I got the acceptance letter and decided to move with Kat, my dad had gotten his diagnosis shortly after. I made a last-minute decision not to go and told my parents I hadn't gotten in.

My dad had thrown a fit about it and ended up calling the admissions office to tell them what a mistake they had made, which is when they informed him that I *had* gotten in. He reamed me out and made me follow my dreams, but I left a piece of my heart at home with him.

"You stop that," he tells me abruptly. "I wouldn't have changed anything about my life, and nothing makes me more proud than my daughter following her dreams, so you just stop that train of thought right in its tracks."

I nod, but the guilt stays put regardless of his words.

Moments later, my mom walks in. "Hey, you guys, who won?" she asks.

Dad pipes up and begins giving her a play-by-play of the game, the best he can, adding a lot of drama throughout. The nurse pokes his head in. "Hey guys, visiting hours have been over for a while, so one of you has to head out. I'm sorry." He gives us an apologetic smile.

Standing, I say my goodbyes and head back home, my mind reeling from this new information about Kas.

Chapter Eighty

Kassian

Tuesday, February 20, 2024

As I lie in bed, my mind swirls with thoughts that are seemingly coming from every direction.

I can't stop worrying about Aiyana, wanting to comfort her but also knowing she needs her space more than anything. I've been heading to the hospital to see her dad during the day while she's at work, and it seems he appreciates the company. I also hired a cleaning service to help Zuni out around the house, and I went over to cut the grass once. It had gotten a little long despite the cold weather, and I didn't want them worrying about it.

My heart tells me I need to do something, make a move, or just do anything really. I just need to be heading in the right direction with her, and that isn't happening at the moment. We've become stagnant, just as I thought I was winning her over. It's like the other night when she cried in my arms, she released me with her tears.

My brain, on the other hand, tells me that she needs her space and she'll come back to me in due time. But what does that even mean? What happens if her dad doesn't get a transplant in time? She'll fall apart and refuse to let anyone support her? That doesn't sound like an option as far as I'm concerned.

Giving up on sleep, I grab my phone and text Ale.

Hey man, could we meet for a drink or something after the game on Friday? I need some advice.

Alice

Yeah, of course, I hope I can help with whatever it is.

Alice

To be clear, this is about Aiyana, right?

Yes...

Alice

Good, because you need to lock that down for everyone's sake.

I'm not prepared to get into what that means.

Alice

Goodnight Narvaez.

Night Alice.

Opening another message thread, I text Aiyana because I can't seem to help myself.

Let me know if you need anything. I miss you.

Little Viper

Miss you too.

Goodnight my little viper <3

Little Viper

Night Kas.

I log into Amazon and browse for items I can overnight to her. I know she's in the middle of her period right now, so she probably needs provisions. I send her a ton of snacks, chocolate, and a new set of Bluetooth headphones so she can zen out to her erotic audio. When I'm done, I finally pass out, waking every so often from nightmares about her leaving me forever.

Chapter Eighty-One

Aiyana

Thursday, February 22, 2024

My period is almost over, and for the first time in years, it's not the most painful thing my body's had to go through. My heart is being torn apart every day.

Dad is starting to decline a little more each day, unable to speak in full sentences now and tiring much more easily.

My stomach dropped to my fucking toes the other day when he fell asleep during Kas's game. That has never happened in all the years I've known my father, and it was the first clear sign that he really won't get better without a transplant.

I'm trying to remain hopeful, and Kat does her best to try and boost my mood and quiet my worrying mind, but nothing seems to truly help.

The entire community now knows about my father's condition. Tribal members, particularly the elders, have come to pray around him and perform healing rituals.

Yesterday, Kat was able to talk the transplant surgeon into allowing my father to leave the hospital for the day to perform a sacred healing ritual with the healers. Usually, the person with the illness will enter a sweat lodge, which is essentially an outdoor sauna with hot stones, while the healers say prayers and help them connect spiritually to our ancestors and pull energy from nature. With his lungs in their current condition, a sweat lodge would not be healthy even though my father argued otherwise, or tried to. He believes the ancestors will protect and heal him if he does the ritual, but one of the younger healers advised that the ancestors want him to have faith, but they don't want him to deliberately do something that we know would be harmful.

It was nice to hear that perspective, and I felt a little less horrible knowing Kat would be there with him. She offered to take the day off from work to oversee the ritual and act as his medical liaison if anything were to happen.

When I went in to see him this morning before work, he seemed to be in much better spirits, but he was still having difficulty speaking. I've never tapped into my spirituality quite as much as I've been these last couple of weeks. I find myself saying prayers and buying crystals, herbs, and other medicinal plants to bring to his room. He has a growing pile of items from our friends in the community who bring him things to help him feel more connected with the elements.

Several of our friends and family from North Carolina and Georgia have also come to see him, and the attention and community have helped keep him going.

I get out of the shower and dry off, fighting the urge to call Kas just to hear his voice. I've been avoiding him because he's the only person who manages to break down my walls time and time again. And right now, I need those walls built as high and strong as possible if I'm going to have any chance at recovering from the fallout if my dad doesn't get this damn transplant.

I braid my hair before changing into one of Kas's oversized shirts and climbing in under the covers. My phone vibrates with a text, and I don't have to check to know who it's from.

Every night since I got back to Philly has been the same thing. A goodnight text from Kas that sets off a swarm of butterflies in my gut. But recently, I've just felt guilt for keeping him at arm's length with no explanation in sight.

Kas

Goodnight my little viper <3

Goodnight Kas.

Chapter Eighty-Two

Kassian

Friday, February 23, 2024

Brenda, the waitress at Rocco's, heads back behind the bar after delivering our beer. The moment she's out of earshot, Ale turns back to me, relaxing into his chair and piercing me with his gaze. "Spill it," he tells me.

"Brenda just brought me this beer; I'm not spilling anything," I joke, making him roll his eyes at me.

"Always deflecting." He shakes his head at me. "Do I have to remind you that *you* asked *me* to have this talk in the first place?"

"Fine, I don't know what to do about Aiyana."

"I'm gonna need a little more information than that, especially considering you haven't exactly told me anything about your relationship. Or lack thereof?" he muses.

I huff, leaning back in my chair. "Aiyana and I have been on again, off again since middle school."

His eyes grow wide, and he sits forward, leaning into me with a serious expression. "How the hell is this the first I'm hearing of this? Kat doesn't know about this, so how the hell could that be possible? We've noticed some sketchy shit going on with you two, but we both thought this was pretty recent."

"Well, in middle school, when Kat and I moved next door, she and Aiyana became instant friends, but she and I always shared a special bond. As soon as I realized she wasn't just being nice, she was *flirting,* middle school Kas took that and ran with it. I thought her kindness was extended to everyone, judging by how she interacted with both me and my sister, but that couldn't have been further from the truth. Even as a teen, Aiyana has always been a fucking menace to society." I chuckle.

He nods slowly. "Okay, so you pursued her then?"

"No, she made the first move, actually." A smile spreads broadly across my face at the memory. "Aiyana was my first everything, and I was hers. I was too shy to do anything about my crush. So one day, when we were working on a science experiment in her parents' garage, she grabbed my face and assaulted me with those ruby-red lips as the baking soda concoction erupted out of that damn volcano. I've been fucking gone for her ever since," I admit.

"Jesus Christ, then why didn't you guys make it official when you got older?"

"She told me she wasn't sure if Kat would approve, and by the time we had this conversation, we were just months from graduating high school, and my world had very recently crashed down around me. Aiyana was the only person I spoke to for months as I dissociated and barely passed my classes. She helped me bring my grades up and pushed me to pick myself up and just get that shit done. There was just so much going on at the time. When we got to undergrad, we became even closer, and things developed into what felt like a real relationship. Apparently, that was one-sided because when we graduated, she applied to school in San Diego to be with Kat, and she never even spoke to me about it. I didn't even get the closure of a breakup because Aiyana insisted we weren't a couple, so when she left, a massive piece of my heart went with her."

Ale assesses me, waiting to speak until after he's had a moment to fully process my words. "Didn't her dad get sick just before she moved with Kat? Have you ever considered that maybe that had something to do with her abrupt change in actions? Maybe she just needed to get away from her reality for a while and ended up being gone longer than she had anticipated?"

I consider what he's said but shake my head. "That would be completely out of character for Aiyana to run when someone she loves needs her. If anything, she'd have found a way to stick around for him."

"Alright, well, you would know better than I would, but I just feel like there's something missing here. I think there's another explanation, but I'm also not convinced it even matters anymore. I'm so madly in love with your sister, it isn't even funny. It's fucking ridiculous, and I wouldn't change a single thing, but if I had known Kat as long as you've known Aiyana, absolutely nothing would have stood in my way. I'd have killed to have all that extra time with her, but I didn't, and in some ways, that's for the best. I wouldn't have been the man she needed me to be as I navigated my mother's illness and my own diagnosis, but *you* are in a uniquely incredible place, Narvaez. You've got to do something."

"I've been thinking about something that might sound fucking crazy, and I need you to tell me if it's *too* crazy." I level him with a stare.

"I think you *need* something crazy, something ridiculous enough to work, that is."

I nod before telling him my plan. "I'm going to ask her dad for his blessing to propose."

A wide grin spreads his lips. "Now *that* is what I'm talking about."

"Do you think it's an okay time though? Weddings should be a happy thing, assuming she even says yes, but right now, things are pretty glum."

"Honestly?" he asks me. "I think we all need some good in our lives right now, Kas. A lot has happened in the last month or so, and I think this would be the perfect distraction for everyone."

My stomach does a little flip of excitement at the thought of Aiyana finally being *mine*. "Alright, let's get to planning then because once I have his approval, I'm going for it before he can change his mind."

We spend the next few hours planning everything out and only leave when Brenda tells us they're closing up for the night. I won't be sleeping much tonight. I've got a lot to get done before tomorrow morning, and I still need to call Kat about it and get my carving kit out from my storage unit.

***

"Thank you for not being mad that we kept this from you," I tell my sister, who was strangely understanding throughout the entire conversation. I really thought this would be the first time she actually lost her shit on me.

"Kas, you and Aiyana haven't exactly been hiding things well, you know. I was just biding my time and waiting for you guys to come to the conclusion everyone else has."

"And what would that be?"

"That you two are made for each other, Kas. Don't be so dense."

"Yeah, well, I hope she sees it that way." I groan, anxiety seeping in. "By the way, what'd you mean about us not hiding things well?" I genuinely thought she hadn't really noticed anything.

"Kas, for months now, you and Aiyana just so happen to be gone or unavailable around the same time as Aiyana says she's out with some mystery man. It wasn't that hard to put two and two together, considering the long looks and sideways glances you have both been shooting at each other since middle school."

"Fair enough. Alright, Kitty-Kat, I've gotta start working on this ring, or I won't finish in time."

"Goodnight, Kas, love you."

"I love you endlessly, Kat, goodnight."

I hang up the phone and get to work.

Chapter Eighty-Three

Kassian

Saturday, February 24, 2024

I managed to get a solid three-hour nap in after finishing the ring for Aiyana. I plan to have her help me pick out her own engagement ring, but I hope she'll want this thin golden viper as her wedding band and stand-in engagement ring for the time being.

When Mom went into the nursing home, she didn't want to take anything with her that reminded her of our father, so she gave Kat her engagement ring and sea turtle necklace, and she gave me her wedding band. I've been holding onto it for years, unsure of what to do with it, but when the thought arose, I knew it was the perfect plan.

The band was thin, but not too thin, so I was able to carve the viper into it without breaking the delicate tail off, and the yellow gold matches all of Aiyana's usual jewelry.

Ale and I decided that I needed to keep things intimate for the proposal. While I just fucking love love and would want a massive public display of my affection for Aiyana so the entire world can know that she's mine, Aiyana's much more private.

She doesn't enjoy PDA and cringes at public proposals, so I've got a plan that I think she's going to love.

I just need to hop in the shower and get over to the hospital to speak with her dad before she gets there.

***

My hands are clammy as I make my way into Qaletaqa's hospital room. He's sitting up, eyes closed, as he recites a familiar prayer asking for healing. I knock gently on the inside of the door to let him know I'm here and pull up a chair beside him. I close my eyes and place my hands on the side of his bed, joining him in the prayer.

I feel his hands take mine, his once strong hands now frail. "May the breeze blow new strength into your being. May you walk gently through the world and know its beauty all the days of your life." We finish the prayer together.[1]

When our eyes open, mine meet his, and he smiles gently at me. "You've come to ask me something." He smirks knowingly. This man has always known exactly what I planned to do before I ever actually did it. "The ancestors spoke to me last night in a dream, and I hope they were right. Before you do, though, could you do me a favor?"

"Anything," I tell him eagerly.

"Could you braid my hair? I haven't gotten a good shower since being here, and I sweat in my sleep. I just want it out of my face, and I can't hold my hands up that long." My heart breaks hearing his words.

In lieu of an answer, I stand, angling my body at the head of the bed so he doesn't have to move as much for me to gain access to his long, graying hair.

I work on crossing the sections of hair one over the other, being meticulous in my actions. When I near the end, he hands me a small band from the table beside him. When finished, I take a seat next to him.

He looks over at the clock on the wall before meeting my eyes again. "It's nearly time for Zuni and Aiya to arrive, so you better start now." He gives me a small grin.

My heart is racing despite being nearly certain he wouldn't seem so happy if he were planning on saying no. I take a deep, steeling breath before finally releasing the words that have been racing through my mind for the last several hours on replay. "I love your daughter more than anything in this world. She breathes life into me and steals my breath away all in the same moment. She's radiant like the damn sun, and I can't imagine spending another day of my life without calling her mine and making sure everyone else knows it too. I've loved her for longer than I care to admit. Longer than I probably even realize, truthfully. Would you give me the absolute honor of your blessing? I know right now isn't a good time, but—" He puts up a hand, stopping the words from leaving my mouth.

"Now is the *perfect* time, Kas. We all need something to look forward to," he tells me, grabbing my hand and looking me directly in the eyes as he says his next words. "I would love nothing more than to see my daughter marry you, Kassian. *Gvgeuyi, uwetsi.*" *I love you, son.*

Tears prick my eyes as he squeezes my hand as firmly as he can. "Now get out of here," he whispers to me just as Aiyana and Zuni head into the room.

I stand abruptly, clearing my throat before heading to the door. "I've gotta head out to run some errands. I'll be back later," I tell them, rushing out without a single glance in Aiyana's direction. I don't trust myself to not just ask her here, and I'll be damned if I ruin what should be a special moment for her by doing it at a hospital.

***

My body is practically shaking with nerves and excitement as I pull into a parking space outside of Meadow Brook Farms. They've got live music playing in the outdoor café area. The lead performer is singing a cover of "All of Me" by John Legend, and it matches my current feelings so perfectly, it's like a sign.[2] From where, I'm unsure.

I head to the concessions counter, and an older gentleman greets me with a friendly smile. "Hey! You play for the Scarlets, don't you? Great game the other day, man," he tells me excitedly.

"Yeah, thanks." I smile politely but hope we can cut this interaction short because I'd rather not have anyone overhearing.

"Hah, well, what can I get for you?" he asks me, and I release a relieved breath.

"Could I get two of those cheese boards you guys make and four soft pretzels, please?"

He nods, ringing me up.

A few minutes later, my arms are full of food, and I'm waiting at a picnic table for Aiyana, Kat, and Ale to arrive.

In the minutes it takes them to arrive, my heart rate has all but returned to normal, but when I see Aiyana's questioning expression as she approaches me, the nerves start up again.

"What's this all about?" she asks me.

"Kat just thought we could all get out for a nice, relaxed night," I tell her, allowing Kat to be the fall guy as we had agreed on.

She quirks a thin, dark brow but takes a seat across from me and immediately starts picking at the food.

***

Thirty minutes later, we're walking through a field that would normally have sunflowers and pumpkins depending on the time of year, but right now, it's just covered in a light layer of snow that started falling moments ago.

Aiyana has her arms wrapped around herself. "It's fucking freezing, Kas," she grumbles beside me.

I take the opportunity to wrap my arms around her, holding her tightly to me as we make our way toward the giant wagon that usually hauls fifty or so people at a time through the Halloween and Christmas lights during the holidays.

One of Alessandro's cousins works here, so he was able to get him to give me the owner's name, and we worked out a deal to make this plan come to life with such short notice.

Once we're at the back of the wagon, I lift Aiyana up and follow behind her. She takes a seat on the blanket-covered bench, and I sit beside her, wrapping my arm around her waist.

"I didn't know they did Valentine's Day lights here," she says with wonder. "My parents used to take me here all the time for the Halloween lights and sometimes for their huge Christmas display too, but I've never heard anyone talk about this."

"Yeah, must be new," I tell her as I peer over at Kat, who's doing her best to hold her composure. Alessandro, on the other hand, looks like he's about to shit a brick at any moment.

Kat calms herself just enough to say, "It must've lost its popularity with the passing of the actual holiday, but I'm really glad I was still able to get us tickets!"

Aiyana gives her a small smile, rolling her eyes, and replies, "Always such a romantic." She chuckles.

"Alright, folks! We're gonna get started!" the driver of the wagon tells us, and soon, we're off.

Aiyana's eyes light up when we make our way through the densely wooded area, and giant glowing hearts hang in every tree. Red, white, and pink lights are strung all over, and several Cupids with their arrows pointed at the wagon glow in the night. The snow starts falling a little heavier down around us, turning the whole place into a romantic wonderland.

"It's beautiful," Aiyana whispers in awe, just loud enough for me to hear.

I tilt my head to her ear, whispering, "*You* are beautiful, my little viper."

She tilts her chin down, a blush creeping across her cheeks that sends a wave of euphoria through me.

The driver starts the playlist I had sent Alessandro's cousin earlier, and my heart rate begins to pick up speed again.

I see Kat and Ale huddled closely together, whispering to one another, their eyes bright and their smiles wide.

We're just moments away from the big surprise, and I couldn't be more nervous.

I'm watching the back of the driver's head intently, waiting for his cue to get down on one knee. The moment I see him scratch the back of his head, I find my body responding for me. I stand as he slows the wagon down to a stop.

Aiyana looks up at me. "What's wrong?" she asks.

I lower to one knee, and her mouth falls open, her eyes wide as she takes me in. The moment the massive sign behind me finally lights up, reading, "Will You Marry Me?" I know it. I can literally see the lights reflecting in her dark pupils.

I reach into my pocket, grab the small velvet box, and open it. I look up into those gorgeous dark eyes, shock still written all over her face, and I know in that moment, *she's going to say no.*

I can't back out of this now, not when I've gone this far. And maybe I'm wrong. *Maybe she's just surprised.*

I take her hand in mine and begin. "Aiyana, I've loved you for what feels like my entire life, or at least, the only moments that have ever counted," I tell her, urging her to understand, to love me back. "I've loved you probably longer than I even realize. Hell," I shake my head, "I might have even loved you since the first moment you stepped foot in my home so many years ago. And I will keep on loving you for as long as I live, and after that, in the afterlife too because there's no life for me without *you.*"

---

1. **Cherokee Blessing**

2. **All of Me – John Legend**

Chapter Eighty-Four

Aiyana

His words are barely making it through the haze in my mind, but when the realization of what's happening hits me, I panic.

"Will you marry me, little viper?" he asks me sweetly, sounding so nervous. The hand he has wrapped around my fingers is shaking, or maybe that's me?

This can't be happening right now.

I bolt upright, wrenching my hand from his, and make a beeline for the back of the wagon, hopping down quickly. I'm pumping my arms and legs as fast as I can, exerting myself more than I have in years.

I'm frantic, running as quickly to my truck as I can. I barely hear Kat calling from behind me, though her voice is growing louder the more exhausted I become.

I finally make it to the parking lot, and several people enjoying their dinner outside are staring at me with confusion.

As I look around, I don't see my truck. My eyes land on Alessandro's SUV, and my heart sinks to my toes.

"Aiyana!" Kat calls, just a few feet behind me. "Get in the car," she tells me abruptly, and my eyes widen.

What the hell does she mean, "Get in the car."

"Just because I don't drive doesn't mean I can't. Get in the freaking car, Aiyana. I won't tell you again. If you want any chance at getting out of here without having to see Kas, you'll get in the damn car and let me do my brother a favor so he doesn't have to see you right now." Her voice is so strained, hurt and confusion laces every word, but she's right. I just crushed her brother with no explanation and yet, she's still helping me.

I get in the passenger side, buckle in, and set my sights out the window, resting my forehead against it. *What the hell has been happening these last few weeks? Has everyone found themselves in some strange, warped version of the space-time continuum or something?* This amount of chaos just can't be normal.

Kat starts the SUV, backs out, and pulls onto the main road, heading in the opposite direction of our home. Before I can ask, she says, "I'm dropping you off at the hospital. Ale and I'll drop off your truck later. I think you need to speak with your dad."

That's all she says. No explanations, and frankly, I'm thankful. I have no desire to relive the last several minutes, but especially not with Kas's twin sister. *My best friend,* who I could have called my sister if I'd just said yes.

But I couldn't.

God, I fucking wanted to. In a perfect world, I'd be able to say yes.

In a perfect world, my dad wouldn't be dying, I remind myself.

We ride the rest of the way in silence, Kat not bothering to fill the empty space with music. When we get to the hospital, she pulls up to the main doors and turns to face me. "Go talk to your dad. I'll have your truck here in the next hour or so."

I have no idea what she wants me to speak to my father about, but it won't be about what just transpired. I don't need a lecture from him, and I definitely don't need to worry him right now.

All I can do is give her a nod as I grip the door handle and make my way out into the frigid weather. The wind chill picks up now that the snow has stopped falling.

The calm before the storm, as they say.

When I arrive at my dad's door, I'm relieved to find my mom isn't here. She'd know something was wrong and wouldn't stop until I finally gave in and explained myself.

As I enter the room, my father's face shines brightly, his smile broad as I approach. "*Edoda*," I greet him.

"Aiyana," he says cheerily but looks past me, his brow furrowing. "You're alone?"

"Um, yeah. Was I supposed to meet Mom somewhere?" I ask, confused.

"No, no. Come, sit." He pats the space beside him as he works to sit upright. He stops, covering his mouth to cough.

"What's on your mind?" he asks me, sounding cautious.

Shaking my head, I tell him, "I just messed something up, and I'm not sure how to fix it or if I even can."

"All things can be fixed with enough care. Tell me what happened."

"I can't," I say, my voice cracking as tears burn my eyes. He wraps an arm around me, pulling me closer.

"You said no," he breathes out, and my heart stops.

"Wh-what?" I stutter.

"Kas proposed, and you said no, didn't you?"

I look at my father, bewildered. "You knew?"

He nods with a small but sad smile. "He asked my permission this morning."

If it were possible to be any more shocked, I would be in this moment. "And he proposed even though you said no?" I ask him.

My father's head jolts back, lips pursed as if I had just slapped him. "Told him *no*? Why would you think I'd say no?"

My mouth hangs open momentarily. *Is he for real?* "Because when you got your freaking diagnosis six years ago, you told me, 'Our culture and way of life is dying; this is why it's important for you to marry within your own.'" I raise my voice slightly.

"You did *not*," my mother shouts from behind me as she enters the room.

My father winces. "It's possible that I, uh, may have said something like that," he admits.

"May have? *Edoda*, you used those exact words. They've replayed in my head every day since."

My mother puts a hand on my shoulder, gripping me firmly. "Your father must have been *really* struggling with his mental health at that time because that is the *only* explanation for why he'd say something like that." She turns her gaze on him. "Isn't that right, my love?" she grits out.

"Yep, must've been having..." His gaze shifts between us. "What do your cousins always call it? A 'menty-b'?" I can't help the laugh that bubbles out of me at that.

"God, how do we fix this?" I ask my parents, frustration settling in.

"You said no to his proposal, so you can't take that back. It'll just tarnish the memory of how you got engaged in the first place. So you've got to propose to *him* instead. Give him some of the power back in this situation, and let him choose you all over again," my mother rushes out.

I look to my father. "And you're *sure* you won't be disappointed in me?" My heart breaks at the thought of losing Kas but also at the idea of my dad ever being disappointed in me.

"Aiya, I could *never* be disappointed in you. And the only reason I ever said those things to you was because I was venting. I was overwhelmed by my diagnosis, and we had recently held an elders meeting where we discussed how few Ani'-Yun'wiya' men and women are still around. It's not an excuse, and I'm sorry it ever happened. I should never have put that on you," he tells me in earnest.

"There's a Cherokee proverb that says, 'A woman's highest calling is to lead a man to his soul so as to unite him with the Great Spirit. A man's highest calling is to protect the woman so she is free to walk the earth unharmed.' I believe this applies to every true relationship, regardless of sexuality. The point is that you and Kas are united, soulmates who have lived many lives before this, traveling the earth with one another, just waiting to be reunited in the next lifetime. And that is something so rare and so beautiful."

"How can you be sure?" I ask him as my eyes prick with tears.

"Because, sweet girl, that's what I share with your mother." He smiles at her lovingly, and my heart clenches in my chest. Soon, my mother may have to walk this earth alone, without him.

"Go. Go home and find your path. Don't return to me without him." He nods his head toward the door, and I make my way outside.

***

She answers on the first ring. "I was wondering when you'd call. I'm out front with your truck. Get in, and we'll figure out what to do."

I hang up, sprinting to my truck parked out front. Kat pushes the door open before sliding into the passenger seat. "Where are we headed?" she asks me.

Tapping my chin for a moment, I think about it and say, "Step one: get a tattoo."

Her brows draw together in shock. "I'm not sure how that's going to change anything. Don't people usually wait until *after* a breakup to change their hair and get a new tattoo? I thought we were fixing things?"

"We are. Just trust me."

"Aiya, I've gotta be honest. It's a little hard to do that after what just happened. I love you, but you've got to let me into that brain of yours."

Her words tear through me, but I know I deserve them. "I'm going to get your brother's name tattooed on me, and while I cry in pain, we're going to plan the biggest, most obnoxious proposal ever."

"But you *hate* those big proposals," she tells me as if I'd forgotten.

"That's because they're cringey as hell. But your brother? He fucking *loves* public proposals. So that's what he's getting. I'm just not sure of all the details just yet."

She pulls out her phone, typing away at the screen. "I'm letting Kas know not to worry about you and asking him to meet me for lunch at a restaurant directly across from Love Park."

"You're a genius, Kat. I could fucking kiss you right now."

"Save that for my brother, girlfriend." She chuckles.

***

"Before I start, you're absolutely sure you want this name *here?*" The tattoo artist asks me—his lips pursed beneath a long, dark beard. The black tattoos inked into his dark skin travel down to his hand as he holds the tattoo gun.[1]

"Don't be so dramatic." I roll my eyes at him. "It's just my clavicle; it's not like you're tattooing my ass."

"At least if it were your ass, you could cover it," he groans, clearly thinking this is a poor lapse in judgment on my part.

"That kind of defeats the purpose. I'm into big gestures today," I tell him, trying to sound confident.

He concedes, getting into position and pulling his tray closer to him.

"Wait!" I yell before he starts. He sits back, rolling his eyes at me. "Can I see that needle?"

"Oh, for fucks sake. Don't tell me you're afraid of needles." He huffs.

"Mind the business that pays you, *Chad.*"

"Aiyana." Kat snickers. "Are you serious? You're afraid of *needles*? How did I not know this?" She laughs.

"Hardy, har har, it's *so* funny. Shut it, woman. Just let me see the damn thing." He brings it close to my face, and my eyes widen at the sight of the hair-thin needles. I almost pass out but do my best to convince myself that it's just a pen. *No needles involved.* Besides, this is for Kas.

"You ready, kid?"

"I'm not a child, but yes," I tell him, lying back in the chair and clenching my eyes shut.

The initial sting of the needles is a shock to my system, but I adjust to the pain quickly, and a few minutes later, he's wiping the cleansing foam away.

Sitting me up, he grabs a mirror from his workspace and hands it to me so I can check out my new, first-ever tattoo. "It's perfect." I smile, taking it in.

Kat leans forward, trying to get a better look. "Oh my gosh! That's so cute!" I snort at her reaction.

***

"I'm glad you told him lunch because I need time to get him a ring!" I realize as we're headed to our floor.

"Don't worry. I had Ale pick something simple up after he left the hospital. I figure you guys will want to pick them out yourselves eventually anyway, so he just got a simple gold band for Kas. And no, you're not allowed to pay him back. His words, not mine," she tells me.

"You're really too good to me, especially after what happened tonight."

"I'll be honest, I was pissed at first, but I've watched you two make googly eyes at each other for years, so I figured there *had* to be a reason why you'd say no. And now that I know? I just feel freaking terrible that you had to carry that weight on your shoulders by yourself for so long."

"I should never have let my fear of disappointing my father get in the way of Kas and me to begin with. It just took me too long to realize that, and I hope it's not too late."

"Stop it. It's not. Kas's love for you didn't suddenly die with your lackluster response," she tells me as we head into the apartment.

"Get some rest. I'll see you in the morning, and we can work out the extra details."

***

Just as I'm finally about to drift to sleep, the realization that Kas hasn't texted me goodnight hits me like a freight train, knocking the wind from my lungs.

God, I really fucking hope this works.

I can't live without him.

---

1. **Girl With The Tattoo Enter.lewd – Miguel**

Chapter Eighty-Five

Aiyana

Sunday, February 25, 2024

"Fuck, I'm glad the sun is at least out," I mutter to Kat as she stands beside me, watching as I pace nervously.

"Well, you're the one that chose to wear that off-the-shoulder sweater." She rolls her eyes at me.

"Big gestures, Kat! *Big gestures*. If I didn't wear this, he wouldn't be able to see the damn tattoo!"

"Okay, whatever," she says, brushing me off.

"Are you sure this is going to work?" I ask her, needing as much reassurance as possible.

"Aiyana, my brother is understandably upset, but he's *obsessed* with you. Of course it's going to work. Now stop asking me that. I'm just trying to focus on mentally rehearsing my parts. You know I can't really dance," she whines.

"You'll be fine. You're not the one proposing," I remind her.

"Yeah, because that would be gross," she jokes, trying to clear some of the tension.

Chapter Eighty-Six

Kassian

Sunday, February 25, 2024

This must be some sick joke, or maybe she *really* didn't realize her mistake. Because seriously? Lunch at the café *directly* across from *Love Park* while I wallow in my own misery over my failed proposal.

There's no way Kat would be this intentionally malicious, so she must've just had a craving for something at this café, though I can't imagine what. I'm seated at a table outside, waiting for her to arrive, and this menu looks pretty horrendous. There's not a single thing I could imagine actually eating here.

Maybe I'm at the wrong place?

The waiter brings a couple of glasses of water as I wait, my stomach churning with bile. I don't know why I even agreed to this. I don't want to be out of my apartment today. Then again,

I couldn't sleep last night because everything in my apartment reminded me of Aiyana.

Even thinking her name fucking crushes me.

How stupid could I have been? I know this woman. I *knew* she'd say no, and yet, I still asked, hurting us *both* in the process.

It took everything in me not to bang down their damn door last night and demand she speak with me. Tell me what I could do to change her mind. Give me some sort of explanation for why she can't or *won't* commit to me. Clearly, Kat wasn't against us being together, so she can't keep using that as a reason.

Though I guess she doesn't actually *need* a reason anymore.

She said *no,* and that seemed pretty damn final to me.

Or rather, she took off like a speed train to hell and didn't look back. I was in so much shock that I couldn't get my legs to move me to chase after her. Which is for the best. She clearly wants me to *stop* chasing her.

I guess I don't know her as well as I thought.

Checking my watch, I realize Kat is ten minutes late, and I haven't gotten a text from her. Loud music playing from across the street jolts me from my thoughts.

I look around, trying to figure out who the hell started playing this fucking song while I'm over here trying to recover from the worst proposal in the history of proposals.

As if to add repeated insult to injury, Bruno Mars's voice rolls around me, singing about looking for something dumb to do, which would *almost* be funny if it weren't so goddamn ironic.[1]

And in the next line, he sings about wanting to marry the person he's singing to. *Oh, come the fuck on! You can't be serious right now.*

A couple jump out onto the sidewalk, dancing and twirling. Then a pair of children run toward them, the larger one helping the other into a little hop. Which I'm sure would've been cute if it weren't for the fact that I'm beyond miserable right now.

Hell, even my own sister hasn't shown up for me.

As the thought passes through my mind, several more people dance out across the street, spinning and jumping in front of the giant "LOVE" sign.

Bruno continues singing about a little chapel where he can take this person he's thinking about and marry them in secret.

I feel like banging my skull into a brick wall right now.

Not only is someone proposing, but they're playing one of my favorite songs, *and* they've got a fucking flash mob!

I'm even more pissed that I'd normally *love* this kind of thing. Flash mobs are my jam. Hell, I'd probably try to join in under literally any other circumstances.

The crowd keeps growing, more and more people joining in as hundreds of onlookers watch the spectacle. I look around, trying to pinpoint who the lucky person is because it sure as shit isn't me.

I stand, unable to tell who it could be, but I'm over this shit. Kat still isn't here, and I'm exhausted. I'll just get a hotel across town so I can get some sleep and maybe search for a new fucking penthouse because it doesn't feel like I'll ever recover if I have to think about Aiyana every moment I'm home.

Not that I won't be thinking about her anyway.

Taking one last look over at the crowd, I turn to leave, but my eyes snag on a couple of women whom I recognize. The shorter woman's hair is a pastel-pink color. I couldn't miss it anywhere.

Rose and Charlie are dancing in this goddamn flash mob?

Then I see another familiar face. Gianni?

And a few more. Matt, JJ, and Kyle are with their wives.

My eyes scan the crowd, trying to catch up and decide if this is some sort of fever dream.

The lyrics continue on about being ready when she is.

And the next thing I know, Kat and Ale come into view. Ale is spinning my sister around as she twirls not so gracefully, her face a contorted mess of anxiety.

The shock is slowly leaving my body as I realize that I know most of these faces. The crowd of dancers is filled with all of Alessandro's family; even his mother is swaying from her wheelchair with his father.

Zuni is rushing toward me, her tablet in hand, as she shouts, "Kas!"

"What is going on?" I ask in a rush, confused and overwhelmed.

She puts a firm hand on the center of my spine and pushes me across the street toward the spectacle in front of us.

Just as my feet make it to the edge of the sidewalk, *"Who cares, baby? I think I wanna marry you,"* floats through the speakers. The crowd parts, and there, positioned in the center of the "LOVE" sign, is Aiyana, down on one knee.

My body takes over, rushing to her despite my shock and confusion.

My heart is fucking bounding out of my chest as she grabs my hand, and I fight the urge to wipe away the tears slipping down her cheeks. "Kas, for years, you've loved me unconditionally even when I couldn't do the same," she tells me, her voice strained. "You've shown me what it's like to be so fucking obsessed with a person that all other words lose their meaning. You've been nothing but incredible to my family, and for reasons we'll have to discuss when there isn't a huge crowd around, I had convinced myself we couldn't be together. And I am so damn sorry," she cries, her voice cracking on the sob. Her words are barely making it in, but I think the shock has officially worn off.

She put on a flash mob... *for me?*

"Kas, I don't just 'think' I wanna marry you. I *know* I do. So, if you haven't changed your mind, will you marry me?" she asks me expectantly, her eyes glistening with unshed tears.

My heart heaves in my chest, all eyes on me.

I drop to the ground in front of her, my palms cupping her cheeks. "Yes, my little viper, every day of the week, I'll choose you," I tell her urgently.

A laugh bubbles out of her, but it's partly a sob. The emotions warring inside her are begging to come out.

I lean in to kiss her, but she pushes me back. "Your ring," she chokes out, grabbing my left hand and sliding the metal band on.

"I thought only women got an engagement ring?" I ask, quirking a brow at her.

She smirks at me. "I'm all about equality, but you can feel free to swap that for something else later."

I chuckle. "*Now,* can I kiss you?"

"There's one more thing," she tells me as she slides her sweater down her shoulder a bit more.

My eyes widen. "Is that *my name*?" Written in black cursive lettering, my name is etched into the delicate tan skin on her collarbone, the skin surrounding it a bit red and puffy, and a thin layer of ointment is layered overtop.

"Aiyana! You got a tattoo!" her mother exclaims from behind me, reminding me that she's still there.

"She *what*?" her dad's voice shouts from the tablet she's holding up.

"Oh, shut it." Aiyana chuckles at them, leaning into me. "*Now* you can kiss me."

I don't hesitate, pulling her to me and pressing my lips to hers in a desperate kiss. Hoots and hollers erupt all around us, but they fade away as pure joy settles into my bones.

I got the girl.

1. **Marry You – Bruno Mars**

Epilogue: Part One-Aiyana

Thursday, August 22, 2024

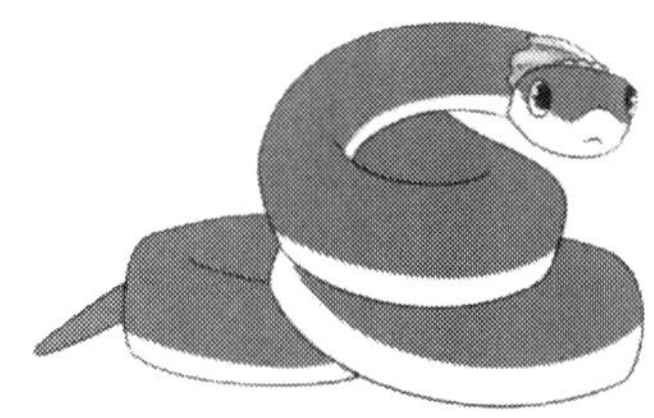

"Alright, are you ready to see your favorite child?" Audrey, our wedding planner, asks.

"Of course I am! Now, can I turn around already?"

"Absolutely," she tells him. I'm standing, hidden behind a large tree as I watch. My dad turns, his warm brown eyes already shimmering with tears, but when he sees Kas standing in front of him, he releases a full-bellied laugh. My cheeks ache from smiling so much, my throat raw from laughter these last few days.

"You look beautiful, sweet girl," he tells Kas jokingly.

"He really is a pretty princess," Kat agrees.

Kas does a little twirl in his white wedding dress. It fits so snuggly over his suit that he couldn't zip it all the way.

He curtsies and takes my dad's hand in his, pressing a joking kiss to his knuckles before standing and wrapping an arm around his shoulders. "You ready to see our girl?" Kas asks my dad, his voice full of adoration.

"Absolutely!"

"Now get out of that cheap dress before we do this, or you'll ruin the pictures," Audrey tells them, her chin held high as she bosses these men around. *I love her already.*

My mother's petite hand grasps my bicep. Turning toward her, I see her standing before me in a cream-and-red, traditional garment made of cloth. Her dark eyes shine brightly as she smiles at me, her ruby-red lips upturned.

"I know this isn't a tradition we would normally take part in, but I wanted to give you something that would cover the old and borrowed," she tells me, referencing the good-luck tradition widely practiced in the States. Luckily, I'm wearing several *new* items, and my garter for later is blue, so I'm all set.

She presents a small golden broach, holding it up for me to see. "This was your grandmother's from your father's side. It's been passed down for many generations."

It's a small serpent with bright, golden amber eyes. "As you know, 'Kaan' means 'serpent,' so even though you may decide to take Kas's last name, I wanted you to have this piece of your family heritage on this special day."

Tears prick my eyes, my throat burning with the effort it takes to choke down the sob threatening to leave it. Grabbing hold of her, I clench her in my arms so tightly I think she might break, but she doesn't complain. Instead, she returns the gesture before pulling back and grasping the waistline of my cream-and-gold garment.

"You look so beautiful, baby. Thank you for wearing this today, even if just for the ceremony," she tells me, referencing the traditional Ani'-Yun'wiya' dress she made me herself, with lots of help from Kas. He's become exceptionally skilled at sewing and insisted he help.

"Thank you, *Etsi*. Can you pin it on for me?"

Bowing her head, she does just that, securing it to my waistline.

I pull her in for another hug, but before I release her, I whisper, "And I'm not changing my name; that's an archaic tradition." I chuckle. "Kas is hyphenating."

My mother's body shakes with laughter. "Of course he is." She smiles, rolling her eyes.

"Hey sweets, you ready to put these men out of their misery?" Audrey asks me, her brown skin glowing in the sun and her golden highlighter radiating her face.

"Eh, I guess," I joke at her vibrant smile.

"Turn the hell around, Kas! Did I say you could look?" she yells at him when he tries to peek.

"No, ma'am," he grumbles at her. She's been running the show for weeks now, and I'm obsessed. She's handling everything exactly how I'd want it without me actually having to do a single thing. I'm so damn thankful for Luca suggesting her to Kas because, frankly, I have zero desire to plan a wedding when I'm in the middle of finishing production on our accelerated vaccines.

Kat comes over, a bright smile lighting up her face. "Come on, gorgeous, let's go make those men cry."

She takes my hand in hers and leads me toward where my father and Kas are standing, facing the incredible mountain range in front of us. The same one Kas took me to before we went skydiving.

When we started thinking about venues, my dad suggested it, and when we got here, Kas realized it was the same place he'd brought me, just from a different entrance with a *much* better view.

The photographers are in position, ready to get video and photos from every angle. "You can turn around now," one of the photographers tells them.

The moment they're facing me, both of them are fighting back tears, grappling to embrace me. Kas playfully elbows my father as he grasps my upper arms firmly in his. "Kassian! You'd stoop so low as to beat up an old, sick man?"

"Stop being so dramatic! In case you've forgotten, you got a lung transplant *six months ago,* so while you're definitely old, you aren't sick," Kas jokes.

My father smiles broadly, turning back to face me. "You look gorgeous, *uwetsiageyv*. I'm so thankful to that family and so stricken for their loss, but their tragedy has allowed me the greatest gift. I get to walk my baby down the aisle and give her away to the most incredible man."

Tears burn my eyes. "No crying! It'll ruin your makeup," Audrey shouts from beside the photographer, easing the tension as we laugh at her abruptness.

He presses a kiss to either cheek before releasing me for Kas, who spares no time scooping me up into his arms, crushing me to his large frame. His lips graze the shell of my ear. "You look incredible, little viper. I can't wait to get you back to our room so I can worship my new wife," he whispers so low that, thankfully, no one else can hear. His words send warmth swimming through me, and those familiar butterflies flap around my stomach.

"You look pretty hot yourself," I whisper in reply as he sets me back on my feet. I take in his tall frame, his broad shoulders stretching the material of his black suit perfectly, tapering at the waist.

"You ready?" he asks me quietly, appraising me as if I'm the most beautiful thing he's ever seen.

"I've never been more ready," I answer honestly. Some people talk about cold feet and nerves before their wedding, but I've never been more certain of anything in my life. *I can't wait to be Kassian Narvaez-Kaan's wife.*

Epilogue: Part One-Kassian

My heart is racing, and my stomach has so many butterflies flapping around that I'm afraid they'll fly out of my mouth. I've never been more excited for any one moment than I am right now. Not even when we won the Stanley Cup a couple of months ago.

Aiyana is standing at the end of the aisle, her hair down with braids throughout, those pouty, round lips of hers are painted a dark red and upturned at the corners. Her father's smile rivals my own as Gianni sits at the piano playing "A Thousand Years" by Christina Perry.[1] Qaletaqa extends his arm for her; she wraps her own around his and begins taking the first steps toward me.

The sun is beginning to set, the clouds taking on a cotton candy quality that I just know will be so damn stunning in our photos, though I'll only ever be able to focus on Aiyana in them anyway. She's always been the most gorgeous person in every room.

As they head down the stone walkway, stepping on the champagne rose petals scattered out by Arlo, Charlie and Rose's eldest, Ale grips my shoulder, leaning in to whisper to me, "Kas, you've gotta rein it in just a tiny bit; your smile is starting to scare the children." He chuckles.

"I can't, man—she's fucking perfect." My voice cracks. Tears are now freely streaming down my face. When she takes the last step before her dad gives her away to me, I suck in a deep breath, wiping the tears away with the back of my hand.

She reaches out, grasping both of my hands in hers, and the music quiets down until it's silent. We're standing hand in hand, our friends and family seated before us as her dad makes his way to stand between us. Not only did his lung transplant save his life and allow him to walk Aiyana down the aisle, but he's also our officiant.

No one else would've been more fitting.

"Alright, you two. We've made Kas wait fourteen long years for this. Let's get this show on the road so we can put him out of his misery," Qaletaqa jokes.

"Please!" I shout, feigning exasperation.

The crowd of friends and family chuckles around us.

He starts by reciting several prayers and proverbs. "It's my understanding that you each wanted to write your own vows, so now is your time to share those." Turning to me, he says, "Kas, would you like to go first?"

Nodding, I grip Aiyana's hands more firmly in mine, not needing to reference my vows as I've recited them a million times over in my head.

"Aiyana, when Kat and I moved in next door to you, I never could have imagined how much my life would change. There had been so many incredible memories and plenty of horrific ones, too, but through it all, you were there every step of the way. The tiny little spitfire showing up at my door, ragging on me while simultaneously shooting googly eyes at me." I pause, allowing everyone's laughter to fade.

"I didn't grasp it then, but I think I've always known deep down that you would be my wife. I was just waiting for you to realize it too." I smile gently at her and pull her hand up, pressing a kiss to her knuckles. "No one knows this besides you, but when everything happened with my parents, I wouldn't talk to anyone. Anyone besides *you,* that is."

I look past her shoulder, seeing the shock on Kat's face before it quickly morphs into an expression of awe, and a single tear slips down her cheek. "I've trusted you with all that I am and work every day to be better for you. I know that I'm not perfect and that I'll make mistakes, but I promise to never hurt you. I can't wait to continue this life with you and the next one after this and beyond. You, Aiyana Kaan, are it for me. I am absolutely *obsessed* with you, and I wouldn't have it any other way, my little viper."

Aiyana's deep brown eyes shimmer under the setting sun, her tawny skin glowing as she holds back tears. "Well," she says, sucking in a breath, "I've got quite the competition to follow."

Our friends and family are dabbing at tears as they chuckle at us.

"Your turn, *uwetsiageyv,*" Qaletaqa urges her.

Aiyana pulls a hand away, shoving it into her bra and digging around for something. The crowd erupts in a fit of laughter. "You need help finding whatever you've lost in there?" I ask her suggestively, not caring who hears, including her dad.

"Oh, stop it. I put my vows in here for safekeeping." She swats my hand away.

"Doesn't seem to have worked, but if you could get your hand out of your bra and stop making your father extremely uncomfortable, that'd be much appreciated," her dad chortles.

"Oh!" she shouts when she finds the folded piece of paper, unfolding it.

"Kas, I'm sorry I was such a shithead," she reads, her eyes growing wide as my smile spreads. "Oops, it looks like I might have brought the wrong copy of these vows." She turns to Kat, handing her the paper. "Hold this for me, will ya, babe?"

Kat rolls her eyes, grabbing the paper as she shakes her head, a small smile tugging at her lips.

Aiyana grips my hands gently in her tiny ones, looking up at me with those endless eyes. "Kassian Narvaez, I've loved you longer than I'd have ever cared to admit, and frankly, all that time you were obsessed with me, I was just as obsessed with you. I was just better at hiding it. I'm sorry I didn't show that sooner, but I'm glad you somehow convinced me or harassed me into it, depending on how you'd like to see it." She giggles.

Again, the crowd billows with laughter.

"I can be *pretty* convincing." I wink at her, and Qaletaqa slaps my shoulder.

"Nasty boy! Can you get through one damn encounter without saying something gross? The ancestors are watching!"

"Sorry, *Edoda*," Aiyana and I say in unison, still snickering between us.

"Please, for the love of gods, finish up," he urges my soon-to-be wife.

"Well, anyway. I love you so damn much it actually hurts sometimes, but I wouldn't change a thing. I promise to love you in every lifetime, and I'll do my absolute best to make my next reincarnated self less of a brat, but no promises there." She smiles brightly at me, her small nose crinkling in the center, eyes bright with humor.

"And as the great Salt-N-Pepa once said, 'What a man, what a man, what a mighty good man,' and he's all *mine*." My heart soars through the damn clouds at her words. I'm finally *hers*.

"Are you done yet? The sun is almost down," her dad complains.

"Yes, *Edoda*, I'm finished." She rolls her eyes in the way that I love so fucking much, crossing her arms over her chest.

"Zuni and Kat will now perform the blanket ceremony."

My sister and Aiyana's mom work together, folding the quilt before standing side by side, circling around us. Aiyana clutches my hands as I bring them to my lips.

"The blanket ceremony is a traditional ritual among the Cherokee or Ani'-Yun'wiya' people," Qaletaqa's voice booms, taking on a faraway quality for this part of the ceremony. "Our ancestors have been performing this ritual for centuries, symbolizing unity and the merging of two souls. On this momentous day, we ask for our ancestors to bless this couple, protect them from evil, and ignite a light within their hearts so bright that it'll act as a calling between their souls, a siren too loud to ignore in any lifetime."

As he speaks, a silence fills the air as if the birds and all small animals have suddenly stopped chattering, listening to his voice. A chill in the air sends goosebumps skating down my arms, and Aiyana's wide eyes look over my shoulder, mesmerized by something. Her mouth is agape as I turn to see what she's staring at.

Dark clouds have gathered behind us, but with her father's last words, they disperse instantly, revealing the brightest rainbow I've ever seen. The chill is replaced by a warmth so calming it coats my entire body in its serenity.

Looking back at Qaletaqa, I see his smug expression greeting me. "The ancestors agree: you *are* soulmates."

At that, Kat and Zuni wrap us in the blanket. "You may now kiss your bride."

And I do.

Boy, do I fucking ever.

My hands instinctively slide behind her, cupping her firm ass and drawing her into me hidden beneath the blanket. A sly smile curves her lips, her arms winding around my neck as I bend forward, closing the gap between us.

Her lips are soft beneath mine, sliding beneath me as I swipe my tongue into her mouth, tasting my cum on her from before we got dressed. The saltiness sends a zap of arousal straight to my cock, which is exactly when her dad clears his throat. As we pull away, our friends and family shout, JJ whistling at us as Kat and Zuni work to fold the blanket back up.

Hand in hand, we turn to face the crowd, our intertwined hands coming up and over our heads.

My gaze searches for Gianni, and the moment his bright-blue eyes meet mine, he gives me a little nod, lifting his guitar.

He begins playing "Steal My Girl" by One Direction.[2] My arms wrap around *my wife,* dragging her into them as I carry her down the aisle. Pressing kisses to her heated skin, I whisper, "Reality is *so* much better than my dreams."

"Same here, Kas, *same here*."

"Now, let's get you out of this dress and into something more you." I smile down at my wife, carrying her off to the cabin we're staying at just down the hill from the reception area on the property.

---

1. **A Thousand Years – Christina Perri**

2. **Steal My Girl – One Direction**

Epilogue: Part One- Aiyana

Friday, August 23, 2024

"Okay, okay, we're going!" I shout to the DJ, who did an incredible job at keeping everyone hyped the entire night. So well, in fact, that we had to pay him extra to stay here doing karaoke with us until now.

It's almost three in the morning, but I have no regrets as Kas clutches my bicep to steady me while we make our way down the dimly lit path to our cabin.

Once inside, he kicks the door shut and hauls me into his arms.

Running his nose along the length of my neck, he breathes me in. "You look so fucking gorgeous in this dress," he growls. Spinning me around, Kas unzips me from behind. "But you'll look so much better without it."

Heat pools in my core as he slides his hands down my back, nudging the black silk gown to the floor.

Kas's fingers wrap around my throat. Leaning in, he whispers, "Get on the bed so I can breed this pretty cunt. My *wife's* cunt."

My back goes rigid and my eyes wide. Turning to face him with flushed cheeks, I say hesitantly, "Kas, I thought we discussed children. And the fact that we don't want them."

His brows crease. "Baby, I just meant I wanted to fill you up. I didn't mean we should have a *child*." His demeanor changes as he takes in my worried expression.

"And you're *sure* you don't want a baby? Because I really, really don't." My heart rate is increasing by the second. We've had extensive conversations about this, and *now* would be just about the worst time for him to change his mind.

Holding my cheeks in the palms of his hands, he gazes at me warily. "There's gotta be something else going on for a breeding joke, of all things, to send you spiraling. What's going on?"

"I'm sorry, I'm overreacting because I have you now, *really have you,* and I don't want anything to come between us."

"Aiyana, there is literally not a single thing that could come between us now. I won't allow it. Now tell me what's going on, please. You're freaking me out."

"You know how I've been trying to get an appointment with someone willing to perform a hysterectomy? And I've had such a hard time after three different providers told me no because I haven't had any children yet, regardless of the fact that I don't *want* any. I know it won't reverse the tissues outside of my uterus that are affected, but if there's even a chance it'll help, I'm more than willing to take it."

He nods slowly, letting his hands fall to his sides.

"Well, I finally found someone, and she's really great. I had the appointment just a few days ago, and with all the wedding craziness going on, I didn't have a chance to really sit down and talk to you about it. And truthfully, I didn't want to jinx it either. But she called me just before our ceremony to tell me she has an opening to get it done next month, and she even said she would perform the surgery while keeping my ovaries. So, I won't struggle with as many hormonal imbalances, and I'm just so freaking happy I could scream."

Kas's concerned expression quickly morphs into one of sheer joy, and all of the anxiety filling me is suddenly flushed out. He grabs me around the waist, carrying me over his shoulder and depositing me on the bed.

"Jesus Christ, woman! You scared the shit out of me!" He laughs, settling in between my legs and pressing kisses up my abdomen as he finds his way to my mouth.

"I'm so fucking proud of you, baby," he whispers, eyes filled with unshed tears. "No one deserves to deal with the pain of endometriosis or the countless treatments you've endured. I'm so sorry it took so long to find someone who respects that we don't want children, but I'll be there every step of the way. No one and nothing could stop me."

"Thank you," I cry, crumbling into his chest. He holds me so tightly, pressing kisses to my skin and whispering warm affirmations.

Children are wonderful, but they aren't everyone's happily ever after. And I'm so glad to have found mine.

Epilogue: Part Two-Kassian

Wednesday, August 22, 2074

I roll over on my side, my bones creaking with the effort, but there isn't a single ache or pain I wouldn't endure to see the way the sun settles across my little viper's gorgeous face each morning.

The same as every morning, Aiyana's eyes crack open, looking up at me with nothing but love glowing in them. "Good morning, Kas," she whispers, her voice rough with sleep.

I gather her wrinkled, tan hands in mine, pressing kisses across her knuckles. "Good morning, my little viper. Happy fiftieth wedding anniversary."

A wide grin spreads across her face, those ruby-red lips of hers crinkling at the edges. "Fifty years already? I'd have thought it was only forty-nine," she tells me with a wink.

"Only fifty in this lifetime, but endless more to go. In this life and the next, I'll always find you," I promise her, not for the first time.

"I hope for your sake that I'm a bit more amenable to being found in the next lifetimes," she says with a chuckle, rolling herself closer to me.

"I don't know, I kind of like the chase," I admit, my throat constricting as the last fifty years with the woman of my dreams flashes blissfully in my mind.

She smooths the pad of her thumb over the skin of my weathered cheek, and our lips meet. Sparks fly in every direction, electricity zipping up my spine. Nothing's changed. Even after all these years, as our bodies age and our skin becomes more wrinkled, the sweet familiarity of being with Aiyana never ceases to lose its thrill.

"I love you, Aiyana," I tell her, nearly choking on the word lodged thickly in my throat as emotion overcomes me.

"I love you too, Kas," she says, her eyes glossy, but that sweet smile remains.

My undoing and my salvation.

The end.

Bonus Scene: Aiyana

Friday, August 23, 2024

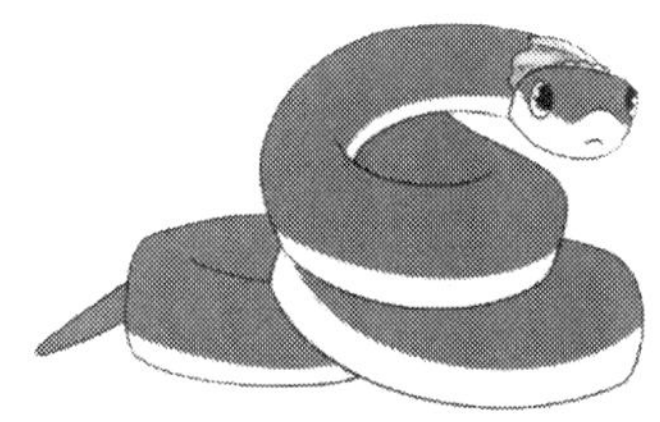

Kas kisses his way up my legs, trailing his tongue along the inside of my thigh before burying his face in my core. "You smell so fucking good, little viper. I can't wait to devour you," he rumbles against my sensitive skin.

"Then get to it, big guy," I urge, pulling his head in closer.

He laughs against me, but *finally,* his tongue darts out, lapping at my needy clit. He pulls away just as my eyes are rolling back. "You're gonna have to beg for it. You sound so sexy when you beg me to eat this sweet cunt."

"Kassian Narvaez-Kaan, eat your wife's pussy, or I'll withhold it from you for a *week*!" I all but screech.

"Yes, ma'am." He chuckles, dipping his head back down. His lips wrap around my clit, sucking it into his mouth. My legs shake from the sensations zipping through me, and my body is alight with arousal.

He runs a finger through my folds, stopping just at my entrance as he twirls his tongue around the sensitive bundle of nerves. "You want this in here?" he asks, his voice low and rumbling.

"Yes," I moan.

"Such a good little slut my wife is, how'd I get so lucky?" he asks me as he slips a finger inside me.

He pumps it slowly, curling it up to hit my G-spot. My core pulls taut, burning from the inside out with searing pleasure.

Kas removes his finger, pressing his nose firmly to my clit as his tongue darts inside me, groaning as he does. "Do you want another finger?" he asks me.

"Uh-huh," I groan as he doesn't wait for a response, inserting them inside me. He stretches his fingers apart once inside, causing my muscles to spasm around him. "Oh fuck, yes." I sigh.

"I'm sorry, baby, but was that you asking for *another* finger?" he asks, not sounding even a little apologetic despite his words.

I moan an inscrutable reply as he continues pumping the first two fingers inside me, my back arching off the bed. "I couldn't quite make that out, so I'm gonna have to assume such a *filthy* little whore like *my wife* would want her pussy stretched around my three fingers. And who am I to deny her on our honeymoon?" he says, toying with me as he removes his fingers before sliding the middle three inside me.

I'm so stretched out, I feel like I might split in two, and it feels fucking delicious.

He continues pumping them inside me slowly as he slurps and sucks on my clit. My muscles tense, fire burning through me as I meet my release, panting as he relentlessly pulls my clit into his mouth, gently nipping on it when he's done.

When he's pulled every last delicious tremble from my body, he sits up on his knees, pressing tender kisses to the tiny scars on my abdomen from my laparoscopic procedure.

"I love you, little viper," he tells me, shifting onto the bed and pulling me against his chest.

"And I love you, Kas."

Afterword

Tremble is obviously a work of fiction, but with that said, there *are* very real people waiting for life-saving measures, including organ, blood, and bone marrow donations. If you feel so inclined, I urge you to join the Be The Match bone marrow registry. They'll send you a test kit where you'll mail back a swab from inside your cheek. This helps match you to someone in need, and while it's very rare that you'd actually be called for donation, it's a possibility that could change someone's entire life and give them the chance of a future they never thought possible. So please, if you're comfortable doing so, join me in the search for bone marrow donors and send in your swab today.

https://bethematch.org/

***

Much like with all the conditions I write about in my "silly little books," Endometriosis is a very real condition that impacts an estimated 190 million women and girls worldwide. And much like all other women's health conditions, Endometriosis is under-diagnosed, and under-treated. If you've ever experienced symptoms similar to Aiyana, or have any reason to believe you may be an Endo warrior, I've linked a resource below to find out more.

"The Endometriosis Foundation of America (EndoFound) strives to increase disease recognition, provide advocacy, facilitate expert surgical training, and fund landmark endometriosis research. Engaged in a robust campaign to inform both the medical community and the public, the EndoFound places particular emphasis on the critical importance of early diagnosis and effective intervention while simultaneously providing education to the next generation of medical professionals and their patients."

https://www.endofound.org/

Furthermore, I'd like to note that not everyone's experience will be the same with any condition I write about. I do my absolute best to represent as many people as possible with my writing, and have the help of nearly one-hundred sensitivity readers, but there are going to be times where your lived experience may be different from that of the characters I've written. This in no way makes your experience any less valid. So in the case of Endometriosis, it's true that many people experience dyspareunia (pain with intercourse), whether this be extremely mild and rarely occurring, severe and persistent or somewhere in between. For the sake of Tremble's narrative, and the type of intercourse Aiyana and Kas enjoy, it was something I did not choose to include, but is a common symptom of Endo, and I hope that if you are impacted by Endo, that Tremble made you feel understood in some way. <3

***

If you'd like to see more of Aiyana and Kas, hold tight for the next couple in the Philia Players series!

Acknowledgements

Thank you to my incredible "Always Smutty In Philadelphia" street team, who have shared my books and relentlessly shoved them down your throats. I appreciate the dedication to having my work seen, and the support you've all shown me has seriously been overwhelming, in the best way possible.

A massive thank you to all the organ donors out there. While many of these amazing individuals aren't alive to read this, what they've done for people and their families is truly unmatched in selflessness. And for those who have chosen to be future organ donors, you're simply incredible. Thank you all for creating circumstances in which I was able to base Aiyana's father's recovery around.

To all the incredible therapists and mental health professionals, thank you for continually working day in and day out to provide these much-needed services in a world that can be so confusing and stressful.

Thank you to each of you who provided sensitivity reading for ***Tremble***. As a non-BIPOC author, it is always my goal to write diverse characters with intention and sensitivity. I wouldn't be able to do that without all of you. The same goes for all health conditions and discussions of therapy. If I'm writing something outside of my lived experience (and sometimes within it for added perspective), I always have sensitivity readers. Each of you are so vital to this process, and I adore you all!

As always, to my readers, who keep me going even when I find it so damn difficult to juggle everything else going on in my life. I'm so thankful for you all.

Xoxo,

Giuliana <3

About the author

Giuliana Victoria is an author based in Pennsylvania who shares her readers' deep love of all things romance. She's a full-time physician assistant student currently in the clinical phase of her program.

When Giuliana isn't writing swoon-worthy book boyfriends, she can be found seeing patients, hiking with her three large breed rescue dogs, and, of course, curled up with a good book beside her husband.

She hopes you'll love ***Tremble*** as much as she enjoyed writing it, and she looks forward to sharing all of her future works with her incredible readers.

Also by

GIULIANA VICTORIA

Philia Players Series

Quiver

Tremble

Book #3 in the Philia Players Series: Coming Soon!

Sign up for my newsletter[1] for a sneak peek at Gianni and Lark's story.

Secret Trials Series

Men's professional rugby, women's college soccer, AND women's college rugby? Sign me up! COMING SOON!

I can't wait for you all to meet Rafael Romero-Castillo and Elise Auclair- I think you're all going to adore them as much as I do <3

Rosa Ranch Series

Western romance with cowboys and a lot of Latin influence: COMING SOON!

1. Newsletter Sign Up

1. Newsletter Sign Up